MY PROTECTOR

BEWITCHED AND BEWILDERED

ALANEA ALDER

www.sacredforestpublishing.com
P.O.Box 280
Moyock, NC, 27958
ISBN:
Digital ISBN-13: 978-1-941315-02-6
Print ISBN- 13: 978-1-941315-03-3
Sacred Forest Publishing

Cover Design and Interior format by The Killion Group
http://thekilliongroupinc.com

DEDICATION

To my readers. Yes you, the one reading right now. This one is for you. Knowing that someone is out there that enjoys my stories helps me to write the next one, so thank you!

-     Alanea

~ Amor Vincit Omnia —
Love Conquers All ~

PROLOGUE

He watched as she pulled her broken body down the alleyway. She had only minutes before well-meaning humans would arrive to help her. She fumbled with a manhole cover, her left arm hanging uselessly at her side. When she finally lifted it out of the way, she gingerly started to climb down the ladder. Her pain filled face turned and for a moment, it was as if she was looking right at him. Suddenly, a look of panic came over her face and she fell from view.

Of course, she had slipped down the ladder.

Gavriel woke with a start, breathing hard. He sat up and tried to slow his heart. His mate had miraculously survived the plummet out of the office window and had managed to avoid detection by the humans, only to possibly fall to her death in a sewer. Groaning, he lay back down. Maybe if he wished hard enough he could start this day over again.

He continually fought the urge to feed. His upper jaw was a constant ache due to his fangs lengthening. He had finally gone to Aiden's brother Adam to ask for more blood. The doctor swore that he would keep his secret and had made the necessary arrangements to triple the blood supply. Yet, no matter how much he drank, it was never enough; the hunger was constant and burned his stomach like acid. When it was evident that he could no longer keep up with the others, Aiden had finally discovered the truth and assigned him to protect Meryn to keep him out of the training courses. He could not fault Aiden his decision; in his weakened state, he put the whole unit at risk. After the reassignment, he had come clean with his fellow unit members about his condition and they surprised him with their unquestioning and unwavering support. During his last transition, he hadn't been with Alpha and had borne it alone.

Knowing that the men had new drills to learn, he sat up and got out of bed. He could not run through the drills with them but he still wanted to see what they were so that he could master them later.

He got dressed and made his way downstairs. When he walked into the dining room, he noticed that the other unit members were sitting on the opposite side of the table from Meryn. The woman in question was sipping her cappuccino with her eyes closed. He made eye contact with Aiden and held up one finger. Aiden shook his head and held up two. Meryn was on her second cappuccino. Smiling, he leaned down and gave her a light peck on the cheek. She opened her eyes, blinked twice, gave a small smile, and closed her eyes again.

It seemed that lately, only he and Ryuu were immune to Meryn's early morning wrath; it was one of the advantages to being at her side most of the day. At first, he had viewed guarding Meryn as an insult. He was disgusted with his own weakness that left him inside with Meryn instead of outside training with his unit. But as the days turned into weeks, he came to look forward to his time with her. He found her to be refreshingly honest and direct. There was no subterfuge or hidden meaning to her words. Her mind was constantly moving and half of the one sided conversations that came out of her mouth had provided him with more entertainment than he had experienced in the past couple centuries.

"Gavriel, you're brave," Colton muttered.

"Meryn adores me, do you not, dear?" Gavriel asked, turning to the lady in question. Meryn merely grunted and kept drinking her caffeine fix. Ryuu walked up with another cup and placed it on the table. Her eyes opened, and she smiled warmly up at her squire. Aiden grumbled under his breath.

"Leave him alone, Aiden, he is Coffee God," Meryn warned.

"I'll be outside if you need me," Aiden said curtly and walked out the back door.

"What has his panties in a bunch?" Colton asked.

"We had a difference of opinion when it came to birth control." Meryn opened her eyes and blinked at the men.

"What do you mean birth control? Are you with child?" Darian asked.

Meryn shook her head. "I don't think so, but it's a possibility. Especially since I'm human, I can get pregnant at any time. Most human women use some form of birth control so they don't become pregnant. Aiden wants babies right away and is upset that I'm thinking about wearing the amulet that Vivian gave me that would slow my ovulation." She took a sip from her cup. "He agrees that I need to wear the amulet so that we have the option to have children a few centuries from now, he just wants to have a baby first." She shrugged.

"Babies are a joy," Darian said.

"Good, *you* have one. Then *you* wake up every two hours and feed and change it. Then *you* spend the next four to five years watching and guarding it's every step until it can walk and talk on its own. After that, it's school, homework, puberty, and attitude. No. Thank. You." Meryn shuddered.

"I'm sure that there is more to it than that, *denka*," Ryuu chided gently.

"Not by much." Meryn set her empty cup down and stood. "Okay peeps, I'll be in Aiden's office if you need me. I'm still helping Adair organize the training programs. Later" She picked up her third cappuccino and walked out of the dining room toward the office.

"Gentlemen, lunch will be ready at noon. We're having tuna fish on whole wheat bread, fresh tavern style chips, and fruit salad." Ryuu gave a half bow.

"I swear; I love this man." Colton pretended to wipe a tear.

"Just don't tease Sascha about what we're having for lunch. I think he's on the verge of snapping you in half," Keelan grinned.

"Our quality of food is the only thing that gets under his skin; of course, I'm going to exploit it," Colton countered.

"Come on, the sooner we do our drills, the sooner we get to have lunch." Darian stood, licking his lips in anticipation. Keelan and Colton stood, and all three waved at Gavriel before walking out.

Gavriel turned to Ryuu. "Did she eat anything?" Ryuu shook his head. Gavriel sighed. "Can you serve an early tea? When she does not eat, she gets...," he fished for the word. "Grumpy."

Ryuu nodded, eyes twinkling. "Of course. Shall I prepare your sustenance as well?"

"Yes, that would be most helpful," Gavriel said and followed Meryn to Aiden's office. Maybe if he were lucky, she would not start pestering him for more paranormal legends until after lunch.

CHAPTER ONE

Turn left in two miles.

"Left? There is no left. Where?" She looked around there was nothing but trees in any direction.

Turn left in one mile.

"There is no left here you daffy contraption!"

You have arrived at your destination.

"Ugh!" Elizabeth Monroe rolled to a stop and put her car in park. Climbing out of her car, she stretched and rubbed her lower back. She had been driving for eight hours and all she wanted was a warm bed. She looked around. She was in the middle of absolutely nowhere.

You have arrived at your destination.

Elizabeth reached in, ripped the GPS off the dash, and threw it into the woods. She looked left down the long dirt road she had come down. Frowning, she turned right. The dirt road seemed to go on forever. She knew that she had guesstimated where Lycaonia's city gate would be since the city wasn't on any known map, but she didn't think she would be this off.

She was about to get back in her car when she heard a low hiss. She froze and looked around her feet for any snake that had yet to go into hibernation. She traced the sound to her back right tire, which was becoming flatter by the second.

"Sugar!" She eyed the mud under her car and sighed. Cussing every step of the way, she stomped back to the trunk to get the jack and spare tire. She opened the trunk and was about to wrestle the spare out when she looked down. She was wearing her new London Fog wool trench. She was not about to get grease on it. She removed her coat and folded it carefully laying it to one side. She removed the tire and the jack and started the process of changing her flat. She was almost finished when she heard a familiar sound.

"You have got to be kidding me!" She dropped the tire iron in defeat. Her back left tire was going flat faster than the right had. This just served as her daily reminder that she had the worst luck in the world.

Wet and cold she grumbled as she threw the flat tire and the tire iron in the trunk and slammed it shut. She reached to her side for her keys when it dawned on her where they were. Turning slowly she looked at her locked trunk that held not only her coat but also her car keys and phone.

"Just freaking great!" She tried to open her trunk she but wasn't strong enough and didn't have the leverage to pry it up.

"What else could go wrong?" she demanded, shaking her fist at the sky. A crack of thunder was her answer as rain began to fall, creating rivulets of water running down her body. Whimpering, she prayed that someone would come by soon.

Two hours later, Elizabeth was thoroughly drenched and shivering. She had already dismissed the idea of shifting since her animal would be just as cold and wet as her human form. If help did come, she didn't want to experience that awkward moment where she shifted back and was naked. She was about to give in to the urge to cry when she heard a car approaching. It slowed down and stopped. She got to her feet and heard a car door open and close.

"Hello there," a male voice greeted.

"Hello," she said.

"How are you?"

Seriously?

"I'm fine and you?" she asked, keeping her voice even.

"I can't complain. What are you doing out here? Don't you have a coat?" he asked.

"Yes. Yes, I do, but it's in the trunk along with my car keys and phone. I have been stuck out here for the past couple hours."

"Sorry, honey! I didn't realize you had been out here so long; I wouldn't have just chitchatted if I had known. Hold on." Elizabeth smiled at the distress in his voice. He was cute.

A minute later, he easily popped the trunk open with the pry bar he had grabbed from his car. She watched him as he walked back toward her with her coat. He was tall and had warm blond hair and bright green eyes. His smile was rueful but kind.

He held her coat. She dug into the pocket and pulled out her keys and phone.

"Thanks. I was about to lose it there," she admitted.

"I can imagine. My name's Colton. Where are you heading?"

"I'm Elizabeth, Elizabeth Monroe. I'm heading to Lycaonia." She stretched and cracked her back.

"We've been on the lookout for you. Let me finish this and you can follow me in. I can swap out your other tire with my spare, which should last you until we can get it fixed. If you don't mind a slight delay, we can go to the Alpha estate, and I can drop off my car and ride into the city with you, to show you around." His smile turned devilish.

She thought about it for a second before nodding.

"That might actually be a good idea. In my current state, I don't know where I would end up." Grimacing, she saw that her new coat was covered in mud from her tire, making her sacrifice seem pointless. Not wanting to get her seats dirty she made sure she had her keys and phone in hand before she threw the coat back into the trunk.

"Great, it won't take me a second. Go warm up in my car." Colton pointed to the car behind them.

"Thanks." She handed him the keys and walked to his car. She climbed in and jacked up the heat. Why did crazy things always happen to her? The only thing she could count on was her bad luck.

True to his word, Colton finished ten minutes later and walked over to the car.

"We're not far from the city gate, from there it's about twenty minutes to the Alpha estate."

Elizabeth got out rubbing her arms briskly. "I'll be right behind you."

Colton grinned and winked. She laughed. He was such a flirt. She walked back to her car. He had left it running with the heat on. What a sweetie. She followed his car down the dirt road. When he turned down an almost undetectable path, she sent up a prayer of thanks that he had found her. She would have never found the city entrance without him.

Twenty minutes later, they were pulling up to a large estate house. She parked behind him and got out. They walked toward the porch.

"I'm just going to let them know that I found you and I'm heading to the city so they can put someone else on perimeter watch." Colton held open the front door for her.

"Sounds good. I still need to find a place in the city to stay and a garage to get these tires replaced, so we'll have to take care of that," she said.

Colton nodded. "No problem. I know a few retired warriors that rent apartments, we'll check with them first."

"That would be a life saver," she smiled up at him.

Colton shut the door behind them. She took two steps forward and tripped over the ornate rug in the foyer. Unfortunately, she landed face first.

"Shit! Are you okay?" Colton gently helped her up and winced when he looked at her face.

She gingerly touched her nose, and her fingers came away with blood. "At least it's not broken. I know how that feels."

"Do you break it often enough to know?" Colton's eyes widened.

"Yup. I'm kind of a klutz."

"That sounds familiar." Colton was now frowning.

"You." A deep male voice said from above them. Elizabeth turned and looked up. At the top of the stairs was the most gorgeous man she had ever seen. He was tall, but lean with broad shoulders that tapered off to a narrow waist. Dark hair fell carelessly around his shoulders in waves. But it was his gray eyes that captivated her; the intensity in his gaze mesmerized her. It was as if she could see the weight of ages in his eyes. When they shifted from eternal gray to red, she swallowed hard.

His movements were a blur as he flew down the stairs. He backed her up against the door caging her in with his arms on either side.

"Gavriel! Man! What the hell?" Colton yelled.

"Leave us!" the dark haired man demanded.

"No way. Get your shit together." Colton said as he tried to wedge himself between them. Her body reacted to Colton's interference. She didn't want to move away from this dark stranger. When she inhaled, it dawned on her that this man was a vampire, and he was her mate.

Gavriel swiped at Colton dragging his claws across his forearm.

Colton cursed and grabbed his arm. "Man! What the fuck?"

"Colton, back off. She must be his mate," a third man said, edging close to them from behind Gavriel.

"Ryuu, are you sure?" Colton asked and started to back away.

"I'm sure. He is my mate," Elizabeth spoke up. Gavriel moved her toward the open door to their left.

"Elizabeth, you don't understand," Colton began.

"He's my mate; he won't hurt me," Elizabeth let herself be herded toward the door. She stepped backward into the empty room and her mate kicked the door shut behind him, never taking his eyes from her.

"You're Gavriel, right?"

He circled her, getting closer with every step. His eyes burned a deep red. Growing up in Noctem Falls, she had only ever seen this once before, when one of the men had been in the midst of his vampiric transition and his more aggressive tendencies had risen to the surface.

"My name is Elizabeth Monroe; I'm your mate." He stopped circling.

"I know. I dreamt of you." His voice sounded deep and raspy.

"What did you see?" she asked.

"You. You falling all the time." He leaned in and inhaled. He closed his eyes, a blissful expression on his face. She realized he could smell her blood.

"Are you in transition?" She watched his face carefully.

He nodded and opened his eyes. "How did you know?"

"I was raised in Noctem Falls."

"Then you know that you need to stay away." He turned his scarlet eyes to her. She flinched. There was barely anything human in that gaze. She looked toward the door, but her animal began to protest. This was her mate; it was her responsibility to take care of him.

He gave an anguished cry and doubled up, wrapping his arms around his torso. Shaking his head, he turned to look at her, his eyes flicking from red back to gray.

"Please go! I do not want to hurt you!" he gasped as she watched the muscles under his skin shift and tremble. She then realized how much pain he was in. He was experiencing blood depravation on top of transition. There was no way she could walk away and leave him writhing in pain. She stepped closer.

"Let me help."

He shook his head. "Please!" he begged.

"No. You're my mate. It is my right and my duty to feed you. I offer all of myself to you," she recited the words that she had heard so many times amongst the couples growing up. To be able to feed your mate was a gift.

"You won't hurt me and I can't stand to see you in so much agony. Please feed." She placed a hand on his back. His head turned, and he stared at her, his eyes shifting from gray back to red.

"I will try to be gentle," he whispered. He stood up, slowly unwinding his arms. When he rose to his full height, he was trembling and near exhaustion. She could see that he was literally fighting to remain lucid.

He took her in his arms and, for a moment, simply stood there with her cheek against his chest. She inhaled, taking his scent deep in her lungs. She would never get enough of him. With every breath, his scent was ingrained on her soul. He lowered their bodies slowly to the rug and tilted her head to one side. He ran his tongue down the column of her neck and she shivered. She had expected him to strike like a starved animal, yet even at his most desperate, he took his time to ensure that she felt as little pain as possible.

When he began to nip and nibble behind her ear, she sighed as her body coiled in expectation. His arms tightened before he sank his fangs deep in her neck.

She had expected pain, but there was very little, just a quick pinch then a flood of pleasure. He held her as if she were the most precious thing in the world as he drank deeply. She could feel his restraint as he took slow, measured sips. Each pull of his lips sent jolts through her body, it felt as if he were licking and caressing her nipples and clit from the inside. Panting, she thrust her hips against him trying to find relief. She felt his lips curve against her neck and he placed his thigh between her legs. The second his firm muscles hit her throbbing flesh, she cried out and ground against him, chasing the pleasure that stayed just out of reach. When his hand reached down to brush against her tightened nipples, she exploded, crying out. Wave after wave of pleasure cascaded through her. She felt the swirling darkness begin to take her. Smiling, she let go. The last thing she remembered was his gentle kiss against her neck.

"Are you certain she is well?"

"She's fine."

"I could have killed her."

"She's a shifter. It would take more than a blood donation to kill her." The male voice sounded amused.

"Listen to Adam, my friend. He doesn't know much, but he does know about healing," another male voice spoke.

Elizabeth blinked and focused on the voices. Of the three, her mate's voice was the sexiest. She froze. Her mate? That's right; she had found her mate.

"Ha-ha. Very funny, Aiden. Be nice or I'll figure out a way to put Meryn on a caffeine IV drip."

"Gods no! Adam, that's not even funny!"

Elizabeth smiled. "That actually sounds good right about now." She sat up to face the men. Two of them towered over her mate and looked enough alike she assumed they were related. Instantly, her mate was at her side, running a gentle hand over her hair.

"How do you feel, *zain'ka moya?*" he asked.

"What's *zain'ka?*"

He leaned in and whispered against her neck. "My sunshine or rabbit. I thought it fitting."

His warm breath against her neck sent renewed shivers through her body.

The two men behind Gavriel cleared their throats. Gavriel stood and kissed her forehead.

"Elizabeth, I know it may be belated, but I am Gavriel Ambrosios. May I introduce to the Unit Commander Aiden McKenzie and his brother Adam McKenzie. Adam runs the clinic for the unit warriors. Gentleman, I finally have the pleasure of introducing my mate, Elizabeth Monroe." Gavriel brought her hand up and kissed it.

"I'm glad she made it to Lycaonia in one piece. Thrice welcome Elizabeth, you couldn't ask for a better mate." Aiden gave a courtly bow. Adam smiled and waved.

She looked at Adam. "You're the doctor?"

"Yes, I am," he replied.

"You and I will be great friends. I am constantly tripping or falling, or tripping then falling over things." She turned to Gavriel when he groaned and covered his face with his other hand. He looked at her, a pained expression on his face.

"So what I saw in my dreams was your everyday life, not just the terrifying moments?" he asked.

"I'm not sure what you saw, but I do get hurt on a fairly regular basis."

"Did you fall out of an office window?"

"Yes."

"Did you fall down the sewer ladder?"

"Yes, that was equal parts painful, humiliating, and disgusting." She shuddered.

"How did you manage to live to adulthood?"

"That's a question for my father. I'm sure he could give you an entire dissertation about my childhood." She grinned up at him.

"I may just have to ask him," he murmured.

"Elizabeth, are you well enough to leave? My mate was curious about you." Aiden said.

She nodded and gently pulled her hand from Gavriel's. Reluctantly, he let go. She swung her legs over the side of the bed and went to hop off, but her right leg became tangled in the blankets. If it weren't for Gavriel's reflexes, she would have spilled onto the floor. Aiden and Adam stared at her open mouthed, Gavriel paled.

"I'm okay, really." She stood and smoothed out her clothes.

"Okay then. I'll drive." Aiden held up his keys.

Gavriel kept a hand on her lower back as they said goodbye to Adam and walked out to the parking lot.

"Do you all live together?" Elizabeth asked once they were on the road.

"Yes, all of the Alpha Unit members live together," Aiden confirmed.

"Even your mate?"

"Meryn has made some changes recently." Gavriel had yet to let her hand go. It was as if he had to be touching her.

"She just couldn't stand to be away from me," Aiden said puffing his chest out. Elizabeth looked over at her mate, who just shrugged.

"What is Meryn like?"

Gavriel shook his head. "Meryn cannot be described, only experienced."

"Now I'm really curious."

"She's one of kind," Aiden said proudly.

"She sure is. I cannot wait for the two of you to meet," Gavriel said.

Aiden laughed.

Elizabeth smiled, but felt a sense of foreboding; she couldn't be that bad. Could she?

"Meryn, this is my mate, Elizabeth Monroe. Elizabeth, this is Meryn, Aiden's mate."

"Is she the unbalanced one?" a voice asked.

Elizabeth stood in the doorway of their front room and watched as spiky brown hair slowly began to pop up from behind the back of the chair, inch by inch, until a pair of bright green eyes watched them unblinkingly.

"What does she mean 'the unbalanced one' and is she all right?" Elizabeth asked, edging behind her mate. Gavriel raised an eyebrow at Meryn. She popped back down disappearing behind the back of the chair, only to reemerge standing at its side. She stared down at the floor.

A handsome man in Japanese style dress stepped forward. "Perhaps some tea?"

Meryn nodded. "Thank you Ryuu, that'd be great." Ryuu bowed and left toward what Elizabeth assumed was their kitchen.

"I hate to leave the two of you and the guaranteed entertainment that is sure to take place as you get to know one another, but Aiden and I need to discuss some things. I would also like to give you some space to take everything in. Things have been moving quickly." Gavriel's eyes were filled with concern when he leaned forward and whispered in her ear. "I will be down the hall in Aiden's office, okay?"

Elizabeth nodded; he was already being considerate of her. As much as she hated to admit it, he was right. Everything felt surreal right now. Maybe some girl talk was exactly what she needed.

"Okay."

"Meryn, be good," Aiden said walking away with Gavriel.

Meryn rolled her eyes. "I'm always good." She turned to Elizabeth "So. Do you know anything about dead bodies?"

So much for girl talk.

Elizabeth blinked and glared at Gavriel's back as he walked away with a chuckling Aiden. Darn that man, he knew this woman was crazy when he'd left her here. She turned back to the tiny human.

"No, not really. Why?"

"I'm trying to compare the damage done to the women killed by that psycho stalker to famous human serial killers to see if I can determine why they were killed, you know, establish a pattern."

"Ahh." Elizabeth couldn't make sense of this human at all.

"So. What kind of paranormal are you?" Meryn sat down on the couch cross-legged, pulling a laptop in front of her.

Elizabeth walked over and sat down in one of the room's chairs.

"I'm a *lepus curpaeums*."

Meryn nodded. "So you're a bunny."

"I'm a *lepus curpaeums...*"

"A bunny. That's cool." Meryn turned back to her laptop.

"What did you mean when you said 'unbalanced one'?" Elizabeth asked, giving up on the bunny comment. She had a feeling it wouldn't do any good to argue with this woman.

Meryn looked up and winced. "Gavriel dreamt about you before you got here. He said you were either mentally retarded or had a severe inner ear imbalance. He broke two of the stress balls I gave him worrying about you."

"I see."

Mental note: Kick mate's ass later.

"He's really nice, so don't hold it against him. He's had a rough couple of weeks. He's been trapped inside with me for a month and not once did he make me feel awkward or like I was a nuisance. He was patient and has been explaining paranormal society to me and telling me stories." Meryn rambled.

Elizabeth smiled. If her mate had been trapped inside during his transition with this woman for a month and hadn't lost his temper, he might be a saint.

"How long has he been in transition?" Elizabeth asked.

Meryn eyed her carefully. "He doesn't want people knowing."

"Meryn, I figured it out on my own; I was raised around vampires. Besides, I'm his mate; normal rules don't apply to me."

Meryn sighed. "I think he's going on two months."

Elizabeth gasped.

Meryn's eyes widened. "What?"

"What do you know about vampiric transitions?" Elizabeth asked as her stomach churned.

"Not much, just that he needs more blood than normal and at the end, he 'levels up' like in a video game."

Elizabeth nodded. "Vampires don't age, but that doesn't mean that they don't change. Everything in this world changes. Vampires go through two different types of transition. One based on their age, usually at the five hundred year mark and then every thousand years or so. Within the age transitions, the one thousand and five thousand year changes are the hardest.

"The second type of transition is one based on need. Those are the most brutal, since it's dire circumstances dictating the changes and not the natural course of events. My Uncle Magnus went through a need-based transition before I was born. They still talk about it in Noctem Falls, he became unstable as his body gained the strength and power he would need to become an Elder.

"Both of these transitions are influenced by age; the older the vampire, the longer the transition, the longer the transition, the stronger they become. Unfortunately, the longer the transition, the more dangerous they become, not only for the vampire, but also for those around him."

Meryn opened her mouth then closed it. She stayed quiet a moment then looked up at Elizabeth. "So if Gavriel has been in transition for nearly two months, he is probably going through that five thousand year transition and a need-based transition since ferals are going bat shit crazy, then what?"

Elizabeth swallowed hard and leaned back in her chair. "Then we could possibly be living with the most dangerous creature on earth, at least until his transition is over."

Meryn grinned. "That is so cool. Gavriel was badass before, but now, he's like Chernobyl badass."

Elizabeth looked at her and blinked. "You're not scared at all, are you?"

Meryn shook her head. "He's surly and grumpy now, but when I first met him, when his transition was just starting, he was charming. He's always been nice to me."

"I kind of like him grumpy," Elizabeth admitted.

"Aiden is like that, I know what you mean," Meryn said running a finger along her laptop skin.

Elizabeth stared at the blue Tardis and smiled. "I like your laptop skin."

Meryn's eyes narrowed. "Do you know the Doctor?"

"Of course."

"Who was the first Doctor?" Meryn asked eyeing her with suspicion.

"William Hartnell. Why?" Elizabeth asked confused.

Meryn let out a breath of relief. "Some people 'say' they love the Doctor, but then when I ask them, 'Who was the first Doctor?' they say Eccleston and I want to scream. You pass." Meryn beamed at her.

She has to be the cutest little thing.

"You're adorable. I'll let you in on a secret. I'm old enough honey, that I watched Doctor Who when it originally aired. My family was visiting London at the time and I became instantly hooked." Elizabeth almost laughed out loud at the reverent expression on Meryn's face.

"That is so fucking cool!" Meryn exclaimed.

Elizabeth laughed. She had never met anyone quite as open and guileless as Meryn. She was childlike and refreshing. "I've been a sci-fi fanatic as long as it's been around."

"I tried to talk Aiden into going to DragonCon, but he said no, that it would be a 'logistical nightmare'." Meryn made air quotes.

"I'll take you next year. I have a standing reservation at a hotel downtown for DragonCon. I can show you the secrets of the Con that most tourists never see." Elizabeth offered.

"No fucking way! I love you!" Meryn bounced in her seat.

Elizabeth had never before met anyone who liked the things she did. In Noctem Falls, science fiction was considered immature or ridiculous. She found herself sharing Meryn's enthusiasm.

"So what do you all do around here to keep from losing your minds? Colton was going to take me into the city, but somehow I don't think that is going to happen now." Elizabeth propped her feet up on the ottoman.

"I'm an internet security expert..."

"Hacker," Elizabeth interrupted.

Meryn nodded, grinning. "I've been working with Adair, that's Aiden's brother who runs the training academy in the city. I'm trying to convince him and the council that it would be more beneficial to assign the trainees to units for more hands-on training than to leave them languishing at the academy until an opening pops up. If my proposal goes through, all thirty of the current trainees will be assigned out to the units here in Lycaonia, and Adair and his trainers can start on the next batch. If it's successful here, they will adopt it in the other three cities effectively tripling the defense force. They're supposed to be making a decision either today or tomorrow," Meryn explained.

"That's actually a very good idea." Elizabeth frowned and wondered why they hadn't done this earlier.

"Don't sound so shocked," Meryn mumbled.

Elizabeth chuckled. "Sorry, I didn't mean to imply you weren't intelligent, it's just that it makes so much sense I was wondering why we haven't adopted this practice before now."

"Oh. That's easy. That's because nobody around here likes change. I swear they wouldn't change their underwear if they didn't have to. Everything is tradition, tradition, tradition. Most of them have forgotten *why* they originally decided to do things a certain way. A lot of practices need to be hauled into the twenty-first century," Meryn said, sounding thoroughly disgusted.

"Tell me about it. I was raised in Noctem Falls; they practically worship the Victorian era there. I still get stares when I wear jeans around the city when I visit my dad."

Meryn's eyes widened. "You were raised in Noctem Falls? I so want to go there. I heard that the vampires carved their city into the cliff face of a deep canyon."

Elizabeth nodded. "I distinctly remember the first time my father took me outside to play. Noctem Falls is actually an underground city. It's a network of caves and caverns deep in the earth."

"Like the dwarves in *Lord of the Rings*?" Meryn whispered.

"Actually, that's a very close representation of Noctem Falls. But instead of dwarves, there are vampires."

"Now I don't know which city I want to visit first. I thought for sure that I wanted to go to Éire Danu first, but now Noctem Falls sounds magical." Meryn chewed on her lower lip.

"Not just anyone can visit Éire Danu. The fae are very protective of their city," Elizabeth warned.

Meryn waved a hand in front of her. "I was invited by their queen. Elder Vi'Ailean is the younger brother of her consort. The Elder likes me." She grinned at her.

Elizabeth blinked. Meryn had already secured an invitation to Éire Danu and by the queen herself? She shook her head. She thought moving to Lycaonia would be boring, just a place to lie low until she could return to the human world without someone figuring out that she could survive a nose dive out of an office building window. She eyed the peculiar little human with renewed interest.

"*Denka*, your tea." The man that Meryn had called Ryuu carried a tray into the room. Immediately, Elizabeth's nose picked up on the faint smell of jasmine.

"Thank you. Ryuu, have you met Elizabeth yet? She's the one that Gavriel has been dreaming about. She'll be moving in," Meryn said, introducing them.

Elizabeth paused. "I'll be moving in?" She thought that Meryn was the exception to the rule about mates living in unit estates.

Meryn blinked. "Yeah, why wouldn't you?"

"It just isn't done, Meryn."

Ryuu chuckled. "You'll soon discover that Meryn often does things that 'just aren't done'." Ryuu poured their tea carefully before stepping back to stand against the wall.

"I do, don't I?" Meryn picked up a small plain cookie and popped it in her mouth before placing one on a napkin on the table. Elizabeth watched in fascination as the cookie lifted all on its own and tiny bite marks appeared.

Meryn caught her staring. "That's Felix. He's a sprite that decided to adopt me. He's super sweet, but not everyone can see him," she explained.

Feeling as if she had stepped into an episode of the *Twilight Zone*, Elizabeth nibbled on a cookie. What had she gotten herself into now?

CHAPTER TWO

"So what do you do, you know, to support yourself?" Meryn asked.

"I'm a personal assistant. I help high level executives stay organized and keep their day running smoothly." Elizabeth was very proud of her work. While working in the background, she had helped many men and women achieve wonderful things.

"Oh my gosh, Aiden needs you! This is so awesome. I have been trying to help, but organization isn't really my thing. I've gotten especially lazy now that I have Ryuu. I swear I don't know how I made it through a day without him. He remembers things like lunch and clean clothes."

Elizabeth laughed. "Those are important things, Meryn. What exactly does Aiden need help with?"

"Everything."

"Really?"

"Yup, really. I think he still hand writes his reports. It'd be a miracle if we found out he was using a ballpoint pen and not a quill and ink." Meryn shuddered.

"It can't be that bad?" Elizabeth scoffed.

The sound of a throat clearing had her turning to look at Ryuu. Elizabeth met his gaze, and he nodded. He was a kindred spirit, serving others as she did, but he served on a personal level, where she served on a professional one.

"You mean to tell me that the man responsible for the defenses of the four pillar cities and the running of all our warrior units still hand writes his reports? How in the hell does he get anything done?" Elizabeth set her cup down.

"Hmmm. Remember what I said about tradition? Routine helps the men remember what to do. If everything is always the same it's easier to remember," Meryn explained.

Elizabeth stared at Meryn in horror. She stood. "Where is his office?"

Meryn's eyes widened before a grin appeared. "I'll show you."

"Meryn, remember what Aiden said about interrupting unit work?" Ryuu warned.

"It's not me this time," Meryn said happily and stood. She led the way out of the room and down the hall. Without even knocking, she turned the handle to a heavy looking wooden door and walked right in.

"Baby, what did I tell you about interrupting?" Aiden growled.

"It's not me. Elizabeth wanted to see your office." Meryn stepped aside and indicated for Elizabeth to walk in.

Not wasting any time, Elizabeth walked in and began to look around. One desk. No computer visible. No wires. No filing cabinets. Surely, they had to be somewhere.

"Where are your files?" she asked.

With a confused look on his face, Aiden pointed to a stack of papers in the corner. Elizabeth walked over. Sure enough everything was handwritten, calligraphy style. The papers were tied together with twine in stacks covered in grime.

Aiden blushed as the finger she ran down the center of the papers came away with a layer of dust. "I don't get to clean much in here," he admitted.

"Computer. Where is your computer?" Elizabeth demanded, feeling a growing panic. She felt like the defense of her people danced precariously on the edge of a sword.

Aiden pointed to a huge laptop on the bottom shelf of his bookcase. Meryn started to snicker behind her. She powered it up and clutched at her chest when the Windows 95 logo greeted her. Meryn, by now, had collapsed into giggles. Sputtering, Elizabeth stepped back then spun to face Aiden and her now concerned looking mate. This could not be happening. Her people's safety now lay in her hands.

"Where are the personnel rosters? Training schedules?"

"I've memorized them," Aiden mumbled.

She stared. "I don't know whether you're a genius or an idiot."

"Hey!" Aiden protested.

"Out!" she screeched.

"What?" Aiden asked. He and Gavriel stared at her as if she had lost her mind.

"You two out, now! Ryuu, I'll need you to take down the list of supplies I'll need to make this office functional. Meryn, I'll need your help in establishing a secure network and databases for personnel management." Elizabeth rolled up her sleeves. The men just stared at her in shock.

"Get out! You can come back in after I turn your sorry excuse for an office into a proper management center. Scoot!" Elizabeth made a shooing motion.

Gavriel walked over and pulled her close. Before she knew what he was doing, he gave her a kiss that scorched her down to her toes. Pulling back, he growled low. "You are sexy when you are being feisty."

"You haven't seen anything yet," she challenged.

"Good. I am feeling better today; I am going out to help Aiden direct the men. If you need me, I will be just outside," he whispered, before kissing her one more time.

"What about me? I need some love before we go outside for drills," she heard Aiden grumble trying to kiss Meryn who was turning her head back and forth giggling. Finally, Meryn let him capture her lips.

After both men had gotten their kisses, they moved toward the door.

"Oh, Aiden," Meryn called.

He turned to her. "Yes, baby?"

"You better read up on how to use a Mac," she warned.

Groaning, he turned around, and both men left to start drill practice.

The rest of the afternoon flew by. By the time she was done, she had racked up quite a shopping list, but damn, the man didn't even have paper clips! Both she and Meryn were exhausted when Ryuu interrupted them, letting them know it was time for dinner.

"You know, when the new desk gets here and everything gets set up, I may take over his office for myself. This is going to be sweet." Meryn shoved her laptop in her little backpack and turned to face her.

Elizabeth thought about it for a second. "Let's order a second desk for you. Let's face it, you'll be in here more than Aiden, there's no reason why the two of us can't share this space while we're getting these cavemen organized."

"Yes! I'll tell Ryuu to order a new monitor and docking station too."

Elizabeth cracked her back. It felt good to be working. She had been afraid that she wouldn't be able to find any projects to work on while in Lycaonia; little did she realize that Fate had a way of giving you exactly what you needed.

"We better hurry. The men won't eat without us and if we make them wait they get snarly." Meryn walked out into the hallway. Together they walked to the dining room. When they entered, five men stood from where they had been sitting at the table. Aiden pulled out the chair next to him for Meryn and her mate did the same for her.

Smiling, she sat down and he scooted her chair in for her. One of the things she always missed when she lived amongst humans was the courtly manners preserved by her people. When Gavriel sat down, she boldly reached over and took his hand. Without changing expression, he turned to look at her. Under the table, he rested their joined hands on his thigh and gently massaged her knuckles.

She had always wondered how matings worked. Whenever she'd asked her father, he always said, "You'll know when you find your mate. There's no stronger force on this planet than that of two mates coming together." He had been right. It wasn't instant love, trust, or intimacy. Just a deep-seated sense of belonging. She had been in a few long-term relationships in her life, but none of those had ever developed the level of comfort that she already had with Gavriel. If she felt this way in the first twenty-four hours, she couldn't imagine how her parents must feel having been mated over one hundred and fifty years.

"You look so serious, what are you thinking?" Gavriel's voice broke her train of thought.

"I was actually thinking about how incredible the mating process is. We were strangers this morning, yet I can't imagine tomorrow without you. Then I thought, if I feel this way in just the first day, I wonder how my parents feel having been mated for over a hundred and fifty years now," Elizabeth explained.

The men around the table smiled at her.

Aiden laughed. "My parents have been mated for over a thousand years. From what they tell me, the bond gets more intense."

Elizabeth swallowed hard. "I may not make it," she muttered.

Gavriel leaned in and nuzzled her neck. "We will be just fine."

Meryn nodded and looked over at Aiden. "I know what you mean. With all the sex, it's almost like I don't get anything else done."

One man dropped his fork. The other turned his head, his shoulders shaking, and the one she recognized as Colton, laughed outright. Aiden just stared at his mate, blushing.

"Meryn!" he exclaimed.

She looked around, confusion on her face. "What? I said 'almost'. I do get a lot accomplished. I'm not sure about you though."

From their intertwined fingers, she felt a tremor. She looked over to see her mate's mouth twitching furiously, but being the conservative vampire he was, he tried to hide his emotion. Elizabeth giggled at Aiden's expression. When Gavriel turned to look at her with a sardonic expression on his face, she couldn't hold back her mirth any longer. She covered her face with her other hand and laughed heartily. The men around the table joined in.

When they settled down, Meryn looked around the table. "I don't know what was so funny."

Elizabeth held her stomach. "Don't Meryn, please; it hurts to laugh so much."

Ryuu, smiling, set two large bowels of pasta on the table. "They were amused at Aiden's reaction to your words *Denka,* nothing more. Laughter is good for the soul," he explained.

"Oh. Okay." Meryn held up her bowl and Ryuu served out a generous portion. He then served Elizabeth before moving on to the men.

"Elizabeth let me introduce you to my fellow unit members. You have already met Aiden McKenzie and Colton Albright." Gavriel pointed to the two men.

Grinning sheepishly, Colton waved.

"On either side of them are Keelan Ashwood and Darian Vi'Alina. Keelan is our resident witch and Darian is our fae brother," Gavriel completed the introductions.

"Hello, I'm Elizabeth Monroe. I just moved from Washington DC, but I was raised in Noctem Falls," she introduced herself.

"Monroe. You wouldn't happen to be any relation to Broderick Monroe?" Gavriel asked apprehensively.

"Yes, he's my father," she said frowning. "Why?"

Growling, Gavriel sat back in his chair.

"What?" she demanded.

"That means your other father is Caspian Rioux, younger brother of Magnus Rioux, the current vampire Elder of Noctem Falls." Gavriel's tone was aggravated.

It dawned on her. Her mate was a vampire, and she had ties to the ruling vampire family. Awkward.

"Wait. Fathers?" Meryn asked, leaning forward her expression intrigued.

"Yes, fathers, as in two of them. My mother and my biological father were best friends. She wanted a baby but hadn't found her mate yet, so my father agreed when she asked him to donate sperm. He figured it would be the only way he would ever have a child. Surprisingly enough, she got pregnant with their first attempt. She was killed in a carriage accident before I was one. My father was heartbroken, so he moved us to Noctem Falls where he could focus on his research in creating an artificial blood source. There he met his mate, my other father Caspian. Caspian became devoted to my father, and it was by watching him act as a lab assistant that I learned how to be a personal assistant. He was always anticipating what my father needed whether it was more tea, his notes, or just being a sounding board. My Uncle Magnus is the vampire Elder. He is somewhat overprotective of me," she said, wincing.

"Wonderful," Gavriel exhaled.

"My dads were so busy in the lab that most days, I followed Magnus around like a lost puppy. I probably know more about the nobles in the ruling vampire houses than anyone, with the exception of Magnus, of course. The vampire court was an interesting place to grow up," she smiled at the memory.

"I need to call your uncle," Gavriel muttered.

"That might not be the best idea."

"It will be fine. I can handle myself. I am not worried, it's just an inconvenience," Gavriel reassured her.

"If you're sure." The more she thought about it, the more she didn't like the idea of Gavriel butting heads with her uncle.

"I am sure. I can handle Magnus." Gavriel picked up his fork and spoon and very elegantly began to twirl his pasta. Though his features remained harsh, his actions were gentle as he held out the fork. She leaned in and accepted the bite.

She chewed and swallowed. "Don't say I didn't warn you."

"We definitely need to visit Noctem Falls now," Meryn said looking up at Aiden.

Aiden paled. "Are you kidding, I'm staying out of Noctem Falls until the fallout of this mating settles."

"But the vampire elder is her uncle, we totally have an in," Meryn protested.

"He might blame me for letting his niece get mated to one of my unit warriors. No. Thank. You." Aiden shook his head.

"E-Liz-A-Beth, you'll take me to Noctem Falls, won't you?" Meryn begged, giving her puppy dog eyes.

"Of course, I will. We can go there after DragonCon next year," she promised.

"Oh no. She talked you into that convention thing." Aiden glared at his mate.

"It's perfectly safe. Think of it this way. It's an event where thousands of people just like Meryn get together for a couple days and live it up," Elizabeth explained. All five men paled.

"Thousands of people," Colton whispered.

"Just like Meryn?" Keelan asked.

Elizabeth looked around. The men had that deer in the headlights looks. "Maybe not *just* like her."

"Thank goodness. One Meryn in the world is enough," Colton teased, looking relieved.

"It's because I'm a 'Limited Edition'. Y'all should be grateful for even knowing me," Meryn huffed.

"We are, my love. We are." Aiden scowled at his men over Meryn's head.

"We wouldn't trade you for a sane version any day," Colton reassured her.

Meryn smiled then frowned. "What do you mean 'sane version'?"

Ryuu walked in holding two baskets. "Here's the bread, fresh from the oven." And just like that, Meryn's attention was diverted. Elizabeth had to hand it to Ryuu; he knew exactly how to handle his charge.

Out of the corner of her eye, she began to see a faint twinkling glow. Without saying a word, she cut up a portion of her pasta into tiny pieces and put them on her bread plate. She pushed the plate toward the little light. Seconds later, the tiny pieces of pasta began to disappear. She watched the entire process in fascination

"I thought life in Lycaonia would be boring," she said under her breath.

"Never, *zain'ka moya,* never," Gavriel said before dropping tiny rolled up bread balls onto the plate next to the pasta. Elizabeth smiled up at her mate as they too began to disappear.

After dinner, the men made their way to their own suites to settle down for the evening. Gavriel, ever the gentleman, offered her his arm. He escorted her as far as the foyer before pausing.

"I had Ryuu get your suitcases and take them to my room. I was not being presumptuous, but I figured that would be the one place I knew where it would not be a problem for them to be there. I have also arranged for a guest room for you, if you prefer." His tone was frosty and his body was tensed.

Her heart turned over. As a little girl, she had dreamed of a handsome prince with courtly manners. Between her own fathers and her uncle, very few men had lived up to her very high expectations. Gavriel had smashed through that glass ceiling and raised the bar infinitely higher.

If she said no, she would have more time to herself. Probably only to think about him and second-guess her decision. If she said yes, she would have to face the fact that she was a mated woman now. She looked up at her mate. His eyes were unreadable. He wasn't pressuring her one way or the other. Not one to shy away from a difficult situation, she realized she knew what she wanted to do.

"I want to stay with you, only..." she hesitated.

"Only what, my mate? Anything you ask for, will be yours," Gavriel assured her.

"Don't expect too much," she blurted out blushing.

He gathered her in his arms and held her close. "Just being here is more than I deserve. There is no way you would fail to meet my expectations, they have been shattered in the face of the beautiful reality that is you."

And there goes my heart, where did it go? Oh yes, in his pocket to carry around for all time.

She sighed and clutched the back of his shirt. He pulled back and kissed her forehead.

"Come, *zain'ka moya*, I will show you to your new home." Gavriel took her hand and led her up the stairs.

"I can stay here, too?" she asked.

"Yes. That was the topic that Aiden and I were discussing before you commandeered his office," he said, sounding faintly amused.

"How could you let your commander function like that? Really? He didn't even have a filing cabinet," she shuddered.

"Now we have you to keep us in line. Between you and Meryn, the unit will be better than ever."

"Are you teasing me?"

"No, my mate, I am sincere. Things have only gotten better since your arrival."

Yup, right there in his pocket.

He led her down a long hallway and turned. They walked until they reached the last door. He opened it and stepped aside to let her walk through. She walked into the dark room and he shut the door behind them wrapping them in total darkness.

"Gavriel..."

"Shh. It is okay," his voice sounded farther away, as if he had crossed the room.

Afraid to trip over any of his furniture she stayed in one place.

"Welcome to my little world," Gavriel said.

Seconds later, tiny lights appeared on the ceiling and walls. Stars, galaxies, whole solar systems swirled around his suite. She gasped and spun around trying to take it all in.

"Vampires are one of the oldest races. There are few secrets of this world that we do not know. But the stars? The stars are still a great mystery. No matter how old I become, I look up and feel like a little boy again when I think about their magnificence," Gavriel said, appearing behind her. He slid his arms around her waist and pulled her against his body.

"Do you think it's the mating pull that makes this feel so right?" she asked, laying her head back on his chest. She felt him shake his head.

"I think the mating pull is there for those who fight their mating. I have seen many couples who have rejected their mates be brought together by the mating pull. It brings them together, but does not ensure happiness. What you feel, what I feel, is when two souls who are destined to be one, come together. I was born for you. My incomplete soul rejoices at finding its other half, and even though it may be jagged and broken, I hope that someday it will be worthy of being the other half of yours."

Elizabeth felt tears well up in her eyes. She turned in his embrace, wrapped her arms around his neck, and squeezed him tight.

"What is this, my mate?" he asked rubbing her back.

"You're just too perfect. You keep saying the most beautiful things and I feel like I will never be good enough to hear them. I know you're old, Gavriel. I don't know how old, but I know you're older than my uncle. Living in Noctem Falls, I've picked up this weird survival sixth sense where I can gauge the age of a vampire and you're pegging off the charts. In all that time, you must have dreamed of your mate. How can I hope to compare to thousands of years' worth of dreams?" she buried her face in his chest.

He pulled back and, in the light of thousands of twinkling stars, she saw the raw emotion in his eyes. The same emotion he tried to keep hidden from others. He spun her around and held her from behind.

"Every year, I added a new star to my story. Every year, I prayed to whoever would listen to send me my mate." His arm lifted, and he pointed to a small bluish light.

"That year, I had to kill my best friend who had turned feral after his mate was murdered by humans. I wept as I added that star as a remembrance to my friend and wished for a soft voice to tell me that it would be okay." He turned their bodies. He pointed to a yellow star blazing bright.

"The year I added that star, I became godfather to the most beautiful baby boy I had ever seen. He was murdered not two months later; he was only been six months old. All I wished for was to have a hand to hold."

When he went to spin them again, she shook her head, weeping. How could something so beautiful contain so much pain? He walked around to stand in front of her.

"I did not tell you this to make you sad. The memories are painful. But it would be even more horrendous if I forgot them completely. Each year, I memorized a new star, so I would not forget. And every year, I made the same plea. 'Please send me my mate. I just want someone to hold'. That is all I wanted. So, even though I have lived thousands upon thousands of years, you fulfill every dream I have ever had for a mate, just by being here. Your compassion and your blossoming love is more than I have ever wanted." He reached down and held her face between his two large hands. She had never wanted someone more in her whole life. She wanted to erase every moment of pain and replace it with one of pure pleasure.

She reached up and pulled him down by the collar of his button-down shirt. She feasted on his mouth, sucking his lower lip until he groaned. Seconds later, he took control. He forced her mouth open and laid his claim. He dipped and teased. He traced her lips and dominated her completely. Shaken by his urgency, she felt her knees give way, and he simply held her to him.

When he pulled back, he was breathing hard.

"I have to stop now, or I will not be able to stop at all," he admitted. She stepped back and he let her. Smiling, she pulled her shirt over her head and his eyes widened.

"Then don't stop," she whispered. She turned to walk to the bed and, in an effort to be sexy, tripped over her own feet, and landed hard.

"Beth!" He was by her side in an instant, helping her sit up.

"Just ignore me. I'll sleep in the bathtub," she mumbled, too embarrassed to look up. She licked her lip and tasted copper. She had busted her own lip open. Perfect.

"My walking disaster," he said, and using his hand, lifted her chin so that she was looking up at him. The second the scent of her blood hit him, she saw his jaw tighten.

"Beth, go! Aiden's suite is down the hall on the left." Breathing hard, he scooted away.

"Not a snowball's chance in hell. You're going to bite me again whether you like it or not. Don't think I've forgotten the pleasure you gave me earlier. That is happening again, mister." Not only was she aching for the pleasure only he could give her, she also needed to feed him. She had noticed how much better he had appeared after he fed from her that morning.

She flipped over on her back and tried to shimmy out of her jeans. When they wouldn't go down any further, she began cussing as it dawned on her that she had forgotten to take her boots off. She tried to pull her jeans down over her boots but they were stuck. She tried to pull her jeans back up, but they were wrapped around the rubber soles of her boots. In a growing sense of horror, she realized how ridiculous she must look.

When she glanced up, she watched as Gavriel's red eyes shifted back to gray. He stared at her with a shocked expression on his face. Feeling completely humiliated, she covered her face with both hands.

"Don't look!" she cried.

The sound of ripping fabric had her looking down. Gavriel had simply shredded her jeans. Two seconds later, he looked up, a savage expression on his face. He reached forward and her body jerked as he ripped her panties from her body. In an effort to save her favorite bra she reached around behind her before his extended claw cut away the fabric between her breasts.

"What were you saying?" he asked, crawling forward on his hands and knees.

"I don't honestly remember," she admitted.

His strong hands easily unzipped her boots, and it wasn't long before he had removed both and her socks as well. Sitting in front of him on his floor as naked as the day she was born, she had never felt sexier. His eyes were flickering between the color of molten mercury and deep burgundy.

"Mine!" he growled. He placed both hands on the inside of her thighs and spread her wide. She opened her mouth to protest but nearly swallowed her tongue instead. He lowered his head and began to make love to her with his mouth. He mimicked what he had just done to her in their kiss. When two fingers speared her deeply, she cried out.

"Do that again!" she demanded.

A masculine chuckle responded. He took her clit between his teeth and curled his fingers deep inside her.

"Gods! Yes! More!" She bucked her hips. He sat up and in a blur of motion began removing his own clothing. When he knelt, his body looming over her, she had a moment to look her fill. The promise of his broad shoulders under his button down shirt had been fulfilled. His entire body shifted under his skin as his muscles flexed. She wanted to lean forward and trace each muscle with her tongue, but he moved with a sense of purpose.

When he was poised between her legs she thought that he would plunge deep and give them both what they were desperate for. Instead, he kissed the inside of each thigh.

"Elizabeth Monroe, Fate may have chosen you for me, but I ask that you choose me for yourself. Will you tie your breath, your heart, mind, and soul to mine? Will you place yourself into my keeping for all eternity?"

There was no hesitation in her heart. "Yes. I want you for all time," she whispered.

"Yes!" he hissed and eased himself forward. Inch by inch, he claimed her. Stretching her completely, he slowly slid past every nerve ending bringing her closer and closer to what she wanted.

Without warning, he pulled back and slammed forward. Again and again, he sunk himself deep, making sure that he pleased her with each thrust.

"You are mine! I am never letting you go!" He rose up over her and struck quickly, sinking his fangs deep into her neck. Her body reacted instantly, throwing her into a whirlpool of pleasure. From the most hidden recesses of her soul, she felt herself lift up. She felt Gavriel's soul answer in response. It wrapped around hers protectively; even in its most primal state, it sought to keep her safe. She experienced the most pure moment of her existence when, for one perfect heartbeat, they were completely one. A second later, they were wrenched apart as their souls unwound and made their way back to their bodies, each carrying a piece of the other with it. Once back in her own body, wave after wave crashed through her. His fangs claimed her from the top down and his cock from the bottom up. He owned every inch of her. Screaming out her pleasure, she rode her orgasm until she had no strength left. She let it take her over. She hung on long enough to hear his roar as he found his pleasure and to feel the warm stream of cum as it filled her. She heard the pounding at the door and didn't even care. Sighing happily, she let the darkness take her

CHAPTER THREE

"Beth, darling, please open your lovely blue eyes," she heard her mate beg.

"No, don't wanna," she pouted. The bed under her was plush, and she wanted to sink down and go back to sleep.

"I need to make sure you're okay. I promised Aiden that if you did not wake after an hour, I would take you to the clinic." She felt a warm finger tap her cheek.

"Aiden? When was he here?" she asked struggling to open her eyes. When she managed to pry them open, she had to blink a few times before he came into focus.

"Umm, right at the end. You're a screamer, my mate." Gavriel tapped her lips.

"Oh. My. Gods. Please tell me he didn't see anything."

"No, I would not let any other male see my mate's beautiful body. I covered you with a blanket and then answered the door. I almost killed that silly cub." Gavriel shook his head. "Though I am grateful at his concern for your wellbeing."

"Cub? I guess he would be a cub to you. Why do you take orders from him anyway? In fact, why aren't you an Elder?" she asked, pulling a blanket up around her chest as she sat up in bed. He propped his head up on his hand. Her eyes traveled down the long length of his body. He wasn't overly hairy, just enough in all the right places. His waist wasn't thin like the pubescent boys that were currently all the rage in advertising in the human world. He had a trim waist, but was solidly built. His well-defined abs made her want to drizzle honey on each crease and make a meal out of him. Even though she was slightly sore from his claiming, she felt herself tighten at the thought of licking every inch of her mate.

"Whatever you are thinking, I like it," Gavriel said, his voice sounding deeper.

"Can you see my thoughts?" she squeaked.

"No, but based on your reaction, I am sad that I cannot. We will be able to feel some emotion and, over the centuries, certain projected thoughts, but that is all," he explained.

"Not all vampires can do that."

"You are right."

"How old are you?" she asked.

He sighed and rolled over onto his back, effectively putting his gorgeous cock on display.

"Stop teasing me." She popped him in the face with his pillow.

Smiling, he pulled the blanket around his waist to cover up and used the pillow to lie next to her. She scooted down until they were eye to eye. He took her hand and simply held it.

"I will be honest with you. I do not know how old I am. I was not lying when I told you I use the stars to remember. Before the invention of the projector I have, I would memorize the position of each star and affix a memory to it. I have forgotten so much, my age is just one of the many things lost to time. To answer your question, I take orders from Aiden because he is our commander. He is strong, fair, and good at being the Unit Commander. I swore an oath to him when he was barely a man, to serve him because I saw the potential in him. He has not let me down yet," he paused, and then frowned before continuing.

"As for being an Elder, I do want that title. If the other elders realized how old I am, they would come to me constantly for answers. The way we rule now works. No one family or person is in charge for very long and it keeps new ideas coming in and prevents any one faction from creating a dictatorship. I like my life the way it is now. That is why I have been hiding my transition; if they discovered my age, it could destroy the precarious balance we have finally attained in our world."

"What you must have seen and done," she said in wonder. "Did you get to see Elvis?" she asked suddenly.

His mouth dropped. "I watched entire empires emerge and fall. Gods rule and disappear. The undocumented miracles of magic and science, kings, queens, wars, and you ask about Elvis?" he asked incredulously.

She smirked. "You totally saw him in concert." She tickled his calves with her toes.

He scowled at her. "Twice," he murmured.

"Ha! I knew it!" she giggled.

"The man was pure genius. His live performances had an element that was never captured by any recording device. I was truly sad when he passed on," he admitted.

"What else?" she prompted then yawned.

"The first time I heard a full orchestra I wept. There were so many beautiful sounds that it overwhelmed me," his eyes softened at the memory. "Tell me something about you," he prompted.

Elizabeth snuggled closer, her eyelids getting heavy. "Much to my family's delight, I refused to date vampires growing up." She grinned at his expression.

"Why?"

"My father has been likened to the Greek legend Adonis and my uncle to an avenging angel. The bar was set kinda high."

"Oh really? And how did I measure up?" He poked her side, making her laugh.

"There is no comparison. You became everything I didn't even know I wanted."

"I think Fate knew you were meant for just one vampire." He kissed her gently.

She pulled back and yawned in his face, then frowned at her own tiredness. He chuckled lowly and pulled her close. He reached up and tapped the light above them sending them out amongst the stars again.

"Goodnight, my mate," he whispered.

"Goodnight, *my* vampire," she quipped back.

My vampire, the one who has completely stolen my heart.

She woke up alone, Gavriel's side of the bed cool to the touch. He had to have gotten up at least an hour ago. At the foot of the bed, he had set up her suitcases so she would see them. She tumbled out of bed and landed on the floor staring up at the ceiling. It looked so plain in the daylight. She frowned at the open curtains and raised blinds. She wanted to lower them to block the sun so she could see his stars again, but contented herself to wait for Gavriel.

Standing, she turned to see she was in front of a full-length mirror. She leered at herself as her body reminded her of the previous night's pleasure. Picking

up the small bag that held her toiletries, she started
looking for the bathroom. The first door she opened
was a closet, the second a small study. When she
opened the third one and discovered a library she was
about to panic. Vampires peed. She knew they did, she
had been raised with them. The fourth and final door
led to an opulent bathroom. She looked around. Was
she really allowed in here? Shrugging, she walked in
and found the shower. The warm colored Italian
stonework made the entire experience decadent.

Wrapped in a towel, she padded over to the mirror
and shook out her long blonde hair. She stuck out her
tongue then crossed her eyes at herself. Surprisingly,
her mate had a wall mounted hair dryer. She smiled,
remembering his long dark hair. She supposed even
vampires didn't like walking around with wet hair in
the winter. She shook her head; the man was too
gorgeous for her sanity. She dried her hair, styling it so
that it fell around her face and down her back in
waves. She applied her normal moisturizer, make up,
deodorant, lotion, and perfume. She walked back out
into the bedroom and knelt by her open suitcase. She
carefully lifted out her favorite cream cashmere
sweater and sighed happily. She loved quality
clothing. It was a by-product of being raised with
tailor-made clothing. She dug out another pair of
jeans, lace boy shorts with matching bra, and socks.
She quickly got dressed and looked from her short
slouch boots to her knee-high, brown leather riding
boots. She chose the knee-high boots to complete her
ensemble. She grabbed her wristlet that held her
phone, money, ID, and lipstick and walked out of the
room.

She retraced their steps from the previous night
until she found the main stairway. She headed down
the stairs and made her way to the dining room. When
she walked in, the men quieted and stood. Aiden

flushed red and Colton gave her a thumbs up sign. Rolling her eyes, she walked over to her mate. He pulled out her seat, and she sat down. He leaned down and kissed her cheek before taking his seat next to her. She placed her wristlet on the table.

"Please tell me that last night wasn't the first time you all heard someone having sex." She arched her eyebrow as Keelan began to choke on his waffle.

"Not true. We thought Aiden put Meryn's head through a wall one night." Colton spoke up.

"You heard that?" Aiden asked, practically shouting.

"Why are you being loud?" Meryn demanded. Aiden gulped and shoveled a huge forkful of bacon into his mouth.

"Please tell me there's coffee," Elizabeth looked around.

"It must be a female thing," Keelan whispered to Colton. Elizabeth turned to the young witch and stared. Both he and Colton turned their attention back to their breakfast.

Ryuu walked in from the kitchen. He set what looked like a second cup in front of Meryn before placing one in front of her. "I prepared a cappuccino since that is Meryn's favorite, but if you let me know what your morning preferences are I can make them for you."

Elizabeth took a sip and shuddered. "Oh Gods, yes!" she took another sip and sighed happily. Gavriel growled at Ryuu.

Aiden nodded waving a fork at his second in command. "Now you know how I feel. It's not right that another male can make our mates sound like that," he grumbled.

"Ryuu is Coffee God. Ryuu can do whatever the fuck he wants." Meryn's gravelly, irritated voice sounded different from the more upbeat personality she had met the day before.

"All hail Coffee God." Keelan and Colton bowed down in their seats reverently to Ryuu who shook his head at their antics.

"What toppings would you like for your waffles, Lady Elizabeth?" Ryuu asked.

"Fresh strawberries with whip cream please," she said without hesitation.

Meryn frowned at her. "You say that like you expected him to ask you."

Elizabeth looked up at Ryuu who shrugged. "He's a squire, Meryn. I was raised being served by a squire. In fact, my father's squire helped raise me to a certain degree. I meant no disrespect."

Ryuu set a napkin in her lap. "None taken. Meryn is still getting used to the fact that I am a servant."

"Of course you are. You're a squire." Elizabeth didn't understand the confusion.

Gavriel took her hand. "Meryn was raised in the human world. She is used to the negative view and contempt that most humans show toward their servants. Since she was not raised in our society, she has not seen the respect and reverence that most squires receive. She is very protective of Ryuu," he explained.

Elizabeth turned to Meryn. "That is just so adorable. That's it; I'm adopting you."

Gavriel nearly dropped his coffee and Aiden inhaled a piece of bacon and immediately began to choke, he pounded on his own chest in an effort to clear his airway.

Gavriel turned to her frowning. "What was that?"

"I said I am adopting Meryn. Evidently, you all haven't been adequate in showing her our world, so I will. From now on she will be my baby sister." Feeling happy with the morning's accomplishments, she sipped her cappuccino.

"Wait. I have a sister, now?" Meryn asked sounding more awake.

"Yes, I have adopted you."

"Does that mean you'll take me to DragonCon and buy me cool tee-shirts and pay for the strippers in the hotel room?" Meryn definitely looked more awake now.

"Of course."

"Whoa, whoa, whoa. Who said anything about strippers?" Aiden demanded, pounding the table.

Elizabeth pointed to Meryn. "She did."

Gavriel nipped at her shoulder making her breath catch. "You do not want to find out how jealous I can be, *zain'ka moya*," he said, his warm breath tickling her sensitized neck.

Meryn smiled at her. "I think I'll like having a sister. Am I related to that Magnus guy now?"

Elizabeth caught Meryn's wink and rolled with it. "Absolutely. I'll call him later to let him know."

"Hey! She is not related to the Rioux, she is a McKenzie!" Aiden growled.

"Technically, I'm an Evans. We're not married, just living in sin," Meryn corrected him.

Elizabeth turned her head before she laughed out loud and ruined everything. Aiden looked like his head was about to explode.

"You are too a McKenzie! We're mated!" Aiden boomed.

Meryn held up her empty left hand. "This says I am single. I'm only mated to you in Lycaonia and that is tee tiny compared to the whole freaking world. Even my driver's license says Evans," she countered.

Aiden stood, his barrel chest heaving. "We'll see about that. Men, move out!" he barked and walked away, fuming. Keelan groaned and Colton pounded his head on the table before looking up to glare at Meryn.

"Can you please, please, *please* not piss him off before a day where we are doing nothing but drills?" Colton complained.

"Now!" was the angry shout from the foyer.

"Fuck me." Colton groaned and stood. He, Keelan, and Darian filed out of the dining room toward the door.

Gavriel stood and kissed her on the cheek. "I am feeling nearly normal today, I think I will see how drills go. Try not to wreak too much havoc today."

"We make no promises," she teased.

"Have fun beating on each other." Meryn grinned at him and waved her fork.

After the front door slammed shut, Meryn let out a breath and put her fork down.

"Okay, what was that all about?" Elizabeth asked.

Ryuu walked in and put a plate of waffles in front of her before going to Meryn. "I'm curious as well. You deliberately baited him; despite your wackiness, you hardly ever upset your mate deliberately." He sat down next to her.

"Aiden asked about children again last night. I wanted to distract him with something else for a while." Meryn shrugged and picked at her waffle.

"Oh, honey, of course he's asking about children, he's a male shifter. What did you tell him?" Elizabeth bit into her waffle and looked down, surprised; Ryuu could really cook!

"I told him I didn't want to be put on any psycho hit list because he knocked me up and that we'd have plenty of time for kids later, like, much, much later. Though I don't know if that's an option anymore." Meryn finally gave up any pretense of eating and put her fork down.

"You don't like kids do you?" Elizabeth guessed.

"Nope. I'm not comfortable around babies. I wouldn't mind if they hatched and were like four or five. You know walking and talking. So they could be like, 'Hey Mom, I gotta pee.' Or, 'Mom, I'm hungry.' At which point I could say, 'Go tell Ryuu'. I never had a mom, I don't think I can be one."

Elizabeth couldn't stand the look on Meryn's face; she looked so dejected and lost. "I never had a mother either you know, and I plan to totally rock being a mom. I mean you get to mold their little minds from the second they are born."

Meryn perked up. "What do you mean?"

Elizabeth continued. "My kids are going to be awesome. I will read to them and make sure they know how to get to Narnia or what to do if the Doctor ever grabs their hand and says 'run!' and they'll know what the one true ring is."

Meryn smiled. "I never thought about it like that. It would be like getting a brand new laptop and you can install whatever new apps you want on it or dress it up with a new skin."

"We can roll with that analogy. Meryn, there's no rule book. As long as the kid is breathing, not hungry, semi-clean, and not rocking in the corner drooling on itself, you're doing a good job." Elizabeth took another bite of her waffle.

"Really? That seems too easy."

"I mean it's a lifelong responsibility, you'll worry about the little bastard until the day you die. But the fun stuff outweighs that."

"And it's not like you'll be alone. I would be more than honored to help. I'll have you know I am an expert at changing diapers." Ryuu ruffled Meryn's hair.

"Thanks, guys. I feel a little bit better about the whole thing. I could be pregnant, it's not like we've been using birth control. I just felt trapped. I wanted more time," she paused then looked up. "What if the ones responsible for killing all those women come after my baby?" she asked in a tiny voice.

And there is the real crux of the issue. She's already afraid for her future child.

"Meryn, how can you say you won't be a good mother when you're already worrying about them?" Elizabeth demanded.

Meryn blinked then smiled.

"*Denka*, I swear to you, no one will ever hurt you or your child. You are under my protection." Ryuu's body practically glowed blue. Elizabeth saw a tiny light hovering around Meryn's ear.

"Plus, you have me, my fathers, my uncle, Gavriel, your mate, and every single unit warrior in the world willing to kill to protect you." Elizabeth motioned to the frantic little light.

"Oh Felix! Thank you!" Meryn cuddled empty air and looked up. "He said he would guard my baby every night."

"See, whenever it happens, you'll have all the support you need." Elizabeth wiped her mouth and sat back with her cappuccino.

"I'll talk to Aiden tonight. But in the meantime, what are we doing today?" Meryn turned to face her.

"I don't suppose you know how to get to the city, do you?" she asked.

"I sure do. Ryuu, will you come with us?" Meryn turned to her squire.

"Of course, *denka*. Just give me a few minutes to finish cleaning up after breakfast." He stood, went to the hallway, and returned with a coat and scarf. He hung it on the back of Meryn's chair and with a bow, left for the kitchen.

"Our order for supplies shouldn't arrive today. Who did you call yesterday to place the order?" Elizabeth asked.

"Ohmigosh, I need to introduce you to Adelaide, that's Aiden's mom. I placed the order with her squire, Marius. He is marvelous." Meryn pulled her backpack onto her lap and pulled out a tiny coat. "Here you go Felix." The coat was visible and suspended for one second, and then disappeared. Meryn turned to her. "Sprites are sensitive to the cold. I also had Adelaide knit me a scarf with a sprite pocket so he could be warm on my shoulder. She made it look like the fourth Doctor's scarf for me." Meryn lifted a brightly colored scarf from the back of her chair.

"That's really neat." Elizabeth paused; her own coat was probably stiff as a board caked in mud, growing mushrooms in her trunk. She eyed the tiny Meryn. She was at least six inches taller than her friend.

"Could we head to the cleaners? My coat is going to need to be cleaned before I can wear it."

"That's cool. I know the witches that run the tailors shop that does cleaning and preserving. It's where Aiden keeps his dress whites." Meryn wrapped the scarf around her neck until her lower face disappeared. Elizabeth smiled at the young woman. By paranormal standards Meryn was still almost a child. Sisterly affection welled up inside her.

"You are too cute!" She laughed as Meryn tried to spit out yarn fuzz.

"I am not cute. I am sexy and alluring," Meryn protested.

"Sorry to burst your bubble, short stack, but you're so cute, it should be illegal."

"You were an only child weren't you?" Meryn asked sourly.

"Yes and I have always wanted a sister. You're it."

"Is it just me or are you teasing me more today than yesterday?"

"Of course, I am. I have adopted you, so gloves are off. You now matter to me, so I don't have to be nice."

"Wait. So, because I'm now family, you can be mean to me? How does that work?" Meryn demanded.

"Meryn, I grew up the only niece to the ruling vampire elder. I was constantly at court. I learned from an early age that it's just easier to be pleasant to the people who don't matter. I don't let them see the real me. But once you're my friend, all bets are off."

Meryn shook her head. "I'm exactly opposite. I don't talk to and am mean to anyone I don't know and am only nice to the ones I do know and like."

"Just different sides of the same coin. Now. What am I going to do about a coat?" Elizabeth frowned. Maybe she could borrow one of Gavriel's.

Ryuu walked in carrying her now immaculate looking full-length gray wool trench coat. "Lady Elizabeth, when taking out your luggage yesterday I noticed the state of your coat. I hope you don't mind that I took the liberty of cleaning it for you." Ryuu held her coat open for her.

Elizabeth looked at Ryuu and smiled. "You're amazing; you do know that, right?" She slipped her arms through the sleeves and inspected the wool. Not a single stain or mark. She stuffed her wristlet in her coat pocket.

Ryuu gave a nod, smiled, and went to help Meryn who was turning circles trying to get her arm in her other sleeve. Once Meryn had her coat on, they headed to her car. She smiled when she saw that someone had changed her back two tires. Living with a house full of men was looking better and better.

"Okay, where am I heading?" Elizabeth asked after they got in. She adjusted her mirrors before turning to look at Meryn.

"Go down this road until we get to the Shifter Elder's estate; you really can't miss it. That's where Aiden's parents live. I want you to meet Adelaide and Marius, from there we can head into the city, and I can introduce you to Sydney and Justice at my most favorite place ever, their café The Jitterbug," Meryn said, sounding slightly muffled from her scarf.

"Looks like we have a plan." Elizabeth put it in drive and rolled out of the driveway. Looking in her rearview mirror, she hoped her mate was having a good day with his pissed off commander.

"Why would she say that?" Gavriel heard his friend ask for the tenth time. The men were standing around the training grounds as Aiden vented.

"I have to admit, it's not like her. She'll tease as good as the next guy, but she never tries to hurt you," Colton agreed.

"Does a wedding mean that much to her?" Keelan asked.

Aiden shook his head. "I asked her about it once, she said there was no point because there wouldn't be anyone to invite from her side of the family. If she had honestly shown any interest, I would have already planned the biggest wedding this city had ever seen." Aiden paced back and forth.

"Maybe she's upset about something else?" Sascha suggested.

"Do you hog all the blankets?" Quinn asked. The men turned and stared at him. "What? My mom is always complaining to my father about that," he said defensively.

"Let's look at this logically..." Ben started. All eyes swung to him. He backtracked. "Okay, as logically as possible when dealing with Meryn. She's pretty surface level when it comes to her emotions. If she's mad, she punches you. When she's happy, she jumps around and tries to kiss your face. So if she said something about matings, maybe she's worried about something else in your relationship."

Aiden gasped and turned to his brother. "I think you nailed it. I..." he hesitated and looked around. The men gathered closer. Gavriel rolled his eyes, the warriors were worse than the old women at the sewing circle when it came to juicy news.

Aiden cleared his throat. "I told her she had to stop interrupting our training sessions, and I asked her about children again," he admitted. The men sucked in their breaths.

"Well, no wonder she was acting out this morning." Darian nodded.

"Why would she act out?" Aiden asked.

"Because, my old friend, she doesn't like being told what to do, and she is terrified of bringing a child into a world where psychotic killers are killing and mutilating pregnant women and their unborn children," Gavriel explained. He paused and let the words sink in. Aiden turned milk white.

"There's no way I'd let anything happen to her or our child," Aiden protested.

"Not to sound like a bastard, but wasn't she attacked at the Alpha estate like a month ago?" Quinn reminded him. All eyes glared at the young witch. He held up his hands defensively. "It's true isn't it?"

"He's right. Of course, she'd be scared. What can we do?" Aiden resumed his pacing.

Gavriel noticed that this had now become everyone's problem. The men all frowned and no one spoke.

"Maybe we could install some sort of alarm system at the house?" Keelan suggested.

Aiden looked at him like he was a genius. "Keelan, that's brilliant! What kind of alarm system?"

"Could we not just get what humans use? They are easy to install and would alert us if anyone tried to break a window or come through a locked door," Gavriel said, suggesting the easiest solution.

"We can do better than humans!" Sascha scoffed.

"We sure can! Oh, I know. What if when the door opens an axe swings down and cuts the intruder in half?" Graham, the bear shifting Delta Unit leader, suggested. Gavriel stared. Keelan, Darian, and Colton looked at each other nervously. They had to live there, too.

"How would the axe know it wasn't one of us?" Keelan asked.

"Good point," Graham murmured, rubbing his bearded chin. The men all nodded.

"Isn't that your mate's car?" Darian asked as the car in question drove down the driveway.

"Yes and unless my eyes are mistaken, Ryuu and Meryn are with her," Darian said.

"That's perfect. We can install whatever protective measures we come up with to the house while they're gone. Okay men. Let's head to the armory and see what we have to work with." Aiden started walking toward the small building that housed all of their weapons.

The men followed behind Aiden talking excitedly. Only he, Darian, Keelan, and Colton lingered back.

"We're going to die, aren't we?" Keelan asked morosely.

"All in the name of love. Come on men, if we're quick enough we can keep them away from the explosives," Colton said.

Gavriel watched the dust cloud settle over the dirt road where his mate had just driven.

I hope your day is going better than mine, zain'ka moya.

CHAPTER FOUR

Oh fuck me! I forgot about the damn sewing circle meeting. Abort! Abort!" Meryn cried from the backseat.

"Too late, we've been spotted," Elizabeth pointed to a woman waving at them enthusiastically in front of the house.

"Damn, that's Horseface. There's no turning back now," Meryn groaned.

"Horseface?" Elizabeth looked at the woman and immediately saw why Meryn had dubbed this woman with the nickname. It wasn't exactly kind, but very accurate.

"I'm terrible with names," Meryn admitted.

When they came to a stop, Ryuu got out of the car and held the door open for Meryn. Elizabeth got out and walked around to stand by her friend.

"Meryn, dah-liiing! We didn't know you would be coming today. How wonderful! I was just saying to Daphne how we missed you at our little meetings. Better late than never, I always say. Who is your friend?" she asked, turning to Elizabeth.

Elizabeth plastered a smile on her face and held out her hand. "I'm Elizabeth Monroe. It's a pleasure to meet you."

"I'm Rosalind Carmichael. Monroe? You wouldn't be any relation to Broderick Monroe would you?" she asked.

"Yes, he is my father."

Rosalind's hand went to her throat in a nervous gesture. "Oh dear, what an honor. Come on girls, this way. I'm sure we can brew some more tea for you two dears." Rosalind picked up the basket she had retrieved from her car and pointed to the door. Ryuu stepped forward and took the basket from her hands. Rosalind tittered at Ryuu, blushing. Meryn rolled her eyes and followed the woman inside. Rosalind waved at them and went into the drawing room excited to be the one to share news that they were coming to their meeting.

"Meryn, what on earth are you doing here?" a soft voice asked, sounding surprised. A lovely woman dressed in a bright yellow dress walked toward them from the hallway carrying a small sewing basket.

"Hey Mom, I kinda forgot what day it was. I wanted to introduce my new friend. We didn't mean to crash your sewing circle meeting," Meryn explained, unwinding her scarf.

The lovely woman turned to her. "And who is your new friend?" she asked, smiling warmly.

"Adelaide, this is Elizabeth Monroe, she is Gavriel's mate. She's adopted me as her little sister because evidently I'm 'too cute'. Elizabeth, this is Adelaide McKenzie, Aiden's mother." Meryn said, introducing them.

Elizabeth was immediately enveloped in a warm hug. When Adelaide pulled back, Elizabeth could see genuine affection in her eyes. "Welcome Elizabeth. Since you have adopted Meryn and she's my daughter that must mean you're mine as well." Adelaide's warm hands squeezed hers before she pulled Meryn into a similar hug. Adelaide pulled back and cocked her head to one side looking down at Meryn with a puzzled expression. She shook her head and grinned.

"I had a feeling you wouldn't be here unless you had forgotten the day," Adelaide teased.

"Mom!" Meryn blushed.

"Might as well come inside. We're just starting a new project. I was on my way back to the drawing room from upstairs. We're switching to a quilting project so I had to change baskets. I'll have Marius make a pot of Honeycup just for you and we'll put out a few teaspoons of warmed honey for Felix." Adelaide looped her arms through theirs and led them to the front drawing room. Ryuu followed. He walked over and handed Rosalind her basket. She giggled and blinked her eyelashes at him. He bowed in a gentlemanly way and walked over to stand next to Marius.

"Ladies, I'm excited to say that my daughter Meryn and the newest member of our family, Elizabeth Monroe, have decided to join us today." Adelaide turned to the tall silver haired man standing against the wall. "Marius, can you prepare Meryn's favorite tea and a treat for our sprite friend as well?"

Marius nodded. "Of course, my lady."

Ryuu turned to Marius. "It would be an honor to help you serve these lovely ladies today."

The women in the room giggled. Elizabeth met Ryuu's eyes; the barest of nods to the woman in the corner was all she needed. She nodded back and sat down, effectively putting herself between Meryn and the garishly dressed woman Ryuu had indicated. Both she and Meryn placed their coats on the backs of their chairs.

"Elizabeth Monroe, a bunny?" the garish woman asked, her tone condescendingly neutral. Elizabeth watched Meryn hunch a little; she could tell that her friend was fighting to keep a scowl off her face. Poor

Meryn. She hadn't been raised around women like this one; luckily Elizabeth had.

"Actually, it's *lepus curpaeums,*" Meryn corrected.

The woman smiled at Meryn patronizingly. "That's just another way to say bunny, dear, why get so wrapped up in the technicalities? Of course, as a human, you wouldn't understand."

Meryn blinked and then smiled. "So, if it's okay to call Elizabeth a bunny, then could I call you a bitch?" Meryn asked sweetly.

Adelaide started choking on her tea. Elizabeth turned to the flustered woman to divert her attention away from Meryn.

"I'm sorry, have we met?" she asked, assuming her most pleasant tone.

The woman looked embarrassed for a moment before she waved a purple handkerchief between them. "You must be new to Lycaonia. I'm so used to everyone here knowing who I am. My name is Daphne Bowers, pleasure to meet you. I have to ask, are you related to that brilliant, handsome scientist working on a blood substitute in Noctem Falls?"

"Pleasure," Elizabeth said, deliberately not answering the woman's question.

After a few moments of silence, Daphne spoke up. "Are you, dear?"

"I'm sorry, there are many scientists working in Noctem Falls, which one were you referring to?" Elizabeth said, being as obtuse as possible. By drawing out this line of questioning she would make Daphne unintentionally highlight her true intentions. Elizabeth had played this game before.

"Broderick Monroe, of course. His assistant, Caspian Rioux, is the vampire elder's younger brother," Daphne clarified.

"Oh yes, you mean my father and his mate, Caspian. Yes, they are working on a blood substitute."

"Oh? Are they mated? I thought Caspian was his assistant. His good looks are simply be wasted being mated to another man," Daphne sighed.

Elizabeth smiled at the other ladies before turning to look at Daphne. "I didn't realize that the ruling houses in Lycaonia were so out of touch. That's just sad," she pouted then continued. "My fathers have been mated for over one hundred and fifty years; to think that you wouldn't know something that is common knowledge everywhere else is, well, forgive the term, but pathetic really." Elizabeth heard the tiniest of sounds and saw that Meryn's eyes were practically bugging out in the effort not to laugh.

Just about that time, Ryuu and Marius walked in carrying two trays. Ryuu immediately went to Meryn and poured her tea and set out the warmed honey for Felix while Marius set a tea service down in front of her. She saw that he was barely concealing a grin. When he straightened he gave a small bow. "Your tea, Lady Elizabeth."

"Thank you Marius, I'm sure it will be perfect." She smirked up at him before he and Ryuu went to stand by the wall.

Visibly agitated, Daphne sipped from her teacup. "Such relationships are subject to opinion," she said, her sweet tone slipping.

Elizabeth turned to Daphne and widened her eyes taking on her most innocent of faces. "Whatever do you mean, Daphne?" she said, deliberately dropping the 'Lady' honorific. She saw Daphne flinch.

"Surely not everyone in Noctem Falls believes in matings between men?"

"Fate chooses our mates for us. Who are we to go against Fate?" Elizabeth asked.

"That's exactly what I'm saying dear, that certain couples must be going against what Fate has planned for them," Daphne nodded to the other women in the room who looked on as the two of them continued to go back and forth.

"So you're saying that my father and Caspian of the House of Rioux are too stupid to recognize that they aren't mates?" she asked keeping her tone even.

"Of course not..." Daphne said.

"Then you must be stating that Fate herself is in error. I have to say I am shocked. I never thought I would encounter such blasphemous opinions here in Lycaonia." Elizabeth clucked and sipped her tea.

"I never knew Daphne felt that way."

"Shocking."

"Who knew?"

The women around them murmured amongst themselves. Elizabeth didn't dare to look over at Daphne; instead she turned to Adelaide.

"Lady McKenzie, I must say your home is one of the finest I have ever seen. My Uncle Magnus has such a sweet tooth, I know that he would be envious of this fantastic tea that you have served." Elizabeth held up her cup and took another sip.

"Thank you, Elizabeth. I'm afraid that tea is one of my vices. My boys give it to me every year for Christmas. I could arrange for some to be sent to your uncle," Adelaide offered. Elizabeth knew that Adelaide offered out of genuine kindness and not as a way to garner favor. The rumors she had heard of this woman were true. She was a rare kind soul.

"Thank you! If you could tell me where to purchase some, I would like to send it home as a present this year. That man is so hard to shop for. I mean, what do you get someone who literally has everything?" Elizabeth gave an exaggerated sigh.

"Lady Elizabeth, I don't mean to be a bother, but, well, is your father truly as handsome as they say?" Rosalind asked, blushing.

"Oh my, yes! Drat the man. Do you know how hard it was for me to find someone to date? None of the men who approached me even compared, that is, until Gavriel," she hid her smile in her teacup as gasps raced around the room.

"Gavriel? Do you mean Gavriel Ambrosios?" a dark haired lady sitting to the right of Daphne asked.

"Yes, Gavriel is my mate. I was claimed yesterday," she replied calmly as chaos broke out around her.

"I can't believe it!"

"Another warrior has mated!"

"How romantic!"

"That means that House Ambrosios and House Rioux are now tied together," one woman whispered and everyone got quiet.

Sugar. Honey. Iced. Tea! Note to self: Call Father to let him know I've mated.

"Adelaide, you must have been mistaken. I could have sworn you said that Elizabeth was a new family member when you introduced her," Daphne said, wiping her brow with her useless purple satin handkerchief.

"Oh, she wasn't mistaken. I have adopted Meryn as my little sister. She is tied to House McKenzie, House Ambrosios and now House Rioux and is under my personal protection."

Elizabeth looked Daphne in the eye as she spoke the last words. She watched as the woman paled. In the background, they heard a tower bell chime.

"I'm sorry to say that is all the time we have for today ladies," Adelaide said, jumping to her feet. Instantly, the ladies were standing and whispering to each other as they made their way out the door.

"Meryn, excuse me for just a moment, I really need to call my father before one of these ladies leaks it out that I am now mated." Elizabeth stood and reached

into her pocket and pulled out her wristlet. Meryn
nodded.

Marius stepped forward. "This way, Lady
Elizabeth."

"Thank you Marius," Elizabeth said and then
followed the man down the hallway to an empty
office. When Marius left, closing the door behind him
she pulled out her phone and called her father.

"Hey pumpkin! I was hoping to hear from you
today. Did you make it to Lycaonia in one piece?" her
father asked as his way of answering the phone.
Elizabeth felt tears prick at her eyes. She could just
imagine her father smiling in the middle of his lab, her
other father would be standing close to the phone,
listening in, both would be wearing lab coats,
whatever experiment they had been working on
forgotten in light of her phone call. She couldn't help
the sniffle that emerged. So much had happened; she
was suddenly very homesick.

"Bethy? Baby? What is it? Are you hurt?" her
father asked, sounding frantic, and no wonder. She
hardly ever cried, not even when she had fallen out of
that dratted office window.

"Bethy is hurt? Where is she?" she heard her Uncle
Magnus demand in the background.

"Magnus hush she has not said anything yet." her
other father, Caspian said.

"I just miss you all so much." She felt her throat
close. This wasn't like her at all; she was not an
emotional person.

"She's crying! She never cries! What has happened,
darling?" her father demanded.

"I'm okay, really. I don't know what's come over
me." She wiped her eyes.

"Do you need us to come to you?" Caspian asked
gently.

"No, really I'm fine."

"You're not fine. You didn't cry when you broke your arm, or your other arm or your leg or your nose or..." her father rattled off. She grinned and laughed between tears.

"I'm mated," she said and then there was silence.

"Papa? Daddy? Unky?" she called out using her childhood nickname for her uncle.

"Has he hurt you? Is that why you are crying?" her uncle asked, his voice dangerously low.

"No, he is the most wonderful gentleman I have ever met. I can't wait for you to meet him. He has completely stolen my heart," she gushed.

"You are really mated," Caspian stated a catch in his voice.

"Yes. Papa, I am."

"We've lost our baby girl," her father sniffled.

"Oh, Daddy!" She wiped her eyes again.

"Boys, you have not lost anything, now buck up. Who is the lucky lad? A bear? A wolf?" Trust her uncle to defuse the situation.

She shook her head even though they couldn't see her. "No, he's a vampire. Gavriel Ambrosios." She heard a gasp and then more silence.

"That sneaky sonofabitch! That cradle robbing bastard!" her uncle exploded.

"Uncle!"

"You do not know him, not like I do. Do not worry baby, I will fix this." She could hear the steel in her uncle's voice.

"Fix what exactly?" she asked putting her hand on her hip.

"He is too old for you, baby," he started.

"No. Now you listen to me Uncle. That man is my mate, and he is just right for me, I won't give him up. Not even for you!" she practically shouted.

"You have always been so damn stubborn!" he shouted back.

"Where do you think I got it from?" she demanded. She didn't relax until she heard his chuckle.

"From me. You get all your best traits from me," he bragged.

"Hey!" she heard both of her fathers protest.

"Okay, my princess, have it your way. But I am still going to call him, just a little chitchat between men," her uncle promised.

"Can you call in a few weeks? He's going through transition right now and not at his best."

"What!" She heard three angry male voices yell.

"Beth, it is not safe. The older we become the harder our transitions get. Not even I know how old Gavriel is; he always goes into seclusion for his transition periods. Something important must be happening in Lycaonia for him to remain there through his transition," Magnus muttered. She heard his voice get louder, then softer. She could just picture him pacing next to her fathers.

"The threat they reported is real. Unit Commander Aiden McKenzie's new human mate was attacked last month. Gavriel wouldn't leave his commander now of all times," she explained.

"You are telling me that you have mated to an ageless vampire going through what has to be a turbulent transition in a hostile city where even the Unit Commander's own mate has been attacked?" her papa asked.

"Yes, that is about right," she winced at the accuracy of the statement.

"Only you. Only you could accidentally find yourself in this kind of situation," she heard her father murmur.

"Do you need Sebastian? I could have him leave immediately," her uncle offered. For a moment, she almost said yes. Sebastian was her uncle's squire and her lifelong ally.

"No. You keep him close. I have a feeling this threat isn't just to Lycaonia. Stay alert," she warned.

"What about you, darling?" her papa asked gently.

"I've adopted the Unit Commander's young human mate, Meryn McKenzie as my little sister. She has welcomed me warmly. She has a squire of her own. It might interest you to know that Meryn's squire is Sei Ryuu." She waited for that to sink in.

"A sister?"

"Adopted?"

"You mean Sei Ryuu of Japan?" they all asked at once.

"Yes, yes and yes. Uncle Magnus, you would love Meryn to pieces! She's so adorable and honest. She reminds me of you, except you've learned political tact. Whatever *she* thinks just pops out of her mouth. I've adopted her because she needs someone to show her how to survive living amongst the ruling houses. It's not as politically charged here in Lycaonia as it is in Noctem Falls, but eventually she will go to other cities and she'll need to be prepared. The fact that Sei Ryuu is her squire and that they have already bonded should tell you a lot about her."

"What in the hell is coming?" her uncle growled.

"Send us pictures, I want to see my new daughter," her papa said, bringing a smile to her face.

"I will."

"Niece, the timing of all of this..."

"I know. It's why I know I'm exactly where I belong and with exactly whom I'm meant to be."

"If you need anything, anything at all..." her father offered.

"I'll call you right away. I promise."

"We love you, honey bunny," her papa teased, using her dreaded nickname.

"I love you all, too. Take care of each other." She squeezed the phone as if she could send them a tight hug.

"Call again, soon."

"I will."

"Bye, darling."

"Bye, Daddy." She hung up the call and held the phone to her chest.

Taking a deep breath, she stuck the phone back in her wristlet. When she opened the office door, she practically ran into Ryuu. He stood leaning against the wall by the doorway his arms crossed over his chest.

"I should have known you'd eavesdrop."

"You haven't been with us long; I had to make sure of your intentions. I apologize for the breech of privacy." He placed a hand over his heart and bowed.

"It actually worked out for the best, I'd rather get this taken care of behind the scenes so we don't worry Meryn," she admitted.

"You see it, too?" he asked.

"What? The improbable number of coincidences that have happened lately? Fate seems to be doing her level best to gather strong allies around Commander McKenzie and his new mate. I'm almost afraid to find out what threat warrants such direct intervention."

Ryuu nodded and looked past her down the hallway. Meryn's laughter echoed toward them. "I've never met anyone like her in all my days. She isn't motivated by greed or power. She doesn't judge people by their race or position. She's very special." He turned his heavy gaze to Elizabeth.

"You mean she's motivated by coffee and nerd gear and judges people solely on whether they're an asshole or not?" Elizabeth grinned.

"Exactly." A smile tugged at his mouth.

"She's so young. I don't think she'll be ready for whatever is coming."

"That is why she has us." Ryuu raised an eyebrow as if daring her to disagree.

"I'll do what I can with the time we have. How do we get her to listen? She isn't the most tractable person," Elizabeth huffed.

Ryuu gave a sly smile. "She is if you know what to say." He winked and indicated for her to follow him.

He led her down the hallway, back to the drawing room. When they entered, Meryn jumped to her feet and raced over to throw her arms around her waist.

"You were awesome! Oh my gosh, when you said she was pathetic, I wanted to do a fist pump. That woman has been an absolute beast to me. It's only a matter of time before I throat punch her." Meryn grinned up at her. Elizabeth turned to Ryuu as if to say, 'see what I mean'?"

Ryuu stepped forward. "Meryn, listen carefully. Elizabeth is not only your new sister; she will also be your Yoda. She will teach you and guide you in the ways of using the force, so that you will master paranormal politics. Learn well, young *padawan*." He clapped a hand on Meryn's shoulder.

When Meryn turned to her, there was reverence in her eyes. "I will try hard, Master Yoda."

When Elizabeth glanced back to Ryuu, he smirked at her and went to pour them a fresh cup of tea. The man was a master at Meryn manipulation. How extraordinary.

"Yes, well. We'll start by learning the history of the Houses, which should help enormously." Elizabeth turned Meryn around and gently nudged her toward the chairs.

Meryn groaned. "Why? That old stuff is boring," she protested.

"Meryn, history for humans and history for paranormals is different. The people you'll be reading about are mostly still alive," Adelaide explained.

Meryn paused and looked at them, a confused look on her face. "Y'all have textbooks about people and all the bad or good crap they have done are in it and they're still alive? Do they let the bad stuff get written about themselves?"

"That's a very astute question. We have scholars who live outside our social norms and pressures. They are completely neutral and record our history with impunity," Elizabeth said, accepting a cup from Ryuu. "We'll pick up some of the more popular volumes when we go out later."

"Will there be stuff about Aiden in there?" Meryn asked.

"I imagine there are stories about nearly everyone you've met in those volumes, darling," Adelaide confirmed.

"Wait. Am I in a book? Like right now?" Meryn looked around a bit wild-eyed.

Adelaide nodded. "As Aiden's mate, your accomplishments will also be recorded."

Meryn paled. "That also means my fuck ups will be in there, too. I don't want to be known for my fuck ups!" she said sounding panicked.

Elizabeth dropped a cookie on Meryn's plate. "That's why I'm here, Meryn. I am your Yoda. I will teach you to avoid public gaffes so that only good things will be recorded about you."

Meryn nibbled her cookie and stared out the window.

Well, that went well.

Meryn suddenly shook her head. "I won't worry about it. What happens, happens. Come on Elizabeth; let's go get some coffee. Tea just isn't cutting it right now." Meryn stood, set her plate down, and started putting on her winter gear. Ryuu was at her side in seconds, helping her with her coat.

Elizabeth sighed and placed her cup back on its saucer. She stood and picked up her coat from the back of the chair. She easily slipped it on and turned to face Adelaide. "It truly was an honor to meet you. I'd like to come back for another visit soon."

Adelaide smiled. "You're welcome anytime."

Elizabeth followed Meryn out into the foyer. She watched, as Adelaide made sure Meryn's scarf was in place before giving her a big hug.

"You girls have fun, don't be out too late," she said a worried expression on her face.

"We won't be. Bye, Mom," Meryn promised.

"Bye darling, be safe."

Once everyone was in the car, Elizabeth put on her seat belt and turned to Meryn.

"Okay shortie, where to now?"

"Go down the road until you get to a three way intersection, keep going straight and follow the signs for the parking garage," Meryn said.

"Sounds easy enough." Elizabeth started the car and pulled out onto the main road. It wasn't long before the intersection came up and she started following the signs to the parking garage. Luckily, she found a parking spot on the ground level and everyone got out.

She looked up at the gorgeous blue sky. Warmer days like this were rare in November.

"Coffee, coffee, coffee. Coffee for me," Meryn sang and led the way down the cobblestone walkway. When they emerged from between two buildings, Elizabeth was surprisingly impressed. The city had an old world charm that reminded her of Noctem Falls, but the open air made her feel very exposed. She was used to the caverns that made her feel closed in and safe.

"This way," Meryn tugged on her arm and practically dragged her down the street. For a tiny human, she sure was strong. Elizabeth made mental notes of all the places she wanted to visit later as she was marched past them. There were so many different shops they didn't have in Noctem Falls; she could just imagine doing all of her Christmas shopping here.

The smell of cinnamon filled the air as they walked past a bakery window that had her mouth watering.

"Meryn, if we could just..." Elizabeth stopped and stared at the assortment of sweets on display.

"Oh, we are definitely hitting this place, but on the way out. They have the best apple fritters I have ever had in my life. But right now, I am dying for some coffee." Meryn looped her arm through hers and they walked down the sidewalk.

Under the open sky, she could feel the sun on her face and the perfumed breezes blowing through her hair. Each alley and turn of the road created small wind tunnels that seemed to collect the wonderful smells of the city and the surrounding forest. It made the city feel alive and so very different from her childhood home.

Even before Meryn stopped in front of a stylish café, she could already smell the rich aroma of freshly ground coffee beans. She inhaled and then sighed happily. When she looked up, she smiled at the cute sign that read The Jitterbug.

"So, what do you think?" Meryn asked.

"I think I have found my new favorite place." Elizabeth smiled.

"Wait until you smell inside." Meryn opened the door and stepped inside.

Ryuu held the door for her and she walked in behind Meryn.

CHAPTER FIVE

"Justice! Look what the wind blew in," a delicate looking man yelled from behind the wide dark wooden counter. The taller dark haired man looked up and smiled.

"Meryn! We haven't seen you in a while. Where have you been hiding?" He waved them over to sit at the counter.

When they sat down, the shorter man practically climbed over the bar to give Meryn a one armed hug.

"Hey Sydney, I want you to meet Elizabeth Monroe. She just moved to Lycaonia and guess what? She's Gavriel's mate," Meryn shared, practically bouncing up and down on her barstool.

The strawberry blond haired man looked at her, eyes wide. "Get out! Congratulations honey!"

"Elizabeth this is Sydney Fairfax and the tall, dark, handsome man behind him is his mate Justice O'Malley. They own The Jitterbug."

Elizabeth couldn't help but smile at Sydney's enthusiastic greeting. "Thank you. Gavriel is everything I've ever wanted in a mate." She winked at him and he threw his head back and laughed.

"He's what a lot of women wanted, if you know what I mean. Now, what can I get you two lovely ladies?" He wiped his hands on a red tea towel and looked at them expectantly.

"I need coffee. Like I really *need* some coffee." Meryn yawned wide.

"Poor thing. Definitely a double strength Bittersweet Mocha for you. What about you Elizabeth?" Sydney asked, reaching for a large cup to get started on Meryn's drink.

"Make it two."

Sydney grinned. "You got it. So while I get these drinks started, tell me all about your yummy mate. Ow!" Sydney rubbed his bottom and scowled at Justice. Justice kept walking toward the supply room.

"I'm mated, not dead!" Sydney yelled. Justice turned and gave his mate a dark, heated look before walking through the double doors.

Sydney turned to them with a shit-eating grin. "I love it when he gets possessive. But seriously, what is Gavriel like? He's always so stoic. All the unit warriors defer to him without question; he just has this commanding air about him."

"He's gentle, and that surprised me, but it's true. Every time he opens his mouth, I lose a piece of my heart," she sighed and smiled, thinking about her mate.

"Look at that face; she's already a goner. But seriously, what can you expect when it's Fate herself bringing the warriors their mates?" Sydney poured a delicious looking chocolatey substance in each cup and stirred in a generous serving of steamed milk. When he was finished, he placed each cup in front of them with a small plate of shortbread cookies.

Meryn took a sip and sighed. "Perfect, as usual."

Elizabeth lifted the cup and took a small sip. The bitter chocolate was perfectly balanced by the espresso and milk. "Pure heaven." She wrapped her fingers around the cup letting the warmth seep into her cold fingers.

"So what have you been up to?" Sydney asked Meryn, settling in on a stool behind the counter.

"Just helping Adair with the trainee program. I got an email this morning that the council is willing to try it out and will give a final decision after a few months. I've also created the online feedback forum that the council wanted and the community message board."

Sydney smiled. "I saw that the kids have taken over the message board. They have been posting our version of urban legends on there for the past two weeks. I hadn't heard some of those stories in decades."

Elizabeth set her cup down. "Did they have the story about the Dark Prince? That one was always my favorite growing up."

Sydney nodded. "And the one about the shifter who couldn't make up his mind whether to be a human or animal."

Meryn looked from Elizabeth to Sydney and back. "I haven't read the one about the Dark Prince, who is he?"

Sydney leaned forward. "He is practically a God amongst vampires. One of their most famous legends of him is how he single-handedly stopped the Great War five thousand years ago. After going berserk and decimating a large portion of the shifter's ranks, he came upon an enemy who was dying, a shifter commander. Supposedly, the shifter expressed a single regret: that he hadn't made it home to meet his newborn son before joining his mate who had died giving birth. His story struck a chord deep in the Dark Prince's heart. He carried the shifter to the vampire medical tent and made his people treat the enemy so that he could live to see his son. That single act of compassion triggered other acts of kindness, on both sides of the fighting by those who longed for peace, until a cease-fire was called."

Meryn leaned forward eyes bright. "I know this story! After the cease-fire, the shifter commander disobeyed orders and abandoned his post. He walked on foot back to Lycaonia to meet his son."

Elizabeth and Sydney both frowned. "That's not part of the story, Meryn. Which thread did you read that from? We may need to take that one down."

Meryn shook her head. "That's the story Gavriel told me when I got bored and wouldn't leave him alone when he was on guard duty."

Sydney laughed. "I imagine he would have done anything to keep you entertained. Anyway, nowadays, vampire parents tell their children to be good or they will tell the Dark Prince that they have been bad."

Understanding dawned in Meryn's eyes. "So like the Boogeyman? Humans do the same thing to their kids. Be good or the Boogeyman will come out of the closet and eat your soul. Though the story of the Dark Prince makes him sound kinda good. I can't really see him eating children's souls." She took another sip of her coffee.

Elizabeth looked at Sydney; they exchanged shocked expressions. Sydney turned to Meryn. "No, the Dark Prince isn't like that. When the parents threaten the children that they will tell the Dark Prince they have been bad, the children stop acting up because they don't want to disappoint him. He is their hero. I've said it before, and I'll say it again, humans can be fucked up." Sydney shuddered.

Meryn stared at them in disbelief. "Come on, you have to have heard of the Boogeyman. Everyone knows about him. He lurks in dark shadows and under beds, and if you're bad, he comes out and either eats your soul or kidnaps you away from your family and eats you while you're still alive. He takes on the form of the child's worst fear."

Elizabeth couldn't believe what she was hearing. "Meryn, human parents tell their children this tale? It's barbaric!"

Poor human babies!

Meryn shrugged. "Well, yeah." She suddenly grinned. "You should hear what they say about werewolves and vampires."

"At least vampires and shifters are real," Sydney countered.

"So are Boogeymen," Ryuu said from behind them.

They all turned to look at him in horror.

"Seriously?" Meryn whispered.

Ryuu nodded. "Boogeymen are derived from the legend of boggarts. Boggarts are said to be evil sprites, which actually makes them sound more harmless than they really are. In all actuality, what you're describing are demons."

Elizabeth scooted closer to Meryn. "But they aren't really real, right?" she asked.

Looking surprised, Ryuu's eyes went to each of them in disbelief. "Yes, but they haven't been seen in our world in over two thousand years."

Elizabeth let out a relived breath. "Thank all the Gods for that."

Ryuu smirked. "Actually, thank your Dark Prince; I'm pretty sure he led that crusade."

She and Meryn stared at the normally quiet squire then looked at each other.

"I don't think I want to know anymore." Meryn turned back to the counter.

Ryuu gave a half bow. "Of course, *denka.*"

Elizabeth agreed whole-heartedly, the less she knew about Boogeymen the better.

Sydney gave a nervous laugh and shook his head. "Okay, on to better news. Did you hear that Elise Bowers found out she's having a girl? She's over the moon! Of course I heard Daphne didn't take it well," Sydney snickered.

Meryn laughed and looked at Elizabeth. "Looks like she's having a bad day all around then, isn't she?"

Grinning, Elizabeth nodded.

"Okay chicks, spill," Sydney demanded.

Meryn told an overdramatized version of that afternoon's meeting. Sydney was laughing and wiping his eyes at the end. He turned to her. "You're welcome here anytime."

"Thanks, I'm already a huge fan of the coffee. This place is stylish and upbeat. I can definitely see myself coming here a lot."

Sydney blushed. "Thank you. Justice and I have put our hearts into this place. It's a dream come true being able to do this with my mate."

"You remind me of my fathers. They also work together."

"Broderick Monroe right? I saw pictures of him and his mate in last year's Midwinter newsletter from Noctem Falls. They're both so handsome. I remember telling Justice that we have to visit Noctem Falls, if only to go to their tailor." Sydney's face took on a happy expression.

"My uncle's squire, Sebastian, acts as their tailor. High quality clothing is my only vice. I was spoiled by his work growing up." Elizabeth pointed to her sweater.

"Lucky girl," Sydney said sounding envious.

"Maybe I should find a tailor," Meryn murmured, looking down at her cartoon t-shirt and long sleeve thermal.

Ryuu spoke up quickly, looking pleased. "I have already contacted three possible candidates. Whenever you decide you're ready for a fitting, I will arrange for them to come to the estate."

"Maybe next week. Around the house, I don't think it matters, but when I go out visiting, I want to look nice." She looked at Elizabeth's sweater and sighed. "That looks snuggly."

"Maybe Father Christmas will get you one this year." Elizabeth winked.

Meryn perked up. "Really?"

"Get your measurements done and we'll see what happens."

Meryn turned to Ryuu. "Okay, call those tailors, tell them any time next week is good."

Ryuu bowed. "Yes, *denka.*"

Elizabeth pulled out her phone and checked the time. "Come on, Meryn, we still need to go to the book store for your history books and that lovely pastry shop before we head back to the estate." She turned to Sydney and held up her empty cup. "Can I get one to go?"

Meryn drained her cup. "Me too, please. When we get back, we have to start on those databases, and if I'm not caffeinated the lines of code blur together."

"I'll make them extra-large." Sydney stood and started their drinks.

"Thanks, Sydney." Meryn turned to her. "What do you think the guys are doing?"

"Probably working very hard at being muscular and training with their clubs and sticks."

Meryn laughed. "They are so boring."

"We put up with them anyway," Elizabeth smiled.

"I installed the spell alarm over the front windows," Quinn said, wiping his hands.

Aiden looked at the small runes in the window frame. "Good work."

Colton walked over to them carrying a large box and handed it to Gavriel with a grunt. Gavriel looked down at the box, then back up to Colton.

"It's C4; can you run it back to the armory? I confiscated it from Graham; I think he's forgetting we actually have to live here. I want to head back before they sneak something else in." Colton turned and hurried back the way he came.

Aiden's eyes widened, and he started walking toward the backdoor. "Graham!"

Gavriel shook his head and decided to take the long way around to avoid that argument. He walked out of the front door and around the house. He was on his way back from the armory when he heard someone call his name.

"Gavriel. Gavriel Ambrosios."

He stopped and looked around. Moving slowly, he reached behind him under his jacket and grabbed his gun.

"Tsk, tsk. No need to get violent, I just wanted to chat."

Gavriel pulled the gun, released the safety, and brought it up.

"Come out where I can see you, then we can talk," he suggested.

"I am out where you can see me; maybe your transition is messing with your eyesight."

Gavriel flinched. The disembodied voice chuckled. "Oh yes, we know about that. You're at your weakest, aren't you? We've been watching you. Every day you're one step closer to becoming like us. I'm here to tell you, you have been chosen."

"I am nothing like you. I have a mate; my soul is anchored. Chosen for what?" he asked.

"You'll see."

"And if I refuse?"

"You won't have a choice. Ta-ta for now."

Gavriel swiveled to the left then to the right; he couldn't hear anything. Cursing, he walked backward to the porch before putting his gun away. The bastards were too close to home for his comfort, especially now that his mate was here.

Walking inside, Gavriel spotted Oron Vi'Eirson and Christoff Du'Prince, the fae and vampire warriors from the Gamma Unit.

"Can you do a full perimeter sweep? Check for any signs of an intruder and report back. Be on alert." Both men saluted.

Oron pulled out his gun and checked the chamber. "You look a bit spooked, sir. Are we checking for anything in particular?"

Gavriel growled, and both men straightened. He knew it was not like him to show emotion, but the transition was making him volatile.

"Another one of those invisible bastards showed up here at the Alpha estate not five minutes ago. Start north and head around east. I'm going to find Aiden and send a second group south. Check in every five minutes."

"Those fucks! I am getting real sick of this shit." Christoff bared his fangs and hissed.

The large fae clapped him on the back. "Cheer up, we may find them this time." Christoff's answering grin was scary. Oron turned to Gavriel, "We'll be back, sir."

Gavriel went inside to search for Aiden. He found him and pulled him and Colton into the hallway. "I just had a feral stop me outside, seemed he wanted to talk. I did not see a bloody thing though." Gavriel ran a hand through his hair.

Colton growled. "Sonofabitch! They are getting bold coming up to the Alpha estate. What did he say?" Colton asked. Gavriel could see his jaw was tight.

Aiden hadn't said a word, but anger was rolling off him in waves.

"Basically that 'they' knew I was in transition and at my weakest." He turned to Aiden. "Maybe these alarms and defense enhancements are not such a bad idea. We also need to check into figuring out a spell that can be used to set a perimeter. I do not like how close they are coming, especially when we cannot see them."

Aiden had to take two deep breaths before he answered. "We need to get a unit out there looking for them."

Gavriel nodded, "I sent Oron and Christoff out; they are heading north."

"Then we'll get the rest of their unit to join them and send Beta south. Tell Keelan and Darian that Alpha Unit is house-sitting for a couple days while we figure out a way to set a perimeter."

Colton nodded and pushed off the wall. "I'll get everyone moving. I can't sit still right now. What if Meryn or Elizabeth had been back there?" he asked quietly clenching his fists.

Gavriel felt his stomach turn. "We cannot think like that, it will be a distraction. Let us concentrate on what we can do."

"I'm going to pull Keelan, Quinn Foxglove from Gamma and Kade Burdock from Beta to start on spell research." Aiden didn't say another word and walked away. Gavriel knew how he felt.

Colton laid a hand on his shoulder. "Thank the Gods they still seem to be afraid of Ryuu's *shikigami*. Don't worry; we won't let anything happen to Meryn or Elizabeth."

"Thank you, my friend."

"I'll be getting Graham and Sascha together if you need me."

Gavriel watched as Colton walked towards the front door. He had only just found his mate; he could not lose her, not when he had just found her.

"What the fuck!"

Gavriel recognized Meryn's voice and went running. He nearly collided with Aiden in the hall as both men ran for the front door. When they got there, they came to a grinding halt. Both women were huddled together and were being shielded by Ryuu; all three were covered in blue flames. Shopping bags lay at their feet. In a perfect circle on the porch, scorch marks showed where the fire spell had gone off around them. Aiden immediately went to the wall by the door and removed the hanging brass ornament. He carefully moved it to the second peg located on the outside of the drawn spell circle disarming the alarm.

He turned to his mate. "Oh my Gods! Meryn! Baby, are you okay? I thought we had disarmed the front door. It shouldn't have been active while you were still out." Aiden rushed forward only to be brought up short by a growling Ryuu. Gavriel had never seen the normally calm squire ever look so angry. Ryuu stepped forward and bumped chests with Aiden.

"Do you know what could have happened if I had not been with her!" he shouted.

"Back off, squire. You don't know what's happened here today," Aiden said, getting in Ryuu's face.

Gavriel pulled a shaken Elizabeth into his arms. Meryn was trying to wedge herself between her mate and her squire.

"Calm down both of you! Aiden, why in the hell is our house booby-trapped? What happened?" Meryn was rubbing her hand up and down Aiden's arm.

Glaring at Ryuu, he pulled Meryn against him and rubbed his chin on her head.

Elizabeth turned to him. "Gavriel, what is it? What's happened?"

He and Aiden exchanged looks. Gavriel sighed; there was no point in keeping them in the dark.

"We had a feral come on to the property today. He got extremely close to the house." Gavriel watched as Ryuu folded his arms over his chest.

Meryn turned to Aiden. "Is that why you booby-trapped the door?"

"It isn't booby-trapped. Initially, I had the men help set alarms through the house for you. So you'd feel safer in our home, but after today, I have Keelan, Quinn, and Kade looking into creating a perimeter spell. I don't even want them close enough to set off an alarm."

Gavriel watched Meryn's face soften. "You're the best husband any woman could ask for."

Aiden looked down at his mate. "Do you really mean that? We can have a real wedding if you want one."

Meryn shook her head. "I was being petty this morning, and I'm sorry if I hurt your feelings. I was scared about something else and took it out on you."

"Come on Meryn, I need to inspect every inch of you to make sure you're okay." He scooped her up and turned to Ryuu.

"Thank you for saving her. Have Colton show you where the alarms are set."

Ryuu nodded. "I'll also work with Keelan, there may be some things I can do to help with a spell." He bowed to Meryn and walked away.

Aiden turned to Gavriel and grinned before he sprinted up the stairs with his giggling mate.

"Never a dull moment around here is there?" his mate asked him. When he looked down, her eyes were twinkling.

"No." He looked around. Everyone else was busy. He held out his arm. "Could I interest you in a mid-afternoon respite?"

Her eyes widened, and she blushed. She laid her hand on his arm. "That sounds lovely."

Gavriel waited until they reached the top of the stairs before he began to grab his mate's rounded ass. The thrill of the chase had his blood boiling. He shut the door and began to strip out of his clothes. Laughing, she jumped on the bed. Unfortunately, momentum carried her off the bed and into the wall. He watched in horror as she slid down out of sight.

"Beth?" He ran over to the bed. There was only a few inches gap between the wall and the bed. He looked up frustrated. The headboard was built into the wall.

"Beth, answer me." He was about to rip the bed away from the wall when he felt something on his foot. When he looked down, a tiny snow white bunny was nuzzling his leg.

Carefully, he picked her up. "You constantly amaze me. My little bunny." His mate licked his face then wiggled in his hands. He set her down on the bed and watched in wonder as she shifted back to human. She shook out her long blonde hair and smiled up at him impishly.

"I've had to shift to my rabbit form on more than one occasion to get out of a sticky situation. Of course, shifting back without clothes is always tricky."

He finished unbuttoning his shirt and let it drop to the floor. Smiling, she turned over until she was on all fours and began to crawl towards the head of the bed.

Gavriel felt his fangs burst through his gums as her ass swayed back and forth, tempting him. He kicked off his shoes and dropped his pants before pulling off his socks. The fabric of his boxer briefs against his cock was almost painful. He shucked out of them and climbed onto the bed. He reached out and pulled on her ankle until she was flat on her stomach. He began to tickle the arch of her foot. Laughing, she thrashed around on the bed.

Gavriel watched her unguarded expression and could not help the joy in his heart. Over the centuries, he had been with many women, but he had never experienced these types of simple moments.

"I'm ... I'm ... so ... gonna ... kick your ass. Just ... as ... soon ... as ... I can ... breathe!" his mate yelled. He took mercy on her and released her leg. She turned over on to her back, breathing hard and smiling. "You're crazy."

"I prefer the term eccentric." He relaxed next to her and lazily ran his fingers down her body. He started at her collarbone; he followed the line of her body between her breasts, down the slope of her stomach until he reached her rounded mound. Watching her expression carefully, he lightly teased the tiny, soft hairs before moving to trace down her leg.

"Humph," she practically growled at him.

He raised an eyebrow at her sour expression.

"Did you say something, darling?" he asked.

"Oh yes, yes I did. I said, please fuck me now."

He rolled and in an instant lay nestled between her legs. When he ran his tongue over his lips, he saw her eyes glaze over with lust at the sight of his fangs. Not many women could orgasm from being bitten; he was a lucky bastard that Elizabeth was one of the rare ones that did.

"Are you ready for me? If I tease you again, will my fingers find you wet?" he growled in her ear.

"Gods yes, please Gavriel, don't make me beg," she panted.

"I would never make you beg my sweet Beth; if anything, I would be the one begging to have one more taste of you." He reached down and rubbed the head of his cock up and down between her folds making sure she was ready before plunging as deeply as he could.

They moaned in unison. Slowly, he glided in and out of her, taking his time. He wanted to make this last. Pushing himself up, he felt the muscles of his arms flex, but it was worth it; he could now reach her neck. Instinctively, she tilted her head, her hands coming up to cup his ass. He felt her fingernails digging into his flesh and loved every second. He thrust deep and she cried out. The look of wild abandon on her face was his undoing. Leaning in, he sank his fangs deep in her neck. She screamed her pleasure and met him thrust for thrust as he increased the pace.

He felt her body spasm around his cock, signaling her first orgasm. Grinning against her neck, he continued to feed. He waited until the spasming stopped before he changed his rhythm. He thrust as deeply as he could and began to hammer into her. When he heard her breath hitch, he reached down and twisted her nipple before immediately moving to her clit. The second he touched her she exploded again.

His own orgasm came in a rush of blood and cum. Lifting from her neck, he watched as her blood dripped onto the sheets. He threw his head back and roared as his balls emptied.

Breathing hard with shaking arms, he leaned down and swiped his tongue over the holes on her neck to close them. Gently, he pulled out of her and collapsed to one side.

"At least I didn't black out this time," she said, yawning drowsily.

"I will have to work on that," he murmured.

"I won't survive. Now, tell me what you didn't want to say in front of Meryn." She rolled over onto her side and pinned him with a knowing look. His mate was far too observant.

"The feral actually made mention that they knew I was in transition and at my weakest. He also said I had been chosen." He heard her gasp. He did not like the fear in her eyes. He pulled her close.

"I will be fine. Even at my weakest, they are still no match for me." He did not dare let her see his face; he knew she would pick up on his lie. She rubbed her nose against his chest before placing a soft kiss against his skin.

"I called my fathers today. My uncle said he would be calling you later for a little 'man to man chat'." She twirled her finger around his belly button.

"I will call Magnus later. I can just imagine what he has to say to me. More than likely the same thing I would say to someone newly mated to a favorite niece, something along the lines of 'if you hurt her, I will skin you alive'." He sighed.

"I'm sorry, but it's because we're so close. Sometimes Daddy and Papa were busy in the lab, so he would watch me. In some ways, I'm closer to him than my fathers, because he wasn't just an uncle growing up, he was my best friend," she confided. He groaned; the man would be gunning for him for sure. She looked up, concern on her face. He kissed the tip of her nose.

"I remember Magnus from my time at Noctem Falls. I respected him as a warrior and I respect him as our Elder. If he feels the need to lecture me about the care of his beloved niece then I will let him."

Gratitude filled her eyes. "Thank you."

"Anything for you. Do you suppose Aiden is looking for me?" he asked, pulling the blanket up around them.

She giggled. "I hope that Meryn wore him out so we can stay like this for a little longer."

"We will check on them in a little bit, for now, let us just enjoy the afternoon."

She snuggled close. He closed his eyes, determined to enjoy this time with his mate despite the threat looming over them.

CHAPTER SIX

Aiden and Meryn. Aiden looked up and grinned at Gavriel before leaning down to kiss his mate on the forehead.

"Okay Meryn, remember what I said. You have to stop interrupting our training; we're still a functioning unit and need to be able to work on our drills. If you need to talk to me, try to come out during a break or lunch."

Meryn sighed. "I'll try, but some stuff can't wait."

Gavriel turned to Elizabeth and kissed her gently before stepping back. "I am going to try to do drills with the guys this afternoon."

"Be careful," she said.

He nodded then both men headed for the door.

Keelan came from the family room looking concerned. "Umm guys, we can take this stuff down right? Guys? Hello? Fireballs?" Keelan trailed after them voicing his concerns.

Meryn laughed. "Poor Keelan." She turned to Elizabeth. "Come on, let's get started."

They walked to the office and looked around at the cluttered mess of stacked papers and the one small desk. They looked at each other.

"Tomorrow?" Elizabeth asked.

"Totally! I don't know how your afternoon went, but I'm wiped. I don't know how Aiden is out there doing drills. I'll work on the databases after dinner when Aiden and I are upstairs relaxing." Meryn stretched and yawned.

"My afternoon was probably similar to yours and I agree; the men must be monsters." They walked to the family room. Meryn collapsed on one of the large leather couches, Elizabeth the recliner. Elizabeth reached over to the side coffee table and picked up the forgotten pastry bag. She pulled out a cookie smiling happily.

"I don't want to move." Meryn curled up into a small ball.

"Me either." Elizabeth kicked back the recliner chewing her chocolate chip cookie. It was scrumptious.

"Ladies, would you like some tea?" Ryuu asked from the doorway.

Meryn opened one eye. "What time is it?"

Ryuu leaned back and checked the foyer clock. "It's one thirty, *denka.*"

"Can you wake us up before the guys come in?" Meryn yawned.

"Of course," he was about to leave the room when the phone rang. He turned and picked up the old-fashioned receiver.

"Alpha Unit Estate, oh yes. How are you today sir? We're fine here. He is outside at the moment, but Meryn is here. Yes, hold please." Ryuu covered the mouth of the receiver.

"*Denka,* Lord Byron is on the phone for you."

Meryn perked up and hopped off the couch. She took the phone from Ryuu. "Hey, Dad. Probably, I'm not sure. I can ask him. Yeah, hold on." Meryn set the receiver down on the sofa table and turned to her.

"I gotta run ask Aiden something." She turned to the door.

"*Denka,* your coat," Ryuu said.

Meryn shook her head, "I should only take a second."

Elizabeth stood. "I'll go with you; maybe the fresh air will wake me up."

Elizabeth followed Meryn out the door to the side of the house. The clearing beside the driveway provided the men the space needed to work in larger groups. They walked up to the open area where the men were sparring with each other. Smiling they waved as she approached.

"Hey Aiden..." Meryn called out.

Aiden turned, a frown on his face. "Meryn, what did I just tell you about interrupting our training? These drills could save your life one day," Aiden practically shouted.

"But I..."

"No. Go back into the house. I'll come to you when we're done." Aiden deliberately turned his back, dismissing her.

"Aiden..."

Aiden ignored her.

"Aiden, please."

Aiden stared down at his clipboard steadily ignoring his mate.

Nostrils flaring, Meryn turned to her. "Wait here."

Oh dear.

Meryn marched back into the house with a determined look on her face.

A few seconds later Meryn walked through the front door and down the porch steps around to the back. A minute later, when she pulled up in a large black Camaro, she had everyone's attention except Aiden's.

Elizabeth watched as Colton jogged up to Aiden. He watched Meryn, his eyes growing wide.

Meryn pulled a gas canister from the trunk and started to douse the car. Elizabeth watched, smiling. Her eyes met Gavriel's. She raised an eyebrow and nodded to where Meryn was gleefully saturating the car. He shrugged. She noticed not one warrior breathed a word to their commander.

Aiden turned to Colton. "Colton, did you spill gasoline in the armory? That could be a potential disaster waiting to happen," he admonished.

Colton shook his head. "No. But Aiden, Meryn..."

"I told her I'd speak to her later."

"But Aiden..." Colton gulped.

"Later," Aiden said in a curt tone.

Meryn threw the gas canister into the car and pulled out a pack of matches. She tried the first match, and it didn't light. Scrunching up her nose, she kept trying.

"Aiden..." Colton tried again.

"I will talk to her later," Aiden said firmly.

Meryn's third attempt worked, she looked up and smiled at everyone before dropping the entire matchbook into the backseat. She stepped back as the entire car erupted in flames.

Colton brought both hands up and threaded his fingers behind his head. Rocking back on his heels, he grinned. "Aiden, what I was going to say was: Meryn is setting your car on fire." Colton jerked his head to the side pointing to the driveway.

"What?" Aiden yelled. He turned to see his car rapidly becoming a small bonfire.

"Meryn! What the hell?" He raced over to stand in front of his mate. He looked at her satisfied smile and back to his car. He pulled at his hair with his hands.

His gaze was furious when he turned back to his mate. "Meryn!" he roared.

She pulled her foot back and kicked him in the shin.

"Fuck! Dammit Meryn!" Aiden dropped down to one knee and rubbed his leg. Elizabeth walked over to stand next to her friend. She might not be a bear, but she was a shifter and Meryn wasn't; she could at least get between them if Aiden needed a second to calm down.

Meryn glared down at her mate. "Shut up! Now *you* listen to *me*." Meryn put both hands on her hips and leaned over her huge mate. "First off, I am not a simpering clingy mate. I don't interrupt you for fun. Usually, if I have to interrupt you, it's something important because guess what? I have my *own* shit to do! In case you hadn't noticed, I'm helping your brother completely restructure the training program and getting computer illiterate elders savvy on message boards. Secondly, my grandmother used to ignore me, and I cannot stress to you enough how much that bothers me. I refuse to be ignored by someone I love again." With tears in her eyes, she headed up the porch steps. She turned back to him. "What I was going to tell you was that your father was on the phone for you." She walked past her squire, whose eyes were shooting daggers at Aiden.

With an evil smile, Ryuu raised his hand and snapped his fingers. The trunk exploded in blue flames. "Actually, Lord Byron saw the smoke from his office window. I informed him of what transpired. He said to call back when you were back in your mate's good graces." He turned and followed Meryn into the house.

Seconds later, Aiden was turning his head back and forth. He swatted his hand in front of his face. "Ow! Meryn come back! Dammit Felix, cut it out!" Aiden lost his balance and ended up on his back. The tiny speck of light struck again and again before it flittered through the door and it slammed shut behind him.

Elizabeth and Gavriel walked up until they stood on either side of Aiden's prone body.

Colton whistled behind them. "Dude, you're so fucked."

Gavriel looked down at his friend, who was now sporting tiny red abrasions on his face and sighed. Looking over at her, he said, "We will be back." He leaned down and pulled Aiden to his feet. "Come on cub, maybe that old man at the store will know of a way to fix this." Aiden nodded absently. Gavriel gave him a gentle shove toward the garage.

"I'll check on Meryn. If you're running to the store, can you pick me up a couple chocolate bars?" Elizabeth asked, trying not to smile. The poor Unit Commander was dazed.

"You can have whatever you want my mate. Thank you for checking on Meryn, she is a little quirky, but we all care about her." Gavriel said.

"You mean *you* care for her, don't you?" Elizabeth teased.

Gavriel nodded. "I have been with her, inside, for the past month since I could not train in the state I was in. She made those long days bearable."

Elizabeth kissed him and nudged him after Aiden's stumbling form. "Go take care of your commander, I have a feeling you and I will be taking care of these two for a long time."

Gavriel ran a hand over her hair. "More than likely, they have a heavy future in store for them." Elizabeth nodded. Gavriel tilted her head up. "You see it, too?" he asked.

"Yes. Remember, I was raised around vampires. I'm used to forward thinking. Hurry back."

He kissed her one last time and followed behind Aiden.

Colton's voice rang out. "Let's make s'mores! Ow!" His head jerked forward from Sascha cuffing him.

Elizabeth laughed at the men's antics.

Gavriel followed behind Aiden as they walked into the store. He wanted to pick up the chocolate for Beth and he was dying to see what advice the old man had for Aiden. Walking behind his commander, they approached the register where the aged man sat flipping through an old *Bass and Guns* magazine. The older man's face brightened when he saw Aiden approaching.

"Well, look what the cat dragged in. Been awhile, son. Surely you don't need more feminine products, considering how much you bought last time you was here."

"Sir, I..." Aiden began. The old man held up a wrinkled hand.

"My name is Bartholomew son, you can call me Bart. I have a feeling I'll be seeing a lot of you, we might as well be on first name basis."

Aiden thrust his hand out giving the old man hand a thorough shake.

"My name is Aiden McKenzie; this is my... friend Gavriel Ambrosios." Aiden pointed in his direction. Gavriel nodded.

Bart nodded back and turned to Aiden. "Okay son, what's yer question?"

"What do you buy a woman to get back on her good side when you've made her really, really angry? Cake? Fudge?"

The wrinkles on the old man's face scrunched together as he frowned.

"How angry did you make her boy?"

"She set my car on fire."

The old man blinked and then began to laugh. He laughed so hard that he began to hack and wheeze. Gavriel thought for sure that Aiden had killed the gentleman. Holding his stomach, the man continued to laugh as he reached for a pen and piece of paper. With a shaky hand, he scrawled something on the paper and thrust it at Aiden. He exhaled and wiped his eyes, still chuckling to himself.

Aiden looked at the paper. "Is this a place that sells good chocolate?" he asked.

"No, son. That is the address where they sell jewelry. Chocolate can fix a lot of things, but it's not the embodiment of kitten angel tears, if you know what I mean. If yer woman set your car on fire, then son, the only thing that can help you at this point is something shiny." The old man rubbed his rounded belly and began to chuckle again at Aiden's chagrin.

"Come on sir, I know that place he is recommending, they do sell nice pieces there. How about you go wait in the car while I buy these candy bars." Gavriel sympathetically pat Aiden on the back before the commander trudged back to the car. Gavriel turned to face the old man.

The old man watched Aiden leave, scratching his stubbled chin. "His woman really that feisty?"

"You have no idea."

"What a lucky bastard."

Gavriel shook his head. "Mine's feistier."

The old man shook his head and rang up the candy bars.

"I have a feeling I'll be seeing more of you boys."

Gavriel picked up the bag. "You're probably right."

Whistling, he walked out of the store to meet up with Aiden.

Elizabeth looked over to where the men were gathered around their unit leaders, getting orders for the afternoon's drills in Aiden's absence.

She walked over and looked at Colton, Keelan, and Darian. Colton was still rubbing the back of his head from where Sascha had thumped him.

"Can I ask you something?" The men nodded. "Aiden is your Unit Commander, how come none of you said anything when Meryn was setting his car on fire? You had plenty of time to stop her." She had been surprised that not one of the warriors had moved to tell Aiden what Meryn had been up to.

Colton looked at Darian and Keelan and all three winced. Colton turned to her with a wry expression on his face. "Because of five words Meryn said to us after she moved in."

"What were they?" Elizabeth asked.

"I. Know. Where. You. Sleep." Colton shuddered.

The warriors standing around them all gulped.

Sascha smiled. "Is this what we have to look forward to when our mates start arriving?" he asked.

Colton laughed. "Mayhem? Not understanding a single word that comes out of their mouths? A new set of rules for conduct and threats of bodily harm?" Colton thought about it then nodded. "Yes."

The men all groaned.

Smiling, Elizabeth patted Colton on the arm. "It gets better. I'll be in the house calming Meryn down if you need me."

"Good luck!" Keelan called.

She waved at the men and then went into the house. She had to listen for a second but quickly identified that the sounds of frustration were coming from Aiden's office. She made her way down the hall and opened the door.

"You okay, sweetie?" Elizabeth asked, walking into the office.

Meryn was slamming things around muttering under her breath. Elizabeth could see an agitated light darting around Meryn's head.

"I'm fine! He's just so damn exasperating! He was so wonderful earlier and then he pulls this shit." Meryn flung one of Aiden's folders across the room. It slammed against the wall and slid down. Elizabeth winced; she would have to organize those papers later.

"Not to sound like I'm taking his side, but I think he got worried that you were outside, especially with the feral sighting so close to the house today. He knows it's just a matter of time before they realize that Ryuu doesn't have a defensive spell up. They are getting bolder." Elizabeth walked over and picked up the folder before setting it on Aiden's desk.

Meryn sat down in Aiden's chair and frowned. Elizabeth waited.

Meryn looked up, a surprised look on her face. "You're not going to ask me what's wrong, are you?"

"No, if you want to tell me you can, but I've discovered that when someone is pressed for answers they seldom reply with the truth." Elizabeth sat down in the leather chair across from Meryn.

"I've been acting just a little bratty this month," Meryn confessed.

"No! Say it ain't so." Elizabeth teased.

Meryn smiled and continued. "Okay, I admit it, I can sometimes be a bit blunt, and I know I'm quirky, but I've been pushing the envelope with the guys. I thought for sure they would have snapped off at me by now, but they haven't. Not once have they ever told me to 'quit acting ridiculous', or to 'grow up'. They haven't made me feel like a nuisance or told me to shut up," she paused.

Elizabeth spoke gently. "Those are someone else's words and responses, aren't they?"

Meryn nodded. "My grandmother was always telling me to 'be quiet' and 'go away'. I figured it would be just a matter of time before the guys got sick of me, too."

Elizabeth got up and walked around the desk; she pulled Meryn up and gave her a hug. "Real family doesn't do things like that Meryn, and that's what we have here. They may be a bunch of chest-banging, cavemen throwbacks, but they're ours. They would never hurt your feelings. Not only do they care about you too much to do that, but they wouldn't risk pissing off your mate, or mine for that matter. Gavriel is absolutely smitten with you. He told me today that you made the long days trapped inside bearable." Elizabeth held the small woman at arm's length.

Meryn sniffled and used her sleeve to wipe her eyes. "That's why it hurt so badly when Aiden dismissed me. I knew that he wasn't doing it to hurt me, but all of a sudden, I was five again and alone."

"You're no longer five and you certainly aren't alone. You have that delightful little sprite that took on someone one hundred times his size for you, not to mention your squire. I thought he was going to deck Aiden when that fireball engulfed us." Elizabeth smiled when Meryn snickered; she was relieved that the human was bouncing back to her normal self.

Meryn looked up at her, eyes dancing. "Did you see their faces when we were covered in blue flames?" she laughed then snorted which made her laugh harder.

Elizabeth laughed right along with her, every time Meryn would snort, Elizabeth would laugh harder. It wasn't long before both women were on the floor under the desk cackling.

"*Denka*, I take it from the laughter that you are feeling better?" Ryuu asked from the doorway.

Meryn stood on her knees to look over the desk but barely cleared it. This made Elizabeth start laughing again. Meryn glared down at her. Elizabeth stuck out her tongue and wiped her eyes. Meryn stood facing her squire.

"Yeah, I'm good. I forgot for a second that I completely kick ass."

Ryuu raised a brow then smiled. "That you do. I was afraid for a moment I was going to have to do something painful to your mate, but since you are laughing and not crying, he is spared."

"Ryyuuu! You can't just knock my mate around like a kid with a toy. He's the Unit Commander for crying out loud." Meryn waved her arms about wildly.

Ryuu just stared at her. "*Denka,* that title means very little to me. Your health and well-being are my only concerns. If his ineptitude leads to another instance where you are almost barbecued then he and I will definitely have words." Ryuu crossed his arms over his chest.

Meryn turned to her. "I can't do anything with him!" she said pointing to Ryuu.

Elizabeth stood and dusted off her jeans. "That is how squires are, Meryn. My uncle's squire has yet to address my uncle with any degree of respect. Sebastian sees my uncle as his charge and nothing more. In a way, I think my uncle needs that. He can always rely on Sebastian to keep him humble."

Ryuu's expression didn't change. "I wouldn't damage him ... permanently." He shrugged.

Meryn smacked her forehead in exasperation. "I give up! And ... I'm hungry." Her concern for her mate forgotten, she looked at Ryuu with puppy dog eyes.

He gave a faint smile and bowed. "I have prepared a snack from the pastries you ladies purchased in the city earlier this afternoon, along with your favorite Earl Grey tea."

"You love me!" Meryn turned to her. "You coming?"

Elizabeth nodded. "For pastries and tea? Of course I'm coming, be there in a moment. I need to ask Ryuu about ordering a certain tea for me, especially considering I'm going to be living here."

Meryn shrugged and walked into the hallway; she paused for a second before turning back to her. "I'm really glad you're here, Bunny," Meryn confessed.

Elizabeth was too touched to rip her cute little face off for calling her 'Bunny'. "Me too, sweetie."

Meryn smiled and walked away.

Ryuu looked out the door and held up a finger. After a few seconds, he lowered his hand and turned to her. "I take it this isn't about tea?"

"I wouldn't mind if you ordered some Fortnum and Mason's English Breakfast tea. I got addicted to the stuff when we visited London. But no, what I was going to ask you is ... have you made sure all the spells have been disarmed? I'm not too proud to admit that this afternoon's fireball scared the hell out of me." She shuddered.

Ryuu scowled. "Don't remind me of that incident. Most are actually still operative, they will only activate if someone tries to open a window and enter from the outside. We can activate the front and back doors whenever we wish with the small, brass charms hanging on the walls by the doors. I have been working with Keelan on what we would need for a permanent perimeter. It's difficult because you can't, for example, ban all shifters. We would need to be very specific, but in doing so, may leave loopholes."

"As long as there's no possibility that either I or my mate will be burnt alive, I'm satisfied. Did you eavesdrop on our conversation?" she asked.

He nodded. "Naturally."

"Can you make sure Aiden understands why she got so upset? I don't think Meryn will say anything, but I think, unless Aiden knows why this impacted her so much, he will inadvertently walk into this blunder again, and it won't be his fault."

Ryuu sighed. "I suppose you're right."

Elizabeth patted him on the arm. "All in a day's work. I hope Meryn hasn't eaten all the apple fritters. She was right, they are delicious." She walked into the hallway toward the family room to wrestle Meryn for some pastries.

"She was crying." Aiden stared down at the jewelry box in his hands and shook his head.

Gavriel knew hurting Meryn enough to make her cry had devastated his commander. He looked from his friend back to the road. "These are the type of things every new couple has to face. All you can do is fall on your sword, beg forgiveness, and then do your damnedest to never hurt her again."

"I knew she had a shitty childhood, but she always made light of it. What was I thinking to ignore her like that?" Aiden beat the small blue gift-wrapped box against his forehead.

"When we get back, grovel, and beg forgiveness." Aiden groaned. Gavriel continued. "And then sit her down and get her to talk about the things that she is insecure about. Let her know you are not a mind reader and that you are not going anywhere."

Aiden turned to him. "You've seen her more than I have this past month, why would she think that I would leave?"

Inwardly, Gavriel sighed. All he wanted was to curl up with his mate and learn more about *her*. When he looked over and saw the absolute confusion on Aiden's face, he knew he had to break it down for him; he owed Meryn that much at the very least.

"Aiden, she lost both of her parents when she was very small. That alone could cause abandonment issues, but when you factor in a grandmother who ignored her existence, I bet she has been waiting for us to tell her to leave or for us to start ignoring her altogether. You really could not have screwed up in a worse way."

When he looked over, Aiden was staring at him mouth open. "Oh Gods, my poor baby."

"You will just have to tell her every day for the next fifty or so years how you feel about her," Gavriel suggested.

Aiden nodded and stared ahead. "Drive faster."

Gavriel nodded. "Yes, sir."

Elizabeth was sipping her tea when she heard a car door slam outside. Meryn turned to her, a look of panic on her face.

"What if he hates me because I torched his car?" she whispered.

"He won't, just talk to him, Meryn. He may be a shifter, but he's still a male. Use small words, not a lot of syllables, and you'll be fine," she suggested.

"Right. Small words. Got it." Meryn twisted her fingers in front of her nervously.

When they heard the front door open and close, Meryn looked like she was going to be ill.

"Breathe," Elizabeth whispered. Meryn nodded.

Aiden walked into the room, Gavriel behind him. Elizabeth had always dated shifters or fae. She liked their larger frames and muscles, but seeing her mate next to the bear shifter, she was suddenly breathless. She remembered the way his sculpted body of lean muscles had looked looming over her, he made the Unit Commander seem clumsy and bulky in comparison.

"Meryn," Aiden said stiffly.

"Aiden." Meryn stared down at her hands.

Elizabeth looked at her mate who shrugged. After another minute of silence, Elizabeth leaned over and whispered. "Remember what I said?"

Meryn nodded before turning back to Aiden. "Want. To. Have. Sex?"

Elizabeth was surprised at how fast Aiden moved, for such a large man he got to his mate in record time. Meryn giggled as Aiden swung her up in his arms and proceeded to kiss every exposed inch of her skin. Aiden turned and nearly sprinted out of the room.

Shaking her head, she picked up her cup and took another sip. "I did tell her to use short words with few syllables."

Gavriel swaggered over and dangled a small white plastic bag in front of her. "For you, my dear."

Elizabeth licked her lips and reached for the bag.

Gavriel jerked it out of reach. "You have to pay."

Elizabeth eyed him suspiciously. "What will it cost me?"

Gavriel gently lowered the bag into her hands. "The rest of the afternoon with me, I would like to get to know my mate much, much better."

"If you can secure us lunch from Ryuu, you have a deal. All I've had today is caffeine and sugar. It may be normal for Meryn, but I'm a shifter and need more sustenance."

Gavriel pulled her out of the chair and into his arms. "Deal. Head up and I will see what I can put together for our lunch."

Elizabeth stood, threw her arms around his neck, and kissed him. She had meant to surprise him, but the trick was on her. He took the kiss over and when he was done, she was panting.

"Sneaky vampire," she muttered, heading for the foyer.

"Of course, and I am sneakier than most," he admitted.

"Hurry with the food."

"As you wish."

Elizabeth turned to stare at him. Did he just quote *Princess Bride*?

Gavriel looked at her, an innocent expression on his face. "What?"

She couldn't determine if he was joking or not.

"Damn vampire."

His chuckle followed her into the foyer.

CHAPTER SEVEN

Gavriel had just reached the kitchen when he heard Beth's startled gasp and then the sound of something or someone tumbling down the stairs.

Beth!

He ran to the foyer to see his mate laid out on the floor, looking up. She blinked slowly then began moving each limb separately. Gavriel knelt at her side checking for any signs of head injury. Colton and Keelan came running from the media room. They looked down eyes wide.

"Shit! Elizabeth are you okay?" Keelan asked, kneeling at her other side taking her hand. He spoke a spell softly and their joined hands began to glow.

"Fine, this is normal. Arms and legs are okay, but I think my ribs are cracked," she said in between shallow breaths.

Keelan nodded. "I can't 'see' the injury, but there's definitely a crack, you're lucky, I don't sense a break. This spell should help you heal faster, but you'll need to rest for a while." He sat back on his heels.

Gavriel picked her up gently and held her close. Keelan stood and brushed off his pants. Gavriel was thankful that Keelan had been home to heal his mate, but what about next time? What if no one had been home? What if she had been seriously hurt? His heart continued to try and climb up his throat. He turned to Colton. "If I could beg a favor? Could you find Ryuu in the kitchen and see if he can put together a lunch for us? I want to take Beth upstairs and put her to bed to rest."

Colton looked at him. "Of course I can. You take care of Beth and I'll be up in a bit." He winked at Beth and turned to head towards the kitchen.

Keelan smiled at Beth and looked at Gavriel. "If you need, me just call. I can do another healing spell in a couple hours that should knit the bones together completely." He cracked his neck. "You know, lunch sounds really good right now. I'm always hungry after doing spells and we've done a lot today." He gave a salute and followed Colton to the kitchen.

"I can walk," Beth protested, blushing.

"If I had my way you would never walk again." He turned and started up the stairs. "I am just going to tie you to my bed where I know you'll be safe." He almost stumbled himself when her pupils dilated.

"That doesn't sound so bad," she whispered, smiling.

Politics. Politics and council meetings. Think of anything but her naked and tied down to the bed.

"If such things interest you, it would be my duty as your mate to indulge you," he murmured against her ear. When they reached the top, he turned left and walked towards their room.

"A duty huh?" she asked, arching a brow at him.

"I am very diligent and thorough when it comes to my duties." He reached down and turned the door knob. He pushed the door open with his shoulder and kicked it closed behind him. Gently, he placed her on the bed and pulled the covers up. The shock on her face soothed his pride. She wanted him as much as he wanted her.

"No, seriously, I'm okay." She went to push the covers back, and he shook his head.

"You rest for a bit. I am going to call your uncle." He pulled the covers back up.

Pouting, she glared at him but then yawned. Blushing again, she snuggled down into the covers.

"Okay, but wake me up for lunch."

"Of course, darling." He leaned down and kissed her temple.

"Best. Mate. Ever," she said and closed her eyes.

Feeling like he could take on the world, he walked out of the bedroom and into his study. He shut the door and walked over to sit down at his desk. He picked up the phone and dialed the number to the vampire leader's main office.

"Elder Rioux's office, may I ask who is speaking and the nature of your call," a crisp female voice asked.

"This is Gavriel Ambrosios calling to speak to Magnus," Gavriel said.

"Mr. Ambrosios, what is your position?" she continued.

Gavriel pulled the phone away from his ear and stared at it. He had dropped out of vampire society for a while, but dammit, she should know his name! As much as he appreciated the fact that his people had structure and weren't aware of his age, he did not like having to dance to someone else's tune.

"I am second in command to Unit Commander Aiden McKenzie of the Alpha Unit in Lycaonia," he explained.

"Oh. Shifters," she sniffed and continued. "Mr. Ambrosios, if you leave a message, Elder Rioux will get to it as soon as he can. Otherwise, I can schedule you a phone appointment. Let's see, his next available opening is March 17th." Her voice was condescending.

March 17th was over four months away!

Grinding his teeth, he took a deep breath. "I cannot wait four months to speak with him. If you would just let him know who is on the phone I am sure he would take my call."

"Mr. Ambrosios, Elder Rioux is a very important man; he does not have time to speak with every person who thinks that they have a problem. I must suggest you take your problem to your local Elder first, if he deems it important enough, I am sure that he will reach out to Elder Rioux," she advised, taking the offer to schedule him a phone appointment off the table.

"What I need to speak to him about is of a personal nature and cannot be discussed with René. Please put me on hold and tell Magnus that I am on the phone. Like I said, I'm sure he will take my call," he explained again. Like hell was he going to go to René to ask about Beth!

"That is Elder Evreux and Elder Rioux to you, sir! I honestly do not know who you think you are, but I will not allow you to speak about our Elders so disrespectfully!" she practically screeched before the line went dead.

Gavriel took a deep breath before he attempted to use his phone again. He didn't want to buy a new one because he had crushed the one in his hand.

He dialed the number again and waited.

"Elder Rioux's office, may I ask who is speaking and the nature of your call," the same female voice asked.

Gavriel didn't even bother with the niceties this time. "Put Magnus on the phone in the next five minutes or you will have to explain to Magnus why he has suddenly lost his council seat. I am Gavriel Ambrosios. I was defending our race before you and your Elders were born. Not only am I old enough to have fathered both René and Magnus, but I also own fifty-five percent of every major vampire holding since the dawn of our people. After you get your Elder on the phone, I suggest you take the time to brush up on our people's ruling houses. House Ambrosios is the oldest and most revered house of the vampire race," he hissed.

"What? I? H ... h ... hold ... please," the woman stuttered.

Breathing hard, he silently cursed himself for losing his temper. His transition was coming to an apex soon, and he was finding it harder and harder to keep himself under control.

"Who in the hell is this? And why is my secretary in tears?" an angry voice demanded.

"Hello, Magnus, it is Gavriel Ambrosios. You might want to make sure your secretary knows who the founding families are before she tells another one of us to leave a message or to go to our local Elder for insignificant issues," Gavriel said acerbically.

"Oh for crying out loud, Gavriel!" Magnus's voice became more muffled. "Yes he is who he says he is. Yes, he is a founding member. I do not know why he is not listed in your literature, you will need to find that out and fix it before coming back here tomorrow. Oh, for goodness sake woman, quit blubbering, and take the rest of the day off."

Gavriel heard a click, silence, and then seconds later Magnus's voice was back and sounding much clearer than before.

"There. I have transferred you to my personal line. You had better be treating my Bethy better than you treated my secretary," Magnus growled.

"Do not, Magnus, just do not. Later. You can berate me later all you wish, just not now." Gavriel brought a hand up and rested his forehead against it.

How was he supposed to keep Beth safe when he could barely function himself?

"Hell, Gavriel, I am sorry. How bad is it? I will not waste my breath asking which transition this is for you, since I know you will not answer, but know that you are family now. I would never do anything that would hurt my Bethy. You have your reasons for keeping your age a secret. If it is important to you, it is now important to me." Magnus's voice sounded sincere.

Gavriel closed his eyes and leaned back in his chair. "I have lost count. But this one, it is the worst it has ever been. I cannot get enough blood. The hunger is always there. The only time it recedes even for a little while is after I feed from Beth. I am not sure if her being my mate is what makes the difference."

"If it is as bad as you say, your body is preparing for a major power increase. It is not even December, Gavriel, how much longer do you have? Most vampiric apexes happen around Long Night."

"My apex should be hitting soon. I do not remember much about my childhood, but I do remember my mother telling me I was special because I was born early, I think my birthday is soon."

"You do not even remember your birthday anymore?" Magnus asked softly.

"I have forgotten more than our entire race remembers." Gavriel opened his eyes; leaning back farther, he stared at the stark white ceiling.

"By the First Blood, you are serious are you not?" Magnus whispered.

"I am afraid so. Let us just say there is much I could correct even within our history books," he said, hoping Magnus would read between the lines concerning his age.

He heard papers being moved and typing. "I am making an announcement to our people regarding your mating with Beth. I am also going to make it known that unless I find a mate of my own and produce an heir, I am naming Beth the heir to my house and you the heir to my council seat. The people here in Noctem Falls know and respect Beth despite the fact that she is a shifter. They will listen to her should something happen to me." He paused and lowered his voice. "I spoke with Beth earlier, something is coming, and I want our Houses to be joined and impregnable before this unknown threat descends upon us. We may avoid possible threats if the enemy has to take on Houses Ambrosios and Rioux combined," Magnus said.

Gavriel heard the sound of more papers rustling. "You do not have to do that, you still have plenty of time to find your own mate. You are not that old Magnus."

Magnus laughed. "Gods, you actually make me feel young and that is saying a lot, my friend. Look at it this way, our enemy may assign me a protection detail to avoid having to deal with you."

Gavriel smiled. "That it probably at least half true."

"You did not call to harass me, did you?" Magnus asked.

"No, actually I called to get Broderick Monroe's phone number."

"I will text you his information so you can add it to your contact list. Are you sure Beth is well?"

"She took a tumble down the stairs, and I almost swallowed my tongue. I was hoping Broderick could provide some insight on how he was able to raise her to adulthood in one piece." Gavriel's phone chimed as the contact information came through.

Magnus started to chuckle. "Neither Broderick nor Beth know, but Caspian came to me right after he mated with Beth's father. She was only about a year old at the time; I do not think he had slept in days. Every time he turned away, she found herself in some new life-threatening situation. What scared us all to death was that she never cried or tried to find help. One day, I found her limping through the palace hallway with her arm dangling broken at her side. Poor Cas was at a breaking point. From the age of two until she was thirty, I had one witch healer and one vampire assigned to her almost around the clock. By the time she was thirty, she knew to find someone or call out for help when she got hurt. I will not tell you how much I had to pay for the severance package for the two on her protection detail, but I will tell you it had to cover PTSD therapy, the poor bastards." Magnus chuckled again and Gavriel put a hand to his stomach, he felt like he was going to be sick.

"Still, despite her unnatural bad luck, I have never had a more dedicated assistant. It took me years to find a replacement after she decided to leave home to see how humans lived. No one was even half as competent as she was. I do not suppose you would be interested in giving up being a unit warrior to move back to Noctem Falls? Beth could go back to pretty much running things for me and you could make sure that our people do not forget what you look like," Magnus wheedled.

"I am afraid not. I am needed here; you will just have to keep replacing your secretaries," Gavriel teased.

"Damn. Keep me posted about what is happening out there. Bypass René and call me directly." Magnus instructed.

"Make sure the secretary knows to put me through," Gavriel said sourly.

"Hah! Give Beth my love."

"I will, thanks again, Magnus."

"Anytime."

Gavriel hung up feeling exhausted. Knowing Magnus, his mate had grown up with the highest level protection detail money could buy and she had still managed to hurt herself on a regular basis. Was she cursed? What had Magnus called it? Unnatural bad luck? Shaking his head, he dialed the number for Broderick Monroe.

Broderick picked up on the second ring. "Hello? Who is this?"

"Hello sir, this is Gavriel Ambrosios."

He heard a chuckle. "I thought I might be hearing from you."

In the background, Gavriel heard a second male voice ask, "Is that him?"

"Yes, Caspian, it's Beth's mate. Gavriel, I'm putting you on speakerphone." After a brief pause, he heard Broderick come back on the line. "Okay we're both here. How did Beth hurt herself?" he asked.

"She fell down the stairs."

"Ahh. Yes, she doesn't get along well with stairs or rugs. Basically, anything that could be a trip hazard is a disaster waiting to happen," Broderick said.

"Flat surfaces are best, but not a guarantee," he heard Caspian chime in.

"She won't want to wear it, but make her reset her 'Alert' necklace. You'll need to change it so that if she activates it, it will reach out to you and local friends instead of us. She absolutely hates it, but it has saved her life more than once," Broderick said.

"We had it made for her sixteenth birthday, a lot of fae magic went into it," Caspian explained.

"How did you not lose your minds with worry?" Gavriel exhaled.

He heard the men laugh. "Who says that we didn't? We still worry?" Caspian asked.

"There were so many nights where we just laid in bed and stared up at the ceiling and prayed to whoever was listening that she would outlive us. We were thankful each and every evening after she went to bed that she had survived one more day. The years she lived out amongst humans were the worst." Broderick's voice cracked.

"She is safe now, love." Caspian murmured.

"Is she? Is she really? Gavriel, she told us you were going through transition and that you have an enemy stalking Lycaonia who has even threatened Unit Commander McKenzie's mate. On top of everything, my precious baby is the type of person who can't even check the mail without sustaining a concussion. Is she safe there with all the dangers and with you?" Broderick asked.

Gavriel moved the phone to his other ear. "All the unit warriors have been patrolling night and day in addition to daily training to keep the city and people safe. We have created new protocols and drills to help us fight this new enemy. Just today, we installed alarm and protection spells here at the Alpha estate to keep our mates safe. Even with this new threat, I honestly feel she is safer here with the Alpha Unit than anywhere else," he said.

"Is she safe with you? My brother's last transition was brutal. The more we gain in terms of abilities and strength, the harder the transition is on us, and this was the transition that put him in position to become our Elder, so you know how perilous it was. Toward the end, right before his apex, he turned savage. We are at our most aggressive right before we gain our new abilities. Given Beth's uncanny bad luck, is she really safe at your side?" Caspian asked, his voice hard.

Gavriel didn't answer right away. He thought about the growing number of instances where he had lost control recently. His first encounter with Beth had been almost violent, and he knew it would get worse the closer he got to his apex. He searched himself for the answer. When the time came, would he recognize his own mate? Finally, he gave the only answer he could.

"I do not know. I want to assure you ... hell, I want to assure myself that I would never hurt her. But I cannot guarantee it. I can swear to you that I would never knowingly or willingly lay a single finger on her in anger. That I would die to protect her, but you may be right, I may be more of a danger to her than our enemy." He covered his eyes with his hand. "Maybe I should send her back to Noctem Falls and to you."

One of the men exhaled loudly. "Safeguard yourself. Right before my brother's apex hit, he knew it was coming, and he asked to be chained. It was the only thing that kept those around him safe, including myself. I want to tell you, 'yes, send her to us', but I know that would be wrong. Mates belong together. If Fate has brought Beth into your life, now of all times, then I have to believe that she is there for a reason. I have to, or lose my mind with worry," Caspian admitted.

"Thank you for that. I've been without a mate for so long, I thought Fate had forgotten me," Gavriel said ruefully.

"If there is one thing I have learned in my short life, it is that Fate has a design of her own weaving. We may only catch a glimpse of the pieces, but there is a much bigger tapestry being woven that we know nothing of. Fate did not forget you Gavriel; she was just waiting for our Bethy to grow up," Caspian said kindly.

"Thank all the Gods you watched over her the way you did, or I may not have gotten her at all. Is there anything I can do to minimize the, um, accidents?"

"Not to make Beth sound juvenile, because she is not childish by any stretch of the imagination, in fact, when she is not actively tripping, falling or tumbling, she is very graceful and poised, but you may want to consider 'baby proofing' the estate," Caspian advised.

"Baby proofing? What's that?" Gavriel got out a pad of paper and pen. At the top, he wrote a reminder to get her alert necklace reset.

"Oh hell, I guess you wouldn't have much experience with children. But doing things like placing pillows around a brick fireplace so that the angled edge isn't exposed or replacing glass furniture with blunt edged pieces. Lots of soft surfaces and padding. Stairs will always be a danger but by now she's learned how to fall down them with minimal damage," Broderick explained.

"If you are together, try to keep one hand on her at all times, you never know when she will just topple over." Caspian added.

"Never, ever let her in the kitchen, *ever*. There are too many ways something can go wrong." Gavriel could almost see Broderick shuddering. He took notes quickly.

"We have a squire living here at the Alpha estate so she should not have to go to the kitchen often," he said.

"Thank the Gods," Caspian murmured.

"Do not let her order fish too often; we had a scare when she choked on some bones that were supposedly removed," Broderick continued.

"Bathrooms are dangerous too, but, well, we had to let her on her own in there for obvious reasons; but you are not restricted in that area," Caspian said then cleared his throat.

"Garages, hardware stores, warehouses, and workshops are especially hazardous." Broderick went on listing the places his mate couldn't go.

Gavriel paused in writing the list. "We have an armory on premises."

"Oh. My. Gods," Broderick whispered.

"No. Just, no! Not only do you need to lock the door you need a biometric sensor to keep her out!" Caspian sounded like he was hyperventilating.

"Easy my love, breathe," Broderick said.

"She is not stupid enough to play with weapons!" Gavriel said heatedly. His mate was not immature or reckless.

"Of course she is not! She is a mature, responsible, and grounded woman. But she will somehow find herself in a situation where she has to go in the armory and then once she is inside something horrible will happen." Caspian said between gasps.

"Gavriel, Beth isn't klutzy; she literally has the worst luck I have ever seen. She'll walk into the armory and for some unknown reason a stack of crates holding grenades, that haven't moved in years will suddenly come tumbling down. In the process, several pins will dislodge and she'll be trapped under the fallen boxes." Broderick paused. "I don't suppose you watch human movies?"

"Meryn has been having us watch them more so we can understand her."

"Have you ever seen *Final Destination*?" he asked.

"Oh fuck," Gavriel whispered.

"Yes, that about sums it up." Broderick sounded defeated.

"Do they make bubble wrap body suits with tracking devices?" Gavriel joked.

"We could start on a prototype," Caspian offered immediately.

"I will just keep her in our room," Gavriel said putting the pen down. That was the only way to keep her safe.

"That's just it; you have to let her walk out on her own. You'll watch her trip and tumble. She will break bones and scrape her skin off. You'll want to cry for her as she's getting bones set and skin stitched back together, but you have to let her fall," Broderick said.

"Why in the hell would I do that?" Gavriel practically yelled.

"If you are constantly holding on to her and guarding her every step, she won't have the strength or confidence to stand on her own. If you tell her how and where to step, she won't be able to walk through life, and if you don't let her walk, you'll never see her fly. And when she is confident and flying through life, she shines." Broderick's voice sounded reverent.

Gavriel felt a deep sense of admiration for these two men. They had been strong enough to watch the one person they loved more than life struggle through so much pain to become the strong woman she is today. "It must have been so hard watching her grow up. I do not know if I will have the strength to watch her get hurt," Gavriel admitted.

Both men laughed. "Growing up? Gavriel, that was last week watching her recover from crashing out of that office window. She fell out of her wheelchair and broke her other arm." Caspian laughed along with his mate.

Gavriel pulled the phone back and stared at it in horror. His mind raced. How could he keep his mate alive? He put the phone back to his ear.

"So, what kind of timeline were you thinking of for that bubble wrap suit?" he asked.

The men just continued to laugh.

Shit!

CHAPTER EIGHT

Beth heard the study door open and close, then the sound of a tray being placed on the dresser. Seconds later the bed dipped down. She opened her eyes and looked at her mate. He looked exhausted and worried. She reached up and pushed his hair away from his face.

"Whatever is worrying you, it will be okay," she whispered.

His smile was forced. "Are you hungry, baby? Colton left a tray for you."

She shook her head and snuggled closer to him.

"Go back to sleep baby, you need your rest. I will wake you up for dinner." He pulled the blankets up around them and curled up behind her pulling her close. She closed her eyes and enjoyed the feel of him. Out of nowhere, the thought hit her that this was her home now.

"Gavriel?"

"Yes, love?"

"Would it be okay if I had my uncle send my things?" Now that she knew she would be living here, she wanted the rest of her wardrobe with her.

"Of course, I will clean out a part of the closet tomorrow." He kissed the back of her head.

Part of the closet? That's so cute. Oh well, he'll find out soon enough.

Smiling, she let herself drift off and return to her nap.

"Beth, honey, time to wake up." She felt a hand on her shoulder. Blinking, she looked up. Her mate was standing beside the bed looking dapper as usual, whereas she could almost feel her bed head.

"Is it morning?" she asked.

He shook his head. "No, it's time for dinner." She could tell he was trying not to smile.

"How bad is it?"

"You may want to stop by the bathroom before we go downstairs." His eyes danced with laughter. She wanted to pull the pillow over her head. Sighing, she got up and walked over to the bathroom. The pain in her side was nearly gone. She reached for the doorknob and noticed he was staying fairly close to her.

Turning, she looked him in the eye. "I don't need a babysitter, Gavriel."

"Maybe I just want to always be near you."

"Fine, but you stay out here while I make myself presentable," she countered.

He nodded and pointed to the bathroom. "I will wait right out here."

She huffed and walked into the bathroom, closing the door behind her. When she looked at herself in the mirror, she gasped. On the other side of the door, she heard his chuckle. Her hair was sticking straight up. Mortified, she turned the water on and wet her hair. She ran a brush through the tangled mess until she looked less like an escapee from an insane asylum and more like the socialite she was. She powdered her face with her compact and added a bit of lipstick. She was so pale; she needed the pop of color the lipstick provided.

"When were you going to tell me about your alert necklace?" she heard him ask. Mentally, she began to curse her fathers. Of course, they would tell him about her magical leash. She opened the door and scowled at him.

"I hate that damn thing. We don't need it."

"I must insist that you re-code it so that should you ever need to use it, it will alert me and not your fathers, who are across the country and not in a position to provide immediate assistance." One look at his face and she knew better than to argue. She had learned growing up; you had to pick your battles and this one she would not win.

"Fine!" she stomped over to her suitcase and pulled out the small velvet pouch that had been tucked away in the corner. She opened the drawstrings and turned it upside down dropping a large pendant necklace and three blue stone key chains into her hand. She turned to him. "This pendant came with six keystones. Both my fathers and my uncle each have one. You will receive the fourth. Who would you recommend to receive the fifth and sixth for here in Lycaonia?"

Gavriel stared down at the small, plain looking flat stones. "Are those worry stones?" he asked.

She sighed. "Yes, the fae warrior who made these for us had a sense of humor. But it actually worked out for the best; since they are small and flat, they're easy to carry." She held one up to him.

He took it and turned it over in his hand. "I would recommend Meryn and Adelaide."

His recommendations surprised her. "Not your commander?" she asked.

He shook his head. "If I was not here, it is almost a guarantee that I would be on a mission with Aiden, so it would be pointless to have two stones with us. If Adelaide had one, you would be able to alert her, Marius, and more importantly Elder McKenzie to the fact that you need help. Any of those three would be able to mobilize assistance in minutes."

She nodded. "And Meryn?"

Smiling he handed the stone back to her. "She is crazy enough to do anything to save you; in addition to that, Ryuu is always with her. I have a feeling there is not much those two cannot do," he admitted.

"Those were the two I'd chosen as well. Okay, give me a moment." She placed the three remaining keystones so that they were touching the large pendant and whispered the spell that she'd learned on her sixteenth birthday. When she opened her eyes, the stones were glowing a deep burnished gold. After a few seconds, the glow faded, and the stones returned to their normal royal blue color. She handed a stone to him and he immediately added it to his key ring.

"I'll give Meryn and Adelaide theirs later." She put the necklace on and sighed.

Her mate surprised her by pulling her in for a kiss. When she looked up at him questioningly, he smiled.

"I know that you hate it, but thank you for wearing it. It will help me worry less when I'm not with you," he said and kissed her on the tip of her nose.

And just like that, she didn't mind the necklace anymore. If it helped her mate worry less so he could concentrate more on himself to avoid getting hurt, then she would gladly wear the stupid leash.

"Come on, let's head downstairs. Tonight Ryuu made one of Meryn's favorites, his own version of Hot Pockets. Each one has a different filling, but you do not know what it is until you eat it. It is actually quite amusing."

"I can't wait." And she meant it. She had had more fun in the past couple days with her mate than in the previous year living alone.

She grabbed her wristlet, and they left the room. As they walked, Elizabeth noticed that he matched his steps to hers perfectly, his hand never leaving the small of her back. She knew he was doing it to prevent a fall, and it made her feel just as rebellious as when her uncle and fathers did it when she was at home. But, she had to admit his touch, though small, felt wonderful. Her animal was practically purring like a kitten. The warmth from his hand was more comforting than controlling. His touch was feather light, acting more like a reminder that he was there, rather than a censure of her. Looking over at him, she noticed that even though his features remained unyielding and stoic, his eyes were warm and almost kind. Just that small touch at her back was enough to put him at ease. Slowly, he was worming his way into her heart. Shaking her head, she reached out and hooked her finger through his belt loop. When he turned to look at her, his rare smile held so much joy that she forgot about her footing and tripped. Laughing, he simply extended his arm and wrapped it around her waist, holding her close. He had a way of making her feel like the most precious thing in his world.

I didn't need my heart anyway; I guess it's safe enough in his pocket.

When they walked into the dining room, Meryn was sitting on Aiden's lap laughing and holding up a square pastry to his mouth. The three other men stood.

Gavriel walked her to their seats and pulled out her chair. She sat, and he scooted her in. He sat down as Meryn continued to fuss at her mate. The men sat down and watched Meryn and their commander.

"No way! You know the rules, if you pick it out, you have to eat it." She swung the pastry back and forth in front of his mouth.

Aiden frowned at his mate. "But I didn't smell the wasabi until it was under my nose. You know I hate that stuff, baby." He looked up at Meryn with sad blue eyes.

Meryn sighed. "Fine, I'll eat it. But if I get one I don't like, you have to eat it." She took a bite and smiled.

Aiden turned to them. "Just in time for the fun." His attention turned to Meryn when she started to wave a hand in front of her mouth. He picked up a glass of water and brought it up to her lips. She took the glass and downed the contents then sat back against his chest.

"Hey Bunny, did you have a good nap?" she asked.

Elizabeth looked around the room and made eye contact with the men whose mouths were twitching. She gave them the same look she used to give Magnus's erroneous aides.

"She can get away with it, you, cannot." The men gulped and nodded.

Ryuu walked in and placed two tall glasses of blood in front of Gavriel.

"Thank you, Ryuu." Gavriel lifted a glass and began to drink. Elizabeth was unfazed. Growing up in Noctem Falls, she was used to seeing blood being served at meals, but if Meryn's reaction was anything to go by Gavriel didn't drink his blood at the table often. She watched him in rapt fascination as he drained the first glass. When she began fidgeting, Elizabeth knew that something was about to pop out of her mouth, poor Meryn looked like she was about to implode from keeping whatever she wanted to say in.

"Do you always drink from a glass?" she finally exploded.

Gavriel shook his head. "Over my lifetime, I have fed in nearly every way imaginable. Drinking from a glass is tame in comparison."

Meryn started to grin. "Would you drink from a man?"

Gavriel nodded.

"Would you drink in a van?" she asked her eyes dancing.

"I don't see why not," he replied.

Elizabeth stared at Meryn as she continued.

"Would you drink from an actor?"

Again, Gavriel nodded.

Laughing, Elizabeth shook her head at Meryn.

"Would you drink on a tractor?" Meryn could barely get the words out she was laughing so hard.

Gavriel frowned. "Maybe from a farmer if the need were dire."

Her mate's serious answers to Meryn's macabre Dr. Seuss questioning made the scene all the more hilarious.

"Don't, please, Meryn." Elizabeth gasped.

The men were staring at them as if they were crazy. When they had both caught their breaths, Aiden frowned down at his mate.

"I can never understand what you say," he complained.

Meryn shrugged. "That's not my fault, I tried to indoctrinate you into the wonderful world of the gamer geek, but it's like you have some sort sci-fi/fantasy narcolepsy. It's weird. The second I try to show you something, you fall asleep."

Aiden grimaced. "I can't help it, it makes me tired."

Meryn looked back at Gavriel. "What does that taste like?" she asked.

Colton laughed, and Darian groaned before reaching into his back pocket for his wallet. He took out a twenty and passed it to Colton.

Colton shook his head and tucked it into his shirt pocket. "I told you she would ask."

Darian scowled at his friend. "I should have known better."

Gavriel regarded Meryn, his eyes kind. Elizabeth knew her mate wasn't mad. Meryn wasn't asking to be rude; she just wanted to know. She had no idea what a huge breach of etiquette it was to ask a vampire about blood.

"It has the viscosity of thick cherry syrup, the intoxicating jolt of your morning cappuccino, and the comforting savory taste of a hearty winter stew," Gavriel held up his glass and winked at Meryn.

She licked her lips. "Can I try?"

Aiden shook his head. "No Meryn, it wouldn't taste the same for you. You've licked a cut finger before right?" he asked. She nodded. "To us blood simply tastes like meat or hamburger, it's nowhere near as enticing as it is for a vampire," he explained.

She blinked at him. "Wait. Your blood tastes like hamburgers? How is that fair? When I lick a cut on my finger, all I taste is copper." She frowned down at her finger.

Aiden looked around the table. "Blood tastes like hamburgers to you guys, right?" he asked.

Elizabeth nodded as did Colton. Keelan and Darian shook their heads.

"To me, blood tastes like earth." Darian was now frowning at his own finger.

"It tastes like ozone to me, the way ozone smells anyway," Keelan contributed.

Elizabeth glanced around the table. Now all the men except Gavriel were staring at their fingers. "How did we not know that? I always assumed it tasted the same for everyone," she asked.

Ryuu walked in and set a platter of fresh pastries in front of them. "That's because our people are so concerned with being proper that they forgot how to be curious. Meryn has no preconceived notions of etiquette, so when she wants to know something she asks. Curiosity is valued and encouraged amongst humans, whereas we value tradition and status." Ryuu's explanation seemed to weigh the room down. Finally, Meryn broke the silence.

"So basically I kick ass, yet again," she said seriously and reached for another pastry.

Elizabeth couldn't help it; she began to laugh. Aiden shook his head smiling and Colton began to flick crumbs at Meryn. Meryn's inborn need to avoid tension and confrontation led her to be slightly silly, but that also meant those around her were usually smiling.

Elizabeth picked up her own pastry and took a bite. She had lucked out; it was a spinach and feta mix. Humming happily, she finished that pastry and reached for another. When she had consumed two more, she noticed that her mate had yet to eat anything, but was instead on his eighth glass of blood. That was more than four times the normal blood requirement and still he drank. Concerned, she tapped his leg and nodded to the red tinted empty glass. Gavriel brought her hand up and kissed her knuckles. Ryuu set another two glasses down and took the emptied glasses away. Gavriel kissed her hand one more time before releasing it to pick up his glass.

"So what would I taste like?" Meryn asked. Aiden growled and pulled her closer to him.

Gavriel shook his head. "Meryn, you're the only one in Lycaonia whose blood isn't enticing to me at all."

Aiden stopped growling, a surprised look on his face. "You never told me that."

Gavriel took another long drink and set the glass down. "I'm not sure why, but even when I'm at my most thirsty, she has no appeal whatsoever to me."

Meryn looked at Gavriel, the insecurity in her eyes was there for everyone to see. "Am I not good enough?" she asked quietly. Aiden immediately nuzzled her neck and rubbed his chin over the top of her head making Meryn's head rock from side to side like a bobble head.

"Meryn, that's not it at all. Trust me, I would rather drink from you than Colton," Gavriel said gently.

"Hey! I resent that. I am irresistible to both sexes, thank you very much," Colton preened.

Meryn smiled at Colton then frowned. "I wonder why I don't seem yummy."

Aiden kissed the back of her head. "You're yummy to me," he admitted.

"Besides, if he's going to drink from anyone, it's going to be me. Sorry, Colton." Elizabeth winked at the wolf shifter.

Colton pouted, then laughed. "I guess you can have him," he teased.

"Thanks, he's the mate of my dreams, and I'm not giving him up." She leaned into Gavriel when he wrapped an arm around her shoulders.

"I have been meaning to ask you, did you dream about me, before we met?" Gavriel asked, looking down at her.

Elizabeth shook her head. "Sort of. I would dream about situations and then they would happen, but you weren't there. Only, I felt like someone was watching and was worried about me. Normally being watched over always made me feel like a child, but in the dream I felt genuine affection and admiration for me."

"That was probably me. I dreamt of you constantly in dangerous situations and I could not do anything about it." Gavriel shuddered.

Colton sat back, his normally jovial face somber. "So what you dream about your mate is true," he said softly.

Elizabeth turned to him. "Have you dreamt of your mate?" she asked and the table got quiet.

He nodded. "It started last week. At first, I didn't see anyone in particular, just random faces, only the place remained the same. Then the same woman started to appear, just her face. Always looking sad, tired, and anxious. I know she's in trouble, but I only get a glimpse each night and then the dream is over."

Gavriel was the first to speak. "I do not think the dreams are meant to scare us. I think they are meant to help us understand what our mates are going through and potential threats so that we can better understand them and keep them safe."

Aiden nodded. "My dream about Meryn didn't come exactly true. She wasn't stabbed to death. But I think because I was so cautious about her safety because of the dreams, that I changed the outcome."

Meryn smiled at Colton. "I know for a fact that the reason I accepted Aiden so easily is because I'd been dreaming of him. I had dreams where we spoke and had fun and scary ones where I was being stalked. But it was the pain on his face as I was dying in my dreams that helped me to take that huge leap of faith in accepting him." Aiden growled low, his face taking on a haunted look hearing about that particular dream.

Gavriel continued. "Every night was hell watching Beth get hurt, but I know that it was not meant to torture me, it was meant to prepare me. I think the dreams are truly meant to help us accept our matings."

"I've dreamt of my mate as well. I think she's one of the cashiers at that grocery store in Madison," Keelan said suddenly. Everyone turned to look at him.

"Then why haven't you gone to claim her?" Darian asked.

Keelan shook his head. "Because she's away at college, about ready to graduate. She'll be back for the holidays. My dreams aren't scary, but I do think Gavriel's right in that they help us get to know our mates better. In my dreams my mate and I joke around and play video games." He smiled widely.

"That doesn't sound very romantic to me," Darian commented.

Keelan shrugged. "She's fun. After she graduates and moves back, I'll head to town and meet her. I can't wait."

Colton smiled at Keelan's enthusiasm, but Elizabeth noticed that it didn't quite reach his eyes. He was still worried about his own mate.

Ryuu stepped away from the wall and began to pick up empty platters. "I still find it odd that so many matings are happening all at once."

Aiden laughed. "You can blame my mother in part for that one and the desire for grandchildren."

Ryuu nodded and continued to clear the table.

It dawned on Elizabeth that Ryuu was right. If something was brewing then it couldn't be a coincidence that the mating spell had been cast. She met Ryuu's eyes and nodded. She would add that to the ever-growing list of things that needed additional follow up.

"Did you remember to contact your uncle about your things?" Gavriel asked breaking her train of thought.

"Sugar! No, I forgot. Good thing they're two hours behind us." She pulled her phone out of her wristlet and sent off a quick text to her uncle's assistant asking him to overnight freight her things.

"Speaking of my things, you weren't actually using that darling little study were you?" she asked sweetly.

Her mate's eyes narrowed. "Why?"

"Because I am commandeering it for my closet."

"Closet? My study is over three hundred square feet." His shocked expression was adorable.

"Good point. Do you use the library as well?"

He stared unblinking. "Yes, actually I do."

"Oh well. I'll need to call in a contractor to remodel the study into functional wardrobe."

"Contractor?" he asked, his face taking on a worried expression.

"You do have contractors and craftsmen in Lycaonia don't you?" She looked around the table.

Aiden was smiling widely. "Of course we do, Elizabeth. In fact I will call them in the morning and have them come by to go over designs with you." He turned to Gavriel. "I knew there had to be something; she seemed too perfect." He threw his head back and laughed.

Gavriel scowled at his friend before turning to her. "The whole study?"

"Yes, the whole study. Do you have any idea how much ventilation quality clothing requires?" she demanded.

Aiden laughed and banged his hand on the table. "Say goodbye to your study," he teased mercilessly.

Meryn sighed. "I wish we had a study."

Gavriel looked at Meryn in surprise before a sly smile crossed his lips. "Aiden does have a study, Meryn." Aiden immediately stopped laughing and glared at Gavriel.

"I know, his office downstairs," Meryn pouted.

Smiling broadly, Gavriel shook his head. "No, he also has one upstairs. Each warrior suite comes with a master bedroom and bath and two additional rooms."

Meryn turned sharply in Aiden's lap to face him. "We don't have a study."

He ran a hand across the back of his neck. "Actually, we do."

"No, we don't."

"Yes, we do."

"Then where in the hell is it? I've been living here over a month, I would have noticed a whole other room!"

"The door to the study is partially covered by the aquarium, you probably missed it."

"We have a study?" She asked again.

"Yes."

"We have our own study?" she asked this time sounding more excited.

"Yes?" Aiden looked down at her confused.

Elizabeth sat back and held up a hand and began a countdown. And in five, four, three, two...

"Holy shit balls, I have my own game room!" Meryn hopped off Aiden's lap and darted out of the room. Seconds later they heard the sound of small feet pounding up the stairs and racing down the hall.

Aiden groaned and dropped his head to the table.

"Serves you right." Darian laughed.

"But I keep my weights in there for when I can't sleep," Aiden complained.

"I am sure that contractor will be more than happy to help you get rid of them," Gavriel said congenially.

A minute later they heard the sound of feet thumping down the stairs. Meryn appeared in the doorway breathless.

"It's so fucking cool! The door is almost hidden, it's like I have my own bat cave. But those weights totally have to go; I'm calling dibs on that room." She walked over and sat down in the empty chair next to Aiden.

Aiden frowned down at her. "How can you call dibs on a room I've been using for the past five hundred years?" he demanded.

Meryn looked up and smiled. "Did you call dibs?"

Aiden shook his head. "Of course, I didn't."

"Ha! Then I get it fair and square," Meryn countered.

Elizabeth turned to her mate. "Do we seem dull and staid in comparison?"

Gavriel shook his head. "I think it is more that Meryn lives in and rules her own world."

"Why would I call dibs on my own room?" Aiden asked.

Meryn ignored him and looked over to Elizabeth. "Will you help me design a game room? I've always wanted one."

Elizabeth nodded. "Sure, I don't know much about games, but I can help you pick out furniture and decor."

"But that's my weight room; I've used it for hundreds of years!" Aiden protested.

Meryn turned to her mate. "Then you've had it long enough and now it's my turn. Be an adult and share. Besides, I called dibs."

"Whatever makes you happy, baby," Aiden said, leaning back in total defeat.

"Sweet! Then later it can be a game-themed nursery." Meryn grabbed the last pastry so that Ryuu could take the empty plate to the kitchen.

Aiden was mindlessly nodding his agreement when her words sunk in. He stood so fast his chair flew back.

"A ... a ... a ... are you? Could you be?" he stuttered.

"What pregnant? Technically... yes. You never did pick up condoms when you raided the grocery store for tampons. Maybe, but I don't think so," she stopped and looked down at her hands and counted. "Yeah, maybe. But if you want to explore the possibility of getting me pregnant, I won't wear the amulet. That is, if you go buy condoms."

"We can have a baby if I go buy condoms?" Aiden asked breathlessly.

"That's kinda contradictory, but yes." Meryn nodded.

Aiden looked the other men.

"Ryuu, I'm leaving my mate with you. Come on, men." He bolted for the front door.

Gavriel kissed her cheek then joined the other men as they followed Aiden out of the room.

Ryuu shook his head as he stacked the plates on his arm. "Meryn, you are terrible."

Grinning, she popped the last bite into her mouth. "That should keep him busy for a while."

Elizabeth chuckled. "Won't you have to get pregnant now?"

Meryn shrugged. "I think I may already be pregnant, it's why I haven't put the amulet on. I'm not sure what it would do to Meryn 2.0."

Elizabeth and Ryuu stared at Meryn. Finally, Ryuu asked the question bouncing around her own head. "Then why did you tell him to get condoms?"

Meryn shrugged and spread her hands. "Because it will be funny watching him try to use them later?"

Elizabeth grabbed her stomach and laughed so hard she thought she was going to wet herself.

"Meryn, I think you're my hero," she said gasping for air.

"I know. I kick ass!"

Laughing, Ryuu leaned down and kissed Meryn's forehead before carrying the plates to the kitchen.

My little sister is very kick ass.

CHAPTER NINE

Gavriel leaned his head back against the headrest as his commander drove at break neck speeds toward the Duck In. What he really wanted was to be snuggled up with his own mate, but he knew that this was important to Aiden. The bear shifter had been dreaming of a family for centuries.

"Okay men. You heard her. We need to buy condoms; I think it may help her to get pregnant," Aiden said, laying out the mission.

"What are condoms? Do paranormals use them?" Keelan asked.

Darian shook his head. "I've never heard of them. Have you Gavriel?" Darian, Colton, and Keelan turned to face him.

"I have a vague idea of what they are. I know the practice of using them started amongst humans hundreds of years ago," Gavriel said. Beyond that, he did not know much.

"Is there a human handbook? Ever since Meryn has moved in, I'm discovering that I don't know as much as I thought I did about their daily lives. It's humbling," Darian complained.

"We don't need a handbook. We have Bart. He's the older gentleman we met at the grocery store the last time we went. He is a great source of knowledge." Aiden said.

"What if he's not there?" Colton asked.

"Good point. Keelan use your phone and go to The Google and see what it has to say about condoms," Aiden ordered.

Keelan took out his phone and its soft, white light lit up his face. As the miles flew by Keelan's frown grew deeper and deeper. As they were pulling into the parking lot, Gavriel noticed that the young witch was blushing and his ears were scarlet.

Aiden turned off the ignition and turned around in the driver's seat to face Keelan.

"Report," he said.

"Umm, sir, can we just go in and check something?" Keelan stared down at his phone unable to meet his commander's eyes.

"Didn't The Google have anything?" Aiden asked.

"Sir, it's awfully hot in here. I'm going inside." Keelan opened the door, practically jumped out, and slammed the door behind him. Aiden stared at the now empty seat, a surprised look on his face.

"What's wrong with him?" Aiden pointed out the window where Keelan waited for them by the sliding entrance door.

"Aiden, according to Meryn, condoms deal with pregnancy, maybe he is embarrassed. He is young, after all," Gavriel suggested.

A look of sympathetic understanding crossed Aiden's face. "Of course. Okay, men. Just like last time. Call out when you find them; my future son depends on us and the success of this mission," Aiden said in a passion-filled voice.

Darian crossed his arm over his chest in salute. "You can count on us, sir."

Colton nodded. "Let's do this." He reached behind him and pulled out his nine millimeter. He checked the chamber, secured the safety, and returned it to the holster.

Aiden hesitated before saying. "Colton, I don't think we'll be attacked at the Duck In."

Colton raised an eyebrow. "And until today, I wouldn't have thought that ferals had balls big enough to approach Gavriel, of all people, next to the Alpha estate either. Things change."

Aiden nodded after a moment. "You men always help me to think when I'm distracted."

Colton grinned and opened his car door. "No extra charge."

Gavriel waited for Darian to get out before he climbed out of the third row passenger seat. He liked sitting back there; it was like he had the entire back of the SUV to himself.

They met up with Keelan who was still the color of a tomato and went inside. They walked in and from across the store they heard a familiar male chuckle.

"I see all your boys are with you now. Wha'd'ya do this time?" Bart chuckled.

"Nothing. My woman asked me to pick something up," Aiden announced across the store.

"Whatcha after tonight boy?" Bart called out.

"Condoms!" Aiden yelled. Several people turned and were staring at them slack jawed. Women started to edge away from them.

Behind the counter, Bart laughed. "I guess yer not in trouble anymore." Under his breath, Gavriel heard the old coot say, "This should be good."

The men spread out and searched the rows. After a few minutes, they heard Keelan whisper.

"Sir, I found them," he hissed, trying to keep his voice down.

"What was that Keelan? Did you say you found the condoms?" Aiden shouted from the aisle that held the soap. Nodding frantically, Keelan didn't answer just pointed. The men gathered around the small display section and stared.

"These boxes are smaller than the tampon boxes," Darian observed.

Colton picked one up and began reading. He laughed, then stopped laughing, stared and then frowned. "Aiden, I don't think this is right."

"Why?" Aiden picked up a box and began reading. "Says right here, Colton, 'Pleasure Pack'. Sounds promising, doesn't it?"

Darian looked down at the boxes. "Aiden, be careful. This one says: 'Twisted, Intense, and Fire & Ice'. Sounds like torture devices to me."

In the background, Gavriel heard Bart burst out laughing.

Gavriel picked up a box and started reading. "Aiden these things *prevent* pregnancy and STDs, whatever they are."

Aiden shook his head. "That can't be right. If Meryn said to get them, I'm getting them. She said if I got these we could have a baby, so I'm not leaving the store without them."

"This one says 'lubricated'; that has to be good, right?" Darian asked, holding up his box.

Aiden nodded. "Do you think they come with instructions?" he turned the box over in his hands.

Keelan leaned in and pulled Aiden down. What he whispered had the men staring at the boxes.

Aiden stood up and glared down at Keelan. "They go *where*?" he demanded.

"Oh stop! Y'all are killing me!" Bart pounded on the counter.

Aiden frowned. "The quicker we get back, the quicker Meryn can explain this to me. Let's just pick some out."

Gavriel stood shoulder-to-shoulder with his unit staring down at the boxes.

Darian rubbed his chin. "If it were me, I would go with the one with the warrior on it."

Colton nodded. "Agreed."

"Okay men, grab the ones that have honored our fallen Trojan brothers and let's go."

From the front counter, Bart called out. "Make sure you get the right size."

Aiden looked over to the old man wide eyed. "They come in sizes?"

Bart nodded. "And considering how they're used, you don't want one that's too big or too small, if you take my meaning." His mouth twitched.

"How do I know what size I am?" Aiden yelled.

"Perverts!" an old woman hissed and walked past with her loaf of bread.

Bart cackled. "Don't mind Ethel, she's just ornery because no man ever went shopping for her, if you know what I mean."

"Bartholomew Macleod, I'll tell your wife you said that to me," Ethel threatened.

Bart shrugged. "Go ahead, she knows you're not getting any, either."

Ethel gasped. "Well, I never!"

Bart laughed. "Probably part of your problem."

Ethel threw the loaf of bread at him and shuffled out as quickly as she could.

Aiden looked remorseful. "I'm sorry you lost a customer because of my inquiry."

Bart waved off his concerns. "She'll be back tomorrow asking which size you bought."

Aiden blushed. "Oh." He turned back to the men. "Is there a chart?"

Keelan shook his head frowning down at the box. "There's no chart. But Aiden, are you allergic to latex?"

"I don't think so, why?"

"These are made with latex, but they say if you're allergic to latex to try some of their lambskin condoms. You don't think they actually use the skin of a lamb do you?" he asked, his eyes looking frightened.

Aiden simply looked over at Bart who shook his head. "Don't be silly boy, that would be a waste of perfectly good leather."

The men breathed a sigh of relief.

"They're made from the lamb's intestines," Bart informed them.

Keelan dropped his box and stood back. "Humans are monsters!" he whispered.

"That's it! Grab the latex ones in the biggest size they have, we're leaving." Flushed, the men grabbed at the boxes and headed to Bart's register.

"That's a lot of condoms boy, and all of them are in extra-extra large. I didn't even know we offered this size." He blew dust off the box. "You sure you're not being optimistic?" he raised an eyebrow.

Grinning, Aiden leaned in and whispered to the old man. The old man sat back. "You're pulling my chain."

Aiden shook his head.

"No wonder yer woman set your car on fire. I would too if someone came at me with that every night. Poor darlin'." Bart rang up the boxes.

"She's no longer angry with me and is talking about having a baby." Aiden said proudly.

Bart stopped mid scan and stared at Aiden. He looked down at the counter of condom boxes and started shaking his head as he resumed ringing up his purchase. "I have got to meet yer woman. Sounds like she has a sense of humor, that one. She reminds me of my wife. Okay boy, here's yer bag." Bart held it out and Aiden handed him the money.

As he was making change, the old man was still shaking his head. "Tell yer woman if she comes to visit me, I'll give her some cake. It would be worth it to meet her." He handed the change back to Aiden.

Aiden accepted his change. "For cake, she'll definitely come. She loved the chocolate one I bought her."

"Good luck son, I think you're going to need it," Bart said sincerely.

"I do, too," Gavriel murmured. The men all nodded.

When they got back to the estate, Aiden immediately went upstairs in search of his mate. The others waved goodnight and went in separate directions to their own suites. Gavriel followed the scent of his mate until he found her curled up in the recliner in the family room covered with a red throw. She had her hand tucked under her cheek and was breathing evenly. The light from the fireplace made her blonde hair glow like a halo. He walked over and gently shook her shoulder.

"*Zain'ka moya,* time to go to bed." He ran a hand over her hair.

She stirred and opened her eyes. She blinked up at him. "Did you accomplish your mission?" she asked smirking.

He nodded. "Yes, though I am not quite sure they are meant to help."

Beth chuckled and pushed the leg rest down in the recliner. When she went to stand, she stumbled and fell forward. He caught her easily and scooped her up. It would be faster and safer for him to just carry her upstairs. Yawning, she rested her head on his shoulder.

"My eyes are so blurry. I could barely keep them open earlier. I think I fell asleep when Meryn was trying to talk to me." She yawned again.

"You were covered with one of our throws, looks like Meryn has taken to you."

"You say that like you're not already wrapped around her little finger," she teased.

He raised an eyebrow. "And you are not?"

"I can't help it; she's so adorable and blunt. She reminds me of my uncle. Keelan seems afraid of her though."

Gavriel smiled wide. "Breakfast times around here can be rough." He set her on her feet when they reached their room and he opened the door. She was already pulling off clothes before the door shut behind him. In only her underwear, she belly flopped onto the bed and tunneled under the covers.

"My poor mate is tired." He removed his clothing laying them across a chair and climbed in next to her.

"Nothing against your virility, but I'm not up to sexy time tonight." Beth yawned again.

"Then what if I were to just give you pleasure?" he asked as his fangs descended.

Her eyes widened for a moment and then she smiled. "Have your wicked way with me."

He groaned when he pulled her body against his. Everywhere their skin touched ignited whirlpools of need. When he leaned over her body and her breasts flattened against his chest he thought he was going to come like an untried youth. Every inch of her was pure sin.

"Please," she whispered and threaded her fingers through his hair; the act lifted her breasts putting them on display beautifully. His heart swelled in his chest. Even exhausted, she looked to his comfort and needs. She had put aside her own tiredness to embrace him and make him feel wanted.

"You already bring me so much joy, the days before I found you seem lifeless and cold. I love you, Elizabeth Monroe, and even if it takes the rest of my days on this Earth, I will thank Fate for sending me the most perfect mate and I will spend each moment showing you how grateful I am for you."

He leaned forward and kissed the tears on her face. She curled her arms around him and pulled him so that he lay flush on top of her body before wrapping her legs around his waist.

"I love you too, my noble vampire. You make me feel like the most precious thing in the whole world, as if nothing else mattered to you but me. I know I'll never be able to thank Fate enough for giving you to me," she whispered.

Unable to speak past the lump in his throat he buried his face in her neck. He could hear the blood thrumming through her veins. He scraped his fangs over her skin and she moaned. When he bit down, she arched her back against him panting. That night at dinner he had drunk over twelve full glasses of blood, but it didn't compare to the richness of her blood. He drank deeply prolonging, her pleasure. When she collapsed back against the mattress shuddering, he carefully and regretfully withdrew and licked the bite marks closed. When he leaned back, he smiled to himself. She had passed out again. He moved carefully to avoid waking her. When he sat back on his knees at the foot of the bed, he could smell her arousal as a slick clear liquid seeped down her thigh. Grinning, he bent down and lapped up the delicacy only his mate could provide. She twitched and laughed in her sleep.

He left the bed and went to the bathroom and wet a washcloth before returning to the bed. Gently, he removed her underwear and cleaned her up. He got up and threw both in the hamper. Carefully, he got in beside her and pulled her close. In her sleep, she automatically wrapped herself around him.

There was nothing he would not do for this woman. If the ferals thought they could come after him when he had finally met his mate, they had another think coming.

When Elizabeth woke the next morning, she felt like she had a sandbox in each eye. All she wanted to do was go back to sleep. But like the day before, she had woken up not long after Gavriel left the bed. It was as if her body was already synchronizing with his. Frowning, she sat up and pushed the covers back. She got out of bed and headed directly to the bathroom.

Catching a glimpse of herself in the mirror, she was horrified. No wonder Gavriel had insisted on carrying her up yesterday. She looked pale and had dark circles under each eye, but what was especially pitiful was the dark bruise that had formed on her forehead from her tumble down the stairs.

"Ugh." She rolled her eyes at herself and started the shower. When steam began to drift from behind the stone wall, she stepped into the shower and let the hot water sluice down her body. She nearly moaned out loud in relief, the water felt wonderful. When she finished, she dried off and wrapped a towel around her hair and body. She started to get ready and easily fell into the beauty routine she had been doing for years, the only difference being she added a bit of bronzer to her cheeks for some color and some concealer on her forehead for the bruise. She decided against drying her hair since she was too tired and, instead, wove her heavy hair into a side braid. She put her hair back up in a towel to soak up any water from the braid.

She went to her suitcase smiling. Picking out her clothes was her favorite part of getting ready. Today, she chose an ankle length black and white plaid skirt with black leggings. She paired that with a merino wool black sweater and used a thin red leather belt to make the entire outfit pop. Instead of heels, she stuck with a low-heeled black leather boot. Best not to tempt Fate with heels today. She removed the towel from her head and hung it up in the bathroom. The braid was almost dry to the touch, which was perfect. She didn't want to get her wool sweater wet.

She grabbed her wristlet and stood up. The room swam for a moment and she had to grab on to the bed. She took a deep breath and let the room stop spinning. What was wrong with her? She walked with deliberate steps to the door and made her way down the hallway. When she got to the stairs, she met up with Colton.

"Good morning, sunshine. I see that you're looking better this morning," Colton said smiling at her.

"Good morning to you, too. Yes, I'm feeling much better." She couldn't help smiling in return; his good mood seemed contagious.

"Great." Colton turned and started to head down the stairs when he noticed that she was hesitating. "You okay?" he asked.

"Actually, could you escort me down? If I take another tumble, I fear Gavriel will lock me in our room," she confessed.

Colton gave her a wolfish grin and bowed ostentatiously. "My lady it would be an honor and a pleasure." He offered her his arm and, when she placed her hand on his forearm as custom dictated, he moved it so that it was tucked in his elbow with his hand over it.

It was more comfortable and casual than the formal way. She squeezed his arm in gratitude. "Thank you,

Colton. You've been very supportive of me since I've arrived."

He shook his head. "Think nothing of it. Ever since you and Meryn arrived, every day has been fun. I never realized how much of a rut we had gotten ourselves into."

"I have a feeling Meryn will keep you on your toes," she said grinning.

He threw his head back and laughed. "You have that right."

They were soon at the bottom of the stairs. Colton kept her hand and continued to escort her to the dining room. When they entered, the men stood, Gavriel's eyes went from gray to red. She felt Colton tense under her hand. She quickly removed her hand from his arm and patted his shoulder in a sisterly fashion. "Thank you for making sure I didn't fall down the stairs again." She walked over to where her mate stood glaring at Colton. When she was close enough, Gavriel snaked an arm around her waist and pulled her close. He grabbed the hand that Colton had been holding and kissed it, putting his scent on her. She noticed that he had six empty blood stained glasses on the table that hadn't been taken away yet. If he was this aggressive now what would his apex be like?

"It was no problem. We wouldn't want you getting hurt," Colton said ignoring Gavriel. He pulled out his seat and sat down. "Oh thank the Gods! Bacon!" With boyish enthusiasm, he began to shovel it onto his plate.

"Hey! Leave some for us," Darian protested and grabbed the platter from Colton, ignoring Gavriel's aggression as well.

Gavriel took a deep breath, his eyes returning to gray. Elizabeth could feel the frustration and regret radiating from him. She leaned in, kissed the side of his neck, and winked at him saucily. Shaking his head, he pulled out her seat for her. She sat down and he scooted her in. He turned to Colton. "Colton, I..." he began.

Colton interrupted him. "So what do you think happened in the Unit Commander suite last night?" he asked, taking advantage of the fact that neither Meryn nor Aiden was downstairs yet. Colton grinned at Gavriel, who nodded his thanks at Colton's understanding before answering. "I have a feeling we'll find out soon enough."

Ryuu walked in from the kitchen with another platter of bacon, which he set in front of Aiden's plate. He placed a cappuccino at Meryn's seat before placing one in front of her.

"Ryuu, I hate to impose, but could you possibly make me a double espresso? Just serve it black," she asked.

He nodded. "Of course. Did you not sleep well?"

"I slept wonderfully. I just can't seem to wake up. I've had more accidents than usual and I think my body is struggling to catch up. Even my bruise from last night hasn't healed yet."

Gavriel turned to her. "Do you need me to take you to the clinic?" He reached up and traced her face with his hand.

She shook her head. "No, I'm fine, just tired. I don't think Adam can do much about that."

Ryuu picked up the empty platter of bacon from between Colton and Darian. "I'll get started on that double espresso right away." He was about to head back to the kitchen when they heard feet running down the hallway and then down the stairs. Seconds later, Meryn burst into the room and flew behind Ryuu.

"Help! He's gonna kill me!" she screeched.

Gavriel, Darian, and Colton jumped to their feet pulling their sidearms out. Over their heads, heavy footsteps thundered down the stairs.

Aiden appeared in the doorway breathing hard. "Where is my mate?" he roared.

The men put their guns away with a sigh of relief and sat down. Elizabeth noticed that none of them pointed to where Meryn was peeking out from around Ryuu.

Ryuu's face was neutral. "What did she do?" he asked.

Aiden flushed. Every second that he didn't answer he grew redder and redder.

Ryuu nodded. "Ah. Yes. Well, think of it as a learning experience. Now, I know that you will be doing your 'Blind man's Bluff' drills today so I've cooked extra bacon. I put the fresh platter by your plate. Would you prefer juice or water with breakfast?" he asked, deflecting Aiden's attention away from Meryn.

Aiden looked at the platter of bacon, looking pleasantly surprised, and sat down without saying a word. He reached out and scraped half the platter onto his plate. "Orange juice will be fine," he grumbled. He looked over at Ryuu, and his mouth twitched when Meryn peeked out again. "Get over here, you little menace, you haven't kissed me good morning yet."

Meryn hesitated, gauging his mood. Ryuu stepped to one side and scooted her forward. Meryn walked over and sat down next to her mate and Ryuu headed for the kitchen. "I'm sorry you got hurt. I didn't know they snapped back like that." She took his hand and brought it to her face and rubbed her cheek against it like Elizabeth had seen Aiden do to Meryn many times.

Aiden's face softened. "It's okay, baby, no permanent damage done."

Colton's head went from Meryn to Aiden and back. Grinning from ear to ear he said, "Please tell me you're talking about what I think you're talking about"

Aiden blushed and scowled at his best friend. Colton and Darian busted out laughing. Aiden, frowning, turned to Gavriel. "I think these two want to do extra drills today."

Gavriel nodded. "I owe Colton so we can let him slide for today. But if you are looking to hand out extra drills, how about Keelan? Is he not late for breakfast?" Gavriel asked.

Colton shot Gavriel a thankful glance before looking at Keelan's empty seat. "Maybe he overslept?"

Darian shook his head. "He's as in tune with the sun as I am, he would never oversleep."

"I'm here," Keelan said from the doorway. When Elizabeth looked up she had to blink. He couldn't be? Why was...?

"Keelan, why in the fuck are you purple?" Colton asked, taking the words out of her mouth.

Keelan groaned and hung his head before walking over to the table. He flung himself in his chair fuming. "Seems Sascha and Quinn decided to set more than alarms. A clever little trap was waiting for me when I got in the shower this morning." The poor witch was a dark plum color from the tips of his hair and over every inch of exposed skin.

Colton continued to laugh as Darian began poking at Keelan's exposed skin. "You're *really* purple." Darian looked impressed.

Keelan looked at him, a sour expression on his face. "No? Really? I hadn't noticed."

Aiden was fighting to keep a straight face. "I'll speak with Sascha this morning."

Keelan brightened. "Are we doing drills with Gamma this morning?" he asked. Aiden nodded. "Perfect," he said, his face taking on a diabolical expression.

Ryuu walked in from the kitchen and stared. "Oh my." He placed the double espresso in front of

Elizabeth and walked over to Keelan. He leaned in and smelled the young witch's hair. "Lavender and Anise?"

Keelan nodded. "Yes, I think that's right."

Ryuu placed his hand on Keelan's head and whispered low. The purple color drained out of Keelan like water through a sieve. Ryuu lifted his hand and, with the other, poured Keelan a glass of juice.

Keelan stared down at his normal flesh colored palms. "How'd you do that?" he asked, twisting to look up at Ryuu.

Ryuu smiled. "What spells did you use to try and remove the color?"

"Fire spells for purification," Keelan said.

Ryuu shook his head. "Lavender and Anise are affiliated with the Element of Air. I used an Air spell to counteract its effects. It was very cleverly done. Let me guess the harder you tried, the darker the stain became?"

Keelan nodded.

"Fire feeds on Air; you basically made the spell stronger." Ryuu walked around the table filling the glasses.

Keelan groaned. "I should have thought of that. Thank you, Ryuu!" Without the pending embarrassment the spell was sure to have caused impeding his appetite, Keelan dug into his breakfast with gusto.

Ryuu smiled at Keelan. "As a squire, I couldn't very well allow someone in my house to remain so afflicted."

"Your house?" Aiden asked. Ryuu ignored him. His eyes narrowed at Meryn for a moment. He stared for a bit longer before he walked over and plucked her cappuccino cup from her hand. "I'll fix you something else." He glided away from the table and headed toward the kitchen.

The men watched as Meryn's eyes widened, her lower lip trembling.

Aiden jumped to his feet. "Well men, better get a jump on our day."

Keelan and Colton grabbed a piece of bread and stuffed bacon in it before downing their juice. Gavriel stood and kissed her on the cheek. "Have fun," he whispered.

Elizabeth eyed the ticking bomb that was Meryn and sighed. She shot back her double espresso and shuddered. She quickly picked up her cappuccino and began to drink. She needed something to chase away that bitter taste.

"I want my coffee, Ryuu!" Meryn yelled.

"Bye," Gavriel said and followed the others out of the dining room.

Ryuu returned with a tall glass. "Here. It's mostly frothed milk with just a little bit of coffee. I'm afraid of what your body would do if we went cold turkey, so we'll be cutting you back in increments." He set the cup down in front of her.

Grumbling, she took a sip. "There's no coffee in here," she complained.

"Yes there is, just considerably less than you're used to. I'll order a decaf version of your espresso bean. You can have the same drinks you're used to, just with no caffeine." He reached over and put a bagel, apple wedges, and cheese blocks on her plate. "You can't go to your office without clearing your plate," he said, his voice stern.

Meryn looked like she was about to argue for a moment before she slumped back. "I am, aren't I?" she asked.

He nodded. "I didn't think to check until you mentioned it yesterday, but your rhythms are different."

"Damn," she muttered.

Elizabeth put two and two together. "But this is happy news! You should tell Aiden right away." Even though she wasn't raised around shifters, she knew of the great importance they put on having children.

"No," Meryn said, biting into her bagel savagely.

"Why not?" she asked.

"Because if he finds out, I won't be able to torture him with the condoms anymore and he will be impossible to live with." Meryn stuffed the blocks of cheese in her mouth until her cheeks puffed out like a chipmunk.

"So when will you tell him?"

"Soon, I promise," Meryn confirmed.

"Oh, Meryn." Elizabeth shook her head.

Meryn looked up. "Don't 'Oh Meryn' me. You don't have to live with him. He already treats me like a glass figurine. If I even so much as sneeze he's hauling me off to the clinic for Adam to check me over. I just want a little breathing room before I tell him. To process it for myself."

"Okay, your call." She stood and stretched. "You finish your breakfast, without choking. I'm going to go get started on the data entry for the unit members. The database you created is going to work perfectly."

"Cool. Be there soon." Meryn frowned down at her apple slices.

Elizabeth smiled. Life was about to get a lot more interesting in the next few months.

CHAPTER TEN

Meryn joined her half an hour later, and they really began to make headway with the personnel files. The more she input, the more concerned she became.

"Meryn, have you noticed anything strange about the files?" she asked.

Meryn nodded gravely. "There are so many that have died. We're adding them so we can track and archive their reports, but there are so many. It's like each unit loses a member at least once every other year." Meryn looked up at her, fear in her eyes. "I had no idea they had lost so many." Her eyes filled. "I don't want to lose anyone."

Elizabeth felt her own tears threaten to spill over. Shaking her head, she deepened her resolve. "We won't lose anyone. They have us now, Meryn, and the mates for the others are on the way. Already you've made changes that will help to keep them safe; just look at your trainee program. That triples the manpower available. We're here for a reason, don't forget that."

Meryn scrubbed at her eyes with the sleeve of her tee-shirt. Elizabeth actually looked forward each morning to seeing what Meryn would wear. Today, she had on a *Ghostbusters* tee-shirt. Meryn smiled at her. "Thanks, I needed that pep talk. I'll stay positive, it's just... I've been targeted before. I still have nightmares; they're so hard to shake because it really happened. It's terrifying when you can't even see your enemy." Meryn wrapped her arms around her midsection as if trying to hold herself together.

Seconds later, Ryuu breezed through the door and was at her side. "What is the matter, *denka*? Your fear was strong enough that I could feel it in the kitchen." He knelt down in front of her and ran a thumb soothingly over a blue dragon tattoo around Meryn's wrist.

"Just remembering the attack. I was telling Bunny that what made it especially scary was the fact that we couldn't see them."

Elizabeth couldn't imagine fighting an unseen enemy. No wonder the men were doing 'Blind man's Bluff' drills. They were conditioning their bodies to move without the benefit of sight, honing their other senses. It must have been a blow to their pride that they couldn't defend Meryn.

"I will do whatever I can to help Keelan and the other witch Quinn to devise a spell to keep them away," Ryuu promised.

A thought struck Elizabeth. "Not to jinx us, but what has kept them from coming back? I mean if we can't see them, why haven't they attacked before now?"

Ryuu stood, crossing his arms, bringing one hand to his chin. He thought about it before answering. "For the first week after the attack, I ordered my *shikigami* to guard the house. They are my spirit servants. I can control them, but it's draining and I can't maintain it. During that first week, whenever they tried to get close to the house the spirits would make them visible. It was enough to keep them away. They are cautious. *This* factor has the men confused.

"Normally, ferals are all about their base desires. They are one step up from shambling zombies. They usually have just enough intelligence to lay basic traps or trick humans. But this new breed, they are patient. They think things through and are leery, this makes them much more of a threat. I have a feeling that the reason why they have stayed out of the house up until now is because of me. I am an unknown to them. I was able to make their assassin visible, and we gained information from him, even in death. They may not want to tip their hand and that is what makes them more dangerous than the typical feral."

"I'm calling Adair. He emailed me yesterday to let me know the program had been approved, and they were starting ranking trials. The sooner we can disperse the trainees the better I'll feel." Meryn reached for her cell.

"Ranking trials?" Elizabeth asked.

Meryn nodded. "Yeah, it's the method they came up with to decide who went to what unit. They were supposed to hold trials and each trainee should have received a score. The highest score got to pick first, then the second highest and so on. Sydney texted me last night, according to the rumor mill, all but one of the top five trainees wanted to be assigned to Alpha. He said the trainee with the second highest score chose to go to Gamma instead to train with Sascha. I didn't realize the amount of prestige that went along with the unit assignments." Meryn put the phone to her ear.

"Hey Adair, what's the news, bud?" she asked.

Elizabeth stepped closer so she could hear his response.

"Hey sweetie. We've completed the rankings and the guys are packing up today. They'll be heading your way tomorrow."

"Tomorrow!" Meryn exclaimed.

"Yeah, didn't I tell you in my email yesterday?" he asked, sounding confused.

"No! No, you didn't. The only thing you said was that you'd be holding trials," Meryn said through clenched teeth.

"Sorry hun, I didn't mean to put you in a bind. I thought you knew that it wouldn't take long to get them ranked. Can you see if Aiden will be ready for them?"

Meryn looked at her watch and chewed on her bottom lip. "They're training now, I'll call you back when they go to their first break."

"Sounds good. Sorry again, kiddo," Adair apologized.

"No worries, I'll figure this out," Meryn said and ended the call.

When she looked up there was panic on her face. "Well, fuckity fuck!"

Elizabeth laughed. "Your word choices are descriptive and surprisingly accurate."

Meryn blinked. "Was that a compliment?"

"Yes, hun."

"Well, I guess we have a couple hours before their first break. Let's get the rest of the personnel files done. I have a feeling the rest of the day will be getting the house ready for the trainees." She looked at Ryuu. "Can you start getting the linens and towels done? I would start emptying the guest rooms but I don't know which ones Aiden has designated for them."

Ryuu bowed. "Of course, *denka*. This program is important to you; I'll do whatever I can to ensure its success. I'll take an inventory immediately." He left closing the door behind him.

Meryn beamed. "He is so cool!"

Elizabeth had a feeling that Meryn had no idea exactly how 'cool' Sei Ryuu could be. But if the man himself hadn't said anything, she wouldn't either. "I bet we can clear this stack and be done before they go on break," she said reaching for the next file.

"I bet we can, too. I can't wait to get rid of these musty old things." Meryn wiggled her nose.

Elizabeth laughed then looked down at her grimy hands. She couldn't wait either.

"*Denka*, it's time for tea. Did you need to go speak with Aiden about the trainees?" Ryuu asked from the doorway.

Elizabeth looked at her watch. The hours had flown by. She looked over to the empty space on the floor where the files had been. Meryn was inputting the last one now.

"Ryuu, could you please dispose of these files in a secure fashion?" she asked, pointing to the neat stacks by the door.

"Of course." He easily lifted three of the stacks and walked away.

Meryn looked at her and she could tell that her friend was just as impressed as she was. Those stacks were heavy!

Meryn stood and stretched. "Okay, let's go crash their training; they should be on break by now."

Elizabeth stood and followed her out to the training grounds. Meryn rubbed her hands over her arms. Neither of them had been smart enough to grab a coat.

"Burr! Damn, it's cold!" Meryn hurried to where the men stood panting, bent over, and trying to catch their breath.

"Meryn! Where is your coat, baby?" Aiden pulled his mate close in an effort to keep her warm.

"Inside, I forgot it. But listen, I called Adair to check up on the rankings and he said that the trainees will be here tomorrow!"

Aiden blinked. "Tomorrow? As in tomorrow, tomorrow?" he asked.

She nodded. "Yup! He said they are packing today and our five will be here tomorrow. I have Ryuu getting the linens and towels together, but I didn't know which of the guest rooms you wanted to designate to the trainees."

"I'll cut training short today so that we can help you get the house ready. That way the other units have time to prepare as well. We'll be in around lunchtime to get started. Thank you for waiting for our break time to tell me."

Elizabeth looked around and didn't see her mate. "Where is Gavriel?"

Aiden's face became grim. "He had a near miss. He's with Colton and Keelan on the back porch getting treated."

Elizabeth's heart picked up. "What do you mean 'near miss'? Treated for what?"

"Colton swung and Gavriel was just a shade too slow. He got clipped by the *bokuto* across the forehead. Keelan is tending to the injury," he explained.

Elizabeth didn't answer; she just started walking toward the back. When she got to the corner of the house, she stopped; she heard the men's voices.

"Thank the Gods you're almost back to normal. If you had been any slower, this could have been bad," she heard Keelan say.

"I'm so sorry." Colton's voice sounded contrite.

"It was not your fault Colton. I think the increase in blood has helped. I cannot wait to get back to normal," Gavriel said, sounding slightly bitter.

"Think of it this way, when you're done, you'll be this new, even more badass version of the Gavriel that everyone already fears," Keelan said, sounding amused.

"It cannot happen soon enough. I do not like feeling out of control," she heard her mate confess.

When the wind shifted, carrying her scent toward the men, she stepped around the side of the house smiling. "There you are! I was looking for you. What happened to your head?" she asked trying to sound nonchalant. She needed to figure out a way to get Gavriel to feed from her again. It wasn't the amount of blood he was taking in that was keeping him safe, it was her blood. If he needed to feed from her three times a day so that he could defend himself then she would force him if she had to.

Gavriel turned to her face neutral. "Just a miscalculation on my part, that and I think Colton was trying to get even with me from this morning."

Colton winced. "I said I was sorry."

Keelan clapped Colton on the back. "Come on, I bet Aiden has figured out some wonderful way to pay you back for nearly taking out his second in command." He steered Colton back toward the training grounds.

"I said I was sorry!" Colton complained loudly.

Gavriel grinned then winced. He brought a hand up and gingerly touched his wound.

She stepped closer and lowered her voice. "Are you sure you're okay?"

He pulled her close and began rubbing her arms. "Yes I am fine, just a nick. It should be healed by dinner. Why are you outside?" he asked.

She rested her head on his shoulder enjoying his simple touch. "Meryn called Adair about the trainees. They will be arriving tomorrow."

"Ah. I bet neither Meryn nor Aiden knew that," he guessed.

"You got it. Aiden said all of you would be helping to clear out rooms after lunch."

"Then let us head back, you need to go inside and I need to help Aiden with drills. I may not be able to spar but I can help correct others." He stood and kept one arm wrapped around her.

When they reached the training grounds, Aiden was trying to get one of the wooden swords away from Meryn who held it up at eye level in what looked to be a samurai stance.

"Okay baby, time to go in now, see here's Elizabeth." Aiden, despite the cold, had sweat beaded across his forehead.

"Size matters not. Look at me. Judge me by my size, do you?" Meryn quipped and brought the sword down making what Elizabeth guessed by the quote, were lightsaber noises.

Aiden looked heavenward. "I still don't understand you!"

Meryn swung the sword around in a mock battle against her invisible opponent. The other men cheered her on. Elizabeth took pity on Aiden. She kissed Gavriel on the cheek. "Be careful." He nodded. She stepped up to the training area. "Much to learn you still have, my old padawan."

Meryn froze mid-swing. "I guess you're right." She handed the sword off to Colton. "Try not to kill any of *our* warriors," she teased. Colton groaned.

Meryn jogged over to her. "Let's go in! I'm freezing my balls off!" Behind her the men erupted in chuckles.

Aiden looked over at the grinning fools. "Ten laps starting now!" he barked. The men jumped to and began jogging.

She and Meryn went inside and, to their delight, Ryuu had stoked the fire in the family room and prepared hot cocoa and oatmeal cookies. When they sat down, Ryuu bundled Meryn up in a blanket.

"He said they'll be in for lunch and after that they'll help us with the rooms," Meryn told Ryuu.

He nodded. "Good. I'll check on lunch now, we're having a thick beef stew with biscuits. Marius sent over the recipe when it began to get colder last month; he said it was a good meal on a cold day." Ryuu bowed and left for the kitchen.

Meryn turned to her, adjusting her hands on her mug. "After our break, can we input the files I have for the missing persons? I was only able to input the basics to run my programs. I want to make sure we capture everything."

"Of course. Even in Noctem Falls, we heard of the murders. I'll do anything I can to help." Elizabeth took a bite of her cookie.

"Thanks. Aiden and the guys do what they can of course, but women think differently than men, we may catch something they have missed."

"I'll do what I can," Elizabeth promised.

After their break, they went back to the office and Meryn showed her the missing person's files.

Elizabeth was shocked at the number. "We can't be missing so many people!" she exclaimed.

Meryn nodded sadly. "Some weren't reported to the council and others were attributed to 'hiking accidents' or 'animal attacks'. But when I started correlating the data, more and more people started popping up."

"Are they all concentrated around Lycaonia? Because we haven't had any missing persons around Noctem Falls," Elizabeth asked.

"I ran as far west as St. Louis, but you're right, they are close to Lycaonia." Meryn pointed to a piece of paper that was a map of the US with little red dots clustered around Lycaonia.

"Does the council know?" Elizabeth asked.

"Yes, Aiden and I told them right away." Meryn nodded her head.

"I'm willing to bet that Magnus doesn't know. He would have discussed this with me and would have barred Noctem Fall's city gates to prevent me from coming here." She put down the map and picked up one of the many pictures of a happy couple.

"Sad isn't it? They were all expecting, too," Meryn whispered.

"Let's scan the pictures in and save them," she suggested.

Meryn nodded and pulled a stack of jagged edged pages out of the scanner.

Elizabeth frowned. "Meryn, what is that?" she asked pointing to the pages.

Meryn turned and smiled. "My history book. The printed copy was so heavy I scanned the pages and made an e-book. Now I can read it on my phone." She pulled her phone out and showed her the reading app.

"I'm impressed. Can you send that to me? Can you do others?" Elizabeth asked, looking at the clear pages on Meryn's phone.

"Yeah, it's easy. The scanner does most of the work. We can create our own collection," she offered.

"This is a really great idea, Meryn. Our most recent generations are better at technology than most of the paranormal world. This would be a great way to get them to read about the history of our people." Elizabeth handed Meryn back her phone.

"I'll put it on the To-Do list. I'm really liking this book though. There's some very interesting stuff in here," she said with an evil grin.

"Gods help us," Elizabeth muttered.

"Mu-wa-ha-ha." Meryn wagged her eyebrows.

"You goof! Scan those pictures and I'll create the database files."

"Okay." Meryn started her project, leaving Elizabeth to her own thoughts.

Why hadn't any of the other council members been informed? Maybe it was just her uncle that had been left in the dark. She worked on creating the files needed so that when she contacted her uncle, she would have all the facts.

Before she knew it, an hour had flown by, and she could hear the sounds of the men coming in. They immediately headed upstairs to shower, meaning lunch would be in the next half an hour.

"I'm going to go jump in with Aiden. Even with the heat on, I haven't been able to get warm from my adventure outside this morning," Meryn said, standing and heading toward the door.

"Not a bad idea, I haven't been able to get warm either," she confessed.

"Better hurry, Gavriel always takes quick showers, though if you joined him, he may take longer," Meryn leered.

"Go on, you nut." Elizabeth shooed her away.

When the door shut, she pulled out her phone. She would have to be quick if Meryn was right. Gavriel would be looking for her soon.

"Beth! How have you been pumpkin?" Her uncle answered on the first ring.

"Fine, how are you?"

"I cannot complain. How is your vampire?"

"Nearing his apex. I can't wait until it's over. I don't like seeing him vulnerable," she admitted.

"Do not worry, darling. Even at his weakest, your mate is still a force to be reckoned with."

"I know, but it still bothers me."

"Is that why you called?"

"No, it's not. I don't know how to put it so I'm just going to lay everything out," she started.

"This does not sound good, Bethy." Her uncle's voice sounded serious.

"It's not, Uncle. Did you know that there have been kidnappings in and around Lycaonia?" she started.

"Yes, that was shared at a council level last month. It's very concerning."

"Did you know that more than twenty couples have disappeared, *all* concentrated around Lycaonia?" she asked.

"What! No one has reported that. Where did you get your information?" he demanded.

"Meryn, the woman I told you about, Unit Commander McKenzie's new mate. She compiled a list of all suspicious disappearances in the area and then cross-referenced them with a list of paranormals living outside the city. Some have been classified as hiking accidents or animal attacks, but shifters don't have hiking accidents and they sure as hell don't experience animal attacks," she said vehemently.

"You are right they do not. Why in the hell has René not reported this?" he asked, his voice filled with anger.

"I don't know, but I also had an interesting conversation today with Sei Ryuu. Evidently, he defended Meryn during her attack and somehow made the enemy visible. They haven't ventured into the house since then. He said this is indicative of a higher intelligence level. This new enemy is cunning and cautious. I've seen the warriors out here, Uncle; they are training to fight blind. I know that Aiden would have cascaded this to the other units around the country, but if the council members aren't aware of everything, I'm afraid that if there comes a time that the warriors need support, and if the council doesn't have the full story, many lives could be lost." And that was her worst fear.

Her uncle's curses filled her ear. "Do you want your name mentioned? I can keep you and Meryn out of this," he offered.

Elizabeth thought about it for a moment. She didn't want to put Meryn at risk especially considering her condition, yet Meryn was one of the few who saw the bigger picture and could explain not only the report's results, but also where the data had come from. She didn't care one way or the other about herself.

"I'll let you use your best judgment. I know that you wouldn't put Meryn or me in danger recklessly."

"Never, my darling girl. I am going to let you go, I have a certain vampire elder in Lycaonia to call." His voice took on a hard edge.

"Give him hell, Unky!" she cheered. She heard his chuckle.

"Miss you every day, Bethy," he admitted.

"I'm doing you more good here than if I were there, pouring your tea," she pointed out.

"That is the Gods' honest truth. Bye, baby."

"Goodbye, Uncle."

She exhaled and grinned. She wished she could be a fly on the wall of René Evreux's office. She loved it when her uncle lit into people; it was truly a thing of beauty. Smiling, she walked out of the office and met up with her mate at the base of the stairs.

"Darn, I was hoping to catch you in the shower." She smiled and wrapped her arms around his neck. She could feel the dampness of his hair and smelled the scent of his soap. He pulled her flush against him. She could feel his growing arousal against her belly.

"I could always take another shower," he whispered behind her ear, sending shivers through her body. Just then, her stomach growled loudly. Chuckling, he pulled back.

"Then again, I need to make sure my mate is fed. I wonder what is for lunch." He placed a warm hand on her back.

"Ryuu said he was making beef stew. I've been smelling it all morning, I can't wait to eat!" she confessed.

Together they went to the dining room. Keelan, Darian, and Colton were already seated and stood as they entered. They all sat down together.

"Now we just need Meryn and Aiden," Colton said, buttering another biscuit.

"They may be a few minutes," Elizabeth informed them.

Colton and Keelan groaned, and both reached for another biscuit.

A few minutes later, a very satisfied looking Aiden and wet haired Meryn walked in. The men stood again.

"Shower sex sucks," Meryn announced loudly.

Colton started choking on his biscuit and Keelan and Darian just stared at her.

Aiden blushed but continued grinning as they sat down.

Elizabeth leaned forward dying to know what prompted that statement. "What happened?"

"Slippery surfaces and not the good kind, one." Meryn started ticking off reasons on her fingers. "Water not a natural lubricant, two. Height differences, three. And I got a freaking charley horse right when..." Aiden covered her mouth at that point.

Ahh. So someone had fun and someone didn't. Poor Meryn.

Aiden removed his hand. "I'll make it up to you later, baby." He said then kissed Meryn's temple.

Meryn just grumbled and savagely sawed her biscuit in half before turning to her mate. "So which rooms are the trainees getting?"

"There are six master suites used by Colton, Darian, Keelan, Ryuu, us, and Gavriel and Elizabeth. On each floor, there are three guest suites so I don't see any reason why each trainee can't have their own room. What that means, gentlemen, is that all of our storage space is about to disappear, so whatever you want to keep needs to be taken to the attic." Aiden turned to the fae. "Darian, can you tape off and designate storage space in the attic for everyone? We need to have the rooms cleared so that they can be made ready to be moved into by tomorrow." Aiden laid out the afternoon's working plans.

Darian nodded. "It's probably a good idea to go through some of our old boxes anyway. I know I have stuff in one of the guest rooms that I probably haven't even thought about in decades. Whatever of mine doesn't fit upstairs I can always ship home to Éire Danu."

"Home?" Meryn asked.

"A fae's true home is always Éire Danu." Darian winked at her.

"Oh." She shrugged.

Ryuu rolled in a cart that held steaming bowls of a dark brown stew. Aiden turned to the squire. "Ryuu, can I ask that you help look after the trainees? They aren't children. They're grown men by human standards, but young in our world."

"Of course. Do I send them to you for discipline?" Ryuu asked as he began to place bowls in front of everyone.

Aiden shook his head. "If they are doing something that merits discipline, go ahead and administer it, then send them to me. Then I can discipline them again. Most are old enough to have outgrown those kinds of hijinks, especially considering they are now assigned to a unit. If I'm not available, you can send them to any Alpha Unit member," Aiden said.

"I'm sure there won't be any issues," Ryuu said grinning.

Aiden groaned. "You just jinxed us."

Ryuu shrugged. "Be that as it may, I will make sure they understand that while they reside in this house they are to respect my rules."

Aiden just nodded. "I trust your judgment."

When Ryuu set the bowl down in front of her, she breathed in the savory aroma. She picked up her spoon and dug in. There was a burst of flavors in every bite.

"Ryuu, this has to be the best stew I've ever had!" she exclaimed and wasn't lying. Growing up in a noble court, she had always been exposed to the world's best, but nothing compared to this simple meal.

Ryuu bowed. "Thank you. I am happy with it."

The table was quiet as everyone devoured their lunch. Elizabeth smiled up at Ryuu when he placed a second bowl in front of her, taking the empty one. When she looked around everyone except Meryn was working on a second bowl.

With a full stomach, she leaned back and looked over at Aiden. She had waited until everyone was nearly done before bringing up the conversation with her uncle. "Aiden, I called my uncle today. I told him about what Meryn has shown me regarding the missing persons. As I suspected, he had not been informed."

The men stopped eating and looked at her.

Aiden frowned. "That can't be right. Meryn and I took that to the council almost a month ago."

"Aiden, if my uncle had known that so many shifters had disappeared around Lycaonia, I would still be sitting in Noctem Falls." She raised an eyebrow at him. He sat back, frowning.

Gavriel turned to her. "What did he say he was going to do?"

"He was going to call Elder Evreux as soon as he got off the phone with me. I imagine it was a one sided conversation," she grinned at the thought.

Colton looked at Aiden. "Can we not even trust our own Elders anymore? What in the hell is going on?"

Aiden shook his head. "I'm sure this is just another gaffe of Evreux's. He probably didn't think it was important to mention since it was shifters being taken and not vampires."

Darian nodded. "I bet you're right, that sounds like him."

Aiden looked at them all. "For now, let's not mention it outside of this room."

The men nodded. Elizabeth noticed that she wasn't the only one who wasn't nodding. Meryn and Ryuu hadn't either.

Aiden stood and clapped his hands together. "Okay people, those rooms won't clean themselves. Let's get started."

Groaning the men stood and began to head upstairs.

Meryn met her eyes. "It's just Evreux being a jerk."

Elizabeth nodded. "I'm sure it is."

They looked at each other. Elizabeth could see it in her eyes. Meryn didn't believe it either.

CHAPTER ELEVEN

Elizabeth shared glances with Meryn as they watched the men walk back and forth carrying boxes to the attic. Even at his weakest, Gavriel was toting weights she would never even attempt. Aiden and Colton were competing as to who could carry the most and Keelan was using spells to float the more awkward sized pieces up the stairs.

Darian had to stop going to the attic as he kept hitting his head on the rafters, so he was carrying boxes from their respective rooms to the base of the attic steps for the others to carry up. Elizabeth and Meryn's eyes followed their mates as they walked by again, bicep muscles bulging.

"Yum," Meryn murmured. Aiden looked at her suddenly and stumbled. Gavriel got caught up in Aiden's legs and he too went down. Both men sat up looking disgusted with themselves.

Ryuu picked up the boxes that Aiden and Gavriel had been carrying effortlessly. Gracefully, he stood and, without saying a word, headed toward the attic.

"Seriously. Damn." Meryn stared.

"You can say that again." Elizabeth nodded.

"Seriously. Damn." Meryn repeated.

Aiden growled and Gavriel hissed low, both men got to their feet and walked over to the women.

"That was your fault," Aiden mumbled rubbing his chin on Meryn's head.

"You don't want me to be sexually attracted to you?" she asked.

Aiden kept his chin on her head and chomped his teeth causing Meryn's head to bounce around. She tried to get away but his quick hands reached out and tickled her ribs. Laughing, she begged for mercy.

Elizabeth's mate had a much more direct approach. He pulled her into his arms and dipped her back. The second he captured her lips she was lost. He teased her until her entire body was vibrating. When he righted them, his grin was satisfied and thoroughly wicked. Damn the man, he knew exactly what he did to her.

"Sneaky vampire," she murmured into his chest.

"I have to make sure I keep your attention." He kissed her temple.

"Oh you have it."

"Are you guys done playing? We have more boxes to carry," Colton called out.

Aiden kissed Meryn before stepping away. "Coming!" he yelled back.

Elizabeth looked at her mate. "Where are all your things?"

"I maintain a home in the city where my things are stored. I like it better here though. Be right back," Gavriel whispered and walked toward their suite.

She shook her head. Her mate had a whole other house, and it hadn't occurred to him that she would want to see it. She stopped. What kind of space did he have there for a closet? Smiling, she continued to count the sheet sets in the linen closet with Meryn. After a few minutes, they noticed the men had been gone a while.

Meryn looked at her. "Where'd they go?"

Elizabeth shrugged and was about to answer when she saw Gavriel walking down the hallway with something large in his hands that was draped with a sheet. The men walked behind him smiling mischievously.

Meryn frowned. "Okay guys, what are you up to?"

Darian stepped forward as spokesman. "We decided to go ahead and do this now before the trainees got here so they wouldn't expect to be spoiled."

Before either of them could ask what he meant, he carefully lifted the sheet.

She heard Meryn gasp and couldn't blame her. Gavriel was holding a very detailed miniature dollhouse. Inside each room were chairs, tables, and other furnishings.

"It's for Felix. Gavriel got the idea after you moved in. Poor Felix always has to eat from a saucer. Nothing in the house fits him, poor little guy didn't even have a chair to sit in, so we made one. Well, Aiden did. He was in charge of furniture." Darian jerked his thumb to his commander.

Aiden blushed and frowned. "No one should have to sleep in a damn shoebox," he mumbled.

Elizabeth noticed that the faint twinkling she normally saw around Meryn was growing brighter and brighter.

Darian continued. "I called a friend that lives in Éire Danu and told her how heroic our Felix had been, braving the cold to come get us when Meryn was attacked. The sprites couldn't do enough for him. They sent sheets, blankets, and practically a whole new wardrobe. Of course, our local sprites didn't want to be outdone. Elder Vi'Ailean has told me that they felt terrible that Felix had to move because he wasn't fitting in. They'll be sending over seedlings in the spring for our own greenhouse that we're building so that he has access to plants year round."

Keelan stepped forward with a small box and opened it. Inside, a tiny necklace lay nestled on white velvet. It was a simple green stone set in silver that hung from a silver chain. Blushing, he lifted it up indicating to Felix that it was his. One second the necklace was there, the next it was gone as Felix put it on.

Keelan cleared his throat. "I've been working with Ryuu to create a perimeter that would make unseen things seen. If you turn the stone in its setting, we'll be able to see and hear you, turn it back and you'll go back to being invisible," he explained.

Elizabeth and the men all stared as the air in front of them shimmered for a second before a small, red haired sprite was revealed. His translucent wings, veined in greens and purples, beat furiously, keeping him hovering between them. Felix was crying silently, his bright green eyes rimmed red. He brought his forearm up to cover his face as he cried.

Elizabeth dabbed at her eyes. Behind her, Elizabeth heard Meryn sniffling as well.

Felix uncovered his eyes and looked at the men. He swallowed hard.

"Thank you. Thank you so much." His tiny voice was clear but conveyed the depth of his feelings. Elizabeth noticed that the men's eyes looked suspiciously misty.

Felix hid his face and fumbled at the necklace, a second later, he was gone again.

"There, there sweetheart, it's okay. You have to stop crying or I'll keep crying, Felix, and when I cry my nose gets stuffed up," Meryn complained, wiping at her own eyes as she comforted the small sprite.

Ryuu stepped forward, reaching for the house to take it to its final location but Colton stepped in front of him.

"Even though you said you didn't need anything, we came up with an idea." Colton reached behind him and took out a blue leather journal from his waistband. He held it out to Ryuu.

"We know that you have been working very hard to master western style cooking, so we all asked around and got some of Lycaonia's best cooks to contribute their favorite recipes, including my own mother, Adelaide and Marius."

Ryuu, looking shocked, took the journal, and very carefully began to flip through the handwritten pages. He closed it solemnly and held it to his chest. "This has to be the finest gift I have ever received. I will cherish it all the days of my life." He bowed low to the men.

Colton laughed and clapped a hand to Ryuu's shoulder gently pushing the man upright. "It's not like we're not getting anything out of it. I can't wait for you to make my mom's pecan pie, it's my favorite," he said, winking.

Ryuu straightened. "Then I shall attempt to make that first."

Without saying a word, Aiden held out a box to Meryn, his face was bright red. "We got distracted yesterday. I got this for you to say I was sorry for ignoring you, but I guess this can be your welcome to the Alpha Estate present instead."

Meryn just stared. Aiden walked over and physically placed the box in her hand.

Gavriel set the house down in the hallway and walked over to wrap an arm around Elizabeth's shoulder. "I did not have time to prepare anything, but the men have all agreed to help me tomorrow to give you the closet of your dreams as your welcome present."

Elizabeth turned in his arms, grabbing the front of his shirt. "Really?"

"Yes, really. Whatever my mate wants, she gets." Gavriel kissed her forehead.

Behind her, Meryn squealed and began to bounce up and down.

"I love it! I absolutely love it! Look, Bunny! He got me a charm bracelet! It has a tiny laptop and coffee mug on it!" Meryn kept jumping, trying to kiss Aiden's face. Laughing, he finally just lifted her up so she could reach him.

Gavriel leaned in. "I told him to leave room for more charms that way he knows what to get when he messes up later."

"Hey!" Aiden protested.

Everyone laughed. Aiden set Meryn down. She put the bracelet on and kept turning her wrist back and forth. She looked up at her mate.

"For a second when I saw the dollhouse, I thought you had found out about Meryn 2.0." She spun the bracelet on her wrist.

"No it was for Felix, we... Meryn 2.0? What in the world is that?" Aiden asked, his eyebrows snapping together. "You better not have hacked something else," he warned.

Meryn laughed. "It's not software! It's our daughter." She grinned up at him.

"Oh dear," Elizabeth murmured. The men grinned at each other.

Aiden's mouth worked like a fish, his previously bright red face quickly drained to become milk white.

"A... a... a..." he stuttered.

Ryuu picked up the dollhouse and headed toward his own suite. "Felix, I think you may prefer to have this with me for a while," he said his mouth twitching. The small light flickered as if Felix were chortling and followed Ryuu.

"A... a... a..." Aiden clutched at his chest and swayed.

Meryn frowned. "I think I broke him."

Colton and Gavriel moved to stand on either side of their commander, laughing. Aiden bent at the waist, wheezing, and put his hands on his knees, gulping in air.

"Ten bucks says he faints," Darian teased.

Darian's words had Aiden's back straightening. He stepped forward, placing his hands on Meryn's shoulders. "Are you certain?"

Smiling, Meryn nodded. "Meryn 2.0 is under development," she said patting her belly.

Aiden turned to them beaming. "I'm going to be a father!" he announced, as if they hadn't been standing there the whole time.

Colton was the first to thrust his hand at his commander. "Congratulations my old friend, I wish your child a lifetime of happiness." The other men stepped forward to congratulate the couple.

"Brightest of Blessings on you and your child," Gavriel said, hugging Meryn.

Elizabeth hugged Aiden. "You're going to make a wonderful father."

"You'll be next." Aiden said.

Gavriel whipped around to stare at her looking startled.

Elizabeth frowned at him. "Next year it is a distinct possibility, you know."

"I never thought about it." Gavriel walked over and pulled her away from Aiden to hold her close.

"Get condoms. They work extremely well," Aiden bragged. Elizabeth had to hide her smile. Meryn just giggled uncontrollably.

"Gods above, we better start stocking up on diapers!" Colton said, grinning from ear to ear.

"I don't do diapers," Meryn informed her mate. Aiden just smiled.

Elizabeth had a feeling that Meryn could have blown up their house just then and he would still be smiling.

The next second Meryn proved her wrong. Without thought, Meryn bent down and picked up a stack of sheets for one of the guest rooms. Elizabeth blinked as Aiden proceeded to lose his mind.

"What in the hell are you doing? Put it down! You can't lift anything!" Aiden swatted the sheets out of her hands.

Meryn's head dropped back on her shoulders and she groaned. "For fucks sake!" Her head snapped back up and she put her hands on her hips. "Already? We're doing this already?" she demanded.

"Should you be standing? Why are you standing?" Aiden pulled at his hair.

"Okay. I can't do you right now." Meryn bent down to pick up the sheets.

Aiden knocked them away again as if they were the greatest threat known to man.

"You are impossible! I have to be able to function over the next nine months!"

Aiden just scooped her up and turned to face them. "Excuse us." He quickly walked toward their suite.

"Neanderthal!" They heard Meryn screech as they turned the corner and disappeared out of sight.

When they were gone, Elizabeth couldn't hold it in anymore. She laughed so hard she thought she was going to rupture something. She wasn't alone, the men around her were laughing as well. Colton slid down the wall gasping for air.

Gavriel smiled as she wiped her tears. "Are they always like this?" she asked.

He nodded. "Pretty much. I was wondering how long she was going to wait to tell him."

Colton exhaled catching his breath. He smiled to himself. "I think everyone knew except Meryn and

Aiden. Her scent and body chemistry changed last week."

"It's no wonder I didn't know, she's always smelled that way to me." Elizabeth said.

"I wonder if she'll get morning sickness, more food for us." Colton gloated and stood, rubbing his hands together.

Elizabeth raised an eyebrow. "You boys do realize that now that's she's pregnant she can't have any caffeine, right?"

All sound ceased. The men froze looking at each other as their terror mounted.

"We won't survive," Keelan whispered.

Darian stepped forward, swallowing repeatedly. "When you say no caffeine, does that mean chocolate, too?"

Elizabeth nodded. She was shocked when Keelan whimpered.

"We're done for the day. I'm going to my room until dinner," Darian said, a blank look on his face.

"Good idea," Colton agreed and started walking toward his suite.

"Maybe an invisibility spell," Keelan muttered to himself as he turned in the opposite direction to his suite.

"You, my love, are a very evil woman," Gavriel said steering her to their room.

She stopped in the middle of the hallway and offered her arm to him. "Can I interest you in a mid-afternoon respite?" she asked, turning his words from the previous day against him.

Not unlike his commander, he easily lifted her in his arms and began to trot to their room. He opened the door and closed it behind him. The room was pitch black. He hadn't raised the light blocking blinds. He put her down and moved away.

"Gavriel?" she called out letting her eyes adjust to the dark room.

She heard a masculine chuckle and saw a pair of red eyes glow from across the room.

"Elizabeth," she heard him call.

She swallowed. "Yes?"

"You're it," he whispered.

Oh Gods.

She watched as the red eyes began to circle her. Her heart began to beat a steady rhythm against her chest. Intellectually, she knew he would never hurt her, but that wasn't the game they were playing right now.

"Gavriel?"

"Your blood is teasing me *zain'ka moya*, it is calling out to me." His voice was low and floated across the room.

"I would never deny you, my mate," she said, turning her head tracking his movements.

"What if I want all of you?"

She swallowed and watched has those red eyes stalked closer. "You already have my heart, soul and body. If there's anything else you want, it's yours," she promised.

"Then I intend to take it." His warm breath on the back of her neck had her shivering.

She turned quickly to face him. He took a step forward, and she took one backward. When the back of her legs hit the bed, his grin became feral. She felt his hands on her shoulders and then she was falling backward and staring at the ceiling. He climbed onto the bed and moved over her until he had a thick, muscular thigh on either side of her legs. Using his strength alone, his bare hands ripped her skirt up the side seam until it stopped at her waistband. She felt the scrape of his claw and her skirt was gone.

When his hands moved up her sweater his claws were gone, but that didn't make him any less dangerous. He jerked the fabric up over her head, but instead of removing it, he twisted the fabric around her wrists. Another jerk of his claw and her favorite bra opened to expose her breasts.

Instead of removing her boots and tights, he simply ripped an opening at her crotch.

"I can smell you, my Beth. I can smell your juices, and I know that if I were to run my tongue down your slit, you would have a feast waiting for me." His voice was low and gravely.

She was about to answer when he did exactly what he said he would do. He lifted the lower half of her body up and slid his tongue as deep as he could inside of her.

"Gods! Gavriel, more, please do that again," she begged. His tongue inside of her swollen flesh was a few degrees cooler than her own body temperature, the difference creating an erotic contrast that had her senses spinning out of control.

One hand left her back and a second later, he had two fingers inside of her, thrusting and curling. She threw her head back panting; she couldn't seem to catch her breath. When he turned his face and buried his fangs into her inner thigh, she was brought up short by a burst of pain. When he drank, he twisted his fingers, and the pleasure returned.

He lifted his head from her leg and stared down the length of her body.

"You belong to me. Every inch of you. Inside and out." He plunged his fingers deep.

"Gavriel," she moaned. Her throat was getting dry from trying to catch her breath.

"That is right my love, scream my name. Let the entire world know that you are mine. If the ferals come, I will destroy every single one; even Death itself will not separate us. I will cover this world in flame and blood before I let you go." He let her lower body fall to the bed where it bounced once. He flipped her and with his hands around her waist pulled her against his body. She could feel the cold metal of his zipper along her opening as his cock pressed against the fabric from the inside.

With a firm hand, he pushed down on the center of her back until her breasts were lowered into the mattress.

"Keep your hands above your head," he ordered, his voice barely human.

Behind her, she heard the sounds of cloth ripping before she felt the hot, hard length of his cock teasing her from behind.

Without warning, he plunged his full length inside of her. She opened her mouth to cry out her pleasure, but her face was forced into the bed. Over and over again, he pounded his flesh deep into her. This was not gentle loving; he was branding her.

When he leaned over her body, his hard chest muscles pushed her further into the mattress, she turned her head to tell him to slow down, but that was when he struck. His fangs sunk deeper than they had before, the pain was nearly unbearable. She was on the verge of calling out for help when the pain morphed into pleasure. Unlike before, the pain didn't disappear entirely it returned again and again keeping her body just on the edge of orgasm.

Just when she thought she couldn't take anymore, the pleasure increased. Each time he swallowed and she felt his lips convulse on her neck, her body would contract the muscles around his cock so that it felt as if he were driving that engorged head over every erogenous zone in her body.

Her sight became blurred, so she closed her eyes; still, he drank.

The sound of his flesh slapping against hers faded; still, he drank.

Her body short-circuited, throwing her into the most intense orgasm of her life; still, he drank.

I wonder if I will wake up after this.

Mindlessly, her body swayed in sync with his thrusts; still, he drank.

It was worth every second.

And then there was nothing.

When she woke, she thought she was blind, but quickly figured out that the sun had set and the only source of light in the room was from the tiny light on the hair dryer plug in the bathroom.

"Gavriel?" she called out. She had to swallow several times to get enough moisture down her throat. There was no response. She reached out and fumbled with the light on the nightstand that simulated the soft, low light of a flickering candle.

She blinked. The sheets were different. He had changed them, but why? She went to sit up, and the room swam in ribbons of color. Slowly, she made it to a seated position. Her neck and inner thigh were sore. She looked down and saw a spreading bruise on her leg. She reached up, and unlike every other time her mate had bitten her, she felt the two holes left behind by his fangs.

"Gavriel?" she looked around the room. The old bedding was in a pile by the door; even from where she sat, she could see the bloodstains. Concerned for her mate, she scooted forward and let her feet drop to the floor.

"Stay there," his voice commanded. She looked around and saw him sitting on the floor under the window. He was naked and his skin was covered in a rusty, flakey layer. Without asking, she knew it was her blood. His legs were pulled up so that his elbows rested on his kneecaps. His arms were crossed and his face, hidden from sight, was buried in his forearms.

"I'm coming to you." She stepped forward, and he didn't raise his head. Slowly she made her way over to him. With little grace, she flopped down beside him. She took a moment to catch her breath.

"I am calling your fathers. I am sending you home," he whispered. The absolute despair and loss she heard in his voice broke her heart.

"No. You're not. You are my mate and I won't leave you," she argued.

When he finally looked up, there was no hope, no life in his eyes. "When I came to my senses, you were barely breathing, I had to give you my blood to get your heart to beat normally. I thought I had killed you." His voice was harsh. The self-recrimination and disgust was in every word.

"But you didn't."

"Look at me! Look!" he yelled, unfolding his body. Nearly every inch of his body was covered in blood. "I did this! I bound you, took you like an animal and nearly drained you dry. You..." his voice broke. "You, my sweet Beth. I should be destroyed."

"First of all, I loved being bound and taken like an animal, though that is a very vulgar way of describing one of the most erotic experiences of my life. I enjoyed every second of it. Would I want to do this every night? No, but I would be disappointed if it never happened again," she freely admitted.

He looked up, shocked. "But I hurt you."

"Yes, but in a good way. When you're taking me like that the pain just takes the pleasure to a whole new level, it's intoxicating to the point of addiction.

You don't have to be in transition for this to happen again do you?" she asked.

He blinked. "You are serious. You would do this again?"

"Except for the blood loss, yes. But I think we can safely attribute that to your transition. Was it a bit scary? Yes. But that made it all the more delicious. Are you listening to me, my mate?" She scooted so that their bodies touched. Both of them shuddered.

"Even now I want to drink from you again." He went to reach out to touch her face but pulled his hand back. She grabbed his hand and placed it against her cheek.

"You're not listening. Did you set out to hurt me?"

"No! Of course not."

"Are you possibly days away from the hardest apex of your life by going through two transitions?"

"Three," he whispered.

"Three? So you are at your five thousandth year. I speculated with Meryn. So you have your natural transition, your fifth millennial, and a power increase due to the ferals." She let his hand drop but kept their fingers intertwined. Their combined hands rested on his thigh.

He turned his head to look at her, his eyes filled with exhaustion. "Not my fifth millennial, my Myriad."

Her heart stuttered. "Myriad? Doesn't that mean..."

He nodded. "Yes. Ten thousand, at least that is as far back as I remember."

Elizabeth sat back covering her mouth with both hands as pieces of the puzzle began to fall into place. The reason why he didn't want power, why he kept his age a secret, why he alone represented the oldest vampiric ruling house and why the version Meryn knew of their legend was different; she had heard it from the man herself.

"Oh sweet Gods above. You're the Dark Prince." She clutched at her chest as the enormity of this reality settled in her mind.

He sighed, closed his eyes, and sat back. "I never wanted you to know."

She could only stare. This was the Dark Prince she had fantasized about as a girl; the invincible warrior that every other man was compared to after her uncle and fathers. And he was her mate. Gone was the golden armor and white plumed helmet. There was no holy sword or fiery steed at his side, just a man. Her man, a man that at the moment believed he had lost everything, including her.

She flicked the side of his leg with her thumb and forefinger.

"Ow!" He looked at her surprised and frowning. "What was that for?"

"I thought you'd be bigger." She made the mistake of glancing down at his groin and giggled.

His mouth dropped.

She leaned against him laughing. He pulled away and righted her before looking into her face. There was disbelief, but also the tiniest ray of light in his eyes. "You thought what would be bigger, *zain'ka moya*?" He asked, his lips twitching.

She cleared her throat and smiled at him. She climbed over his knee until she sat between his legs and snuggled close to his chest. Automatically, his arms circled her.

"Dark Prince, surly warrior, charming gentleman, it doesn't matter. They are just different sides to my mate." She yawned and winced as her neck flexed.

He felt her flinch. "I would take this pain from you if I could," he whispered.

"It's not so bad. Think about it this way, this is the most out of control you'll be for at least another five thousand years; I'm going to enjoy it."

He gathered her against him with one arm and used the other to stand. He walked over to their bed and gently set her down. She didn't feel complete until he slid in next to her.

"You do not see me any differently?" he asked.

"No. I was raised among our ruling houses; as a little girl, you were the prince of my dreams. Maybe Fate was preparing me for you even then."

He kissed the top of her head and whispered his prayers of thanks to the one who watched over them.

"Gavriel?"

"Yes, my love?"

"You're over ten thousand years old right?"

"Yes darling."

"What exactly is in your other home in storage?" she asked unable to keep the excitement out of her voice.

"Nothing compared to the treasure in my arms," he said, squeezing her tight.

"Gavriel?"

"Yes, love?"

"I want to go through your stuff." She bit down on the muscles of his chest playfully.

His laughter was like a balm on her soul.

"Whatever I have, whatever I am, is yours already, *zain'ka moya.*"

Maybe he had stored her heart away with his other treasures from myth and legend.

Smiling, she dreamt of her heart being guarded by her mate in a cavern of gold and silver

CHAPTER TWELVE

The next day, she added a bright teal scarf around her neck to complete her ensemble of a chocolate brown sweater and jeans to hide Gavriel's bite marks. More to keep Gavriel from feeling guilty than anything else. Her neck irritated her every time she turned her head, but it was nothing compared to the on again off again sharp pain from the bite in her thigh. She hadn't lied to him the night before. It had been scary, yes, but one of the most erotic experiences of her life. If she had to give up a little blood to experience Gavriel at his most primal, she would gladly do it again. She grabbed the two remaining keystones and stuck them in her jeans pocket. She would have to remember to give Meryn hers today.

She walked down the stairs slowly and walked to the dining room. The men stood when she walked in. Keelan let out the breath he had been holding. Elizabeth looked to the empty seats where Meryn and Aiden usually sat. Smiling, she walked to her mate. He kissed her gently before she sat down; he pushed her chair in and sat beside her. He immediately reached for her hand. The men resumed their seats.

Ryuu came from the kitchen with a huge platter of egg, bacon, and cheese English muffins, setting it in the middle of the table. Elizabeth guessed he chose something quick that could be reheated later as the men got hungry throughout the day, while everyone pitched in to get the trainees settled. She picked up a sandwich from the platter. It was still warm when she took a large bite. The cheese was melted perfectly.

"Ryuu, these are amazing. Put this breakfast choice at the top of the list," Keelan said, smacking his lips.

"Agreed. Though they are kinda small," Darian said, holding up a sandwich, which in his huge hand looked tiny.

Ryuu smiled. "Don't worry about the size, I made plenty," he assured the fae.

"Good, because I'm on my fifth," Colton said, reaching for another.

Elizabeth stared. Where did the man put it?

He caught her staring and winked. "Growing up, my mother always said I ate as if I were feeding myself and my wolf."

"I can't blame you with this meal, I'll probably have another myself," she admitted.

She noticed that Gavriel's plate was empty but Ryuu kept cycling out glasses of blood. He was drinking even more today.

They all turned when they heard footsteps. Aiden appeared in the doorway alone. He looked around and shrugged. "She said she wasn't going to get up until she was awake. Don't ask, I don't know." He sat down and piled five sandwiches on his plate.

Elizabeth turned to the squire "Ryuu, you might want to go take her a small cup of something. If she thinks she can stay in bed until she wakes up, she's wrong. She'll just go back to sleep and get overtired, which will make her even more evil. Trust me, I know."

Ryuu nodded and picked up the small mug he had placed at Meryn's seat. "I'll be back."

"Lord and Lady, please protect and guide this brave warrior as he faces certain death," Keelan murmured as he began the prayer for the Brave Warrior.

Colton snorted and kept eating.

Aiden nodded. "Go with the Gods' blessings."

Ryuu rolled his eyes and left the room.

"Well, it was nice having a squire while it lasted," Darian sighed.

"You all are just bad." Elizabeth smiled and picked up a second sandwich.

Keelan shook his head. "You don't understand. Meryn is scary in the morning."

She shook her head. "She can't be that bad." She took a bite and looked up. All five men were looking at her solemnly and nodding.

"I need my caffeine in the morning, too," she countered.

"Yes, but you have yet to threaten to castrate and dismember anyone," Keelan pointed out.

"Keelan, she was just kidding." Elizabeth looked at Aiden for support. "Right?"

Aiden shrugged. "You're talking to the mate whose car she set on fire the other day."

Gavriel patted her leg. "She would regret any drastic actions later I am sure."

Ryuu walked back in looking unscathed.

Keelan stared. "How did you do it?" he asked in wonder.

Ryuu let out a breath. "I had to promise her another small cup of coffee." Ryuu quickly walked to the kitchen.

"She'll be fine," Aiden said and bit one of the sandwiches in half.

Halfway through breakfast, Ryuu went back upstairs with another cup of coffee. The men were feeling better since Meryn now had some form of caffeine in her. Elizabeth was sipping her cappuccino when the doorbell rang. The men all looked at each other.

"Well? Someone answer it," Elizabeth laughed.

Everyone stood and walked to the foyer. Aiden opened the door and a group of four tall men stood smiling at them. Behind them stood a smaller young man next to another man in a wheelchair.

"Sir! Trainees for the Alpha Unit reporting in," the man closest to the door announced. He indicated to the others. "Basil Barberry, witch. Kai Anders, tiger. Cedric Ri'Emere, fae and I am Lennox Chevalier, vampire. Our fifth will be joining us later." The four crossed their forearms over their chests and bowed in salute. Lennox straightened and pointed to the two others that waited behind them. "I am not sure who they are."

The young man that stood next to the wheelchair stepped forward. "My name is Noah Caraway, and this is my best friend Jaxon Darrow. We were hoping to speak to Lady Meryn." He spoke very quickly. Elizabeth could tell he was nervous.

Aiden stepped forward and was about to greet them when an irate voice called out from the drive.

"Commander! Commander, I would like a word!"

Everyone turned to see Elder Evreux stalking toward them. The trainees looked surprised and quickly stepped back to let the Elder pass.

"Elder, what a surprise to see you out here." Aiden turned to the others. "Come on in, it's cold outside, might as well get you settled. Where are your things?" he asked Lennox.

"We drove two cars here, sir, our things are in those," Lennox answered.

"Get warmed up first then we'll haul your things in." Aiden opened the door wide.

Elder Evreux walked in as if he owned the place. The trainees respectfully waited and filed in behind him. The two others brought up the rear.

"Elder, what brings you out here?" Aiden asked.

"I came to speak with your mate. Evidently she had information to share with Elder Rioux that I would like to discuss with her," he sneered.

Elizabeth stepped forward. "Actually Elder, I was the one who called Elder Rioux. My name is Elizabeth Monroe."

She noticed that his entire demeanor changed. "Elizabeth Monroe, what a pleasure it is to finally meet you. Your uncle has had nothing but wonderful things to say about you." The change from prickly to pleasant was unnerving.

Out of the corner of her eye, she noticed movement at the top of the stairs. When she saw Elder Evreux's line of sight turning to the stairs she stepped in front of him. "My uncle has spoken of your dedication to our people."

The Elder's eyebrows shot up. "Our people?" he asked.

"Of course. I was raised in Noctem Falls, after all. This is the first time with the exception of my short forays into human cities that I haven't been surrounded by vampires. I find that I miss the caves." She smiled, hoping that she had distracted him. What on earth was Meryn doing?

Elder Evreux preened. "I am dedicated to our race; I am humbled that Elder Rioux has taken notice. I find your manners a refreshing change. Maybe I should visit Noctem Falls sometime soon." He turned to Aiden, his smile dropping. "Where is your mate?" he demanded.

"Meryn! Someone is here to see you!" Aiden called up the stairs.

"Hold on!" was her reply.

Aiden's smile to Elder Evreux was tight. "She'll be right down."

"Ahhh!" Meryn wailed. Everyone turned to look up the stairs.

"What?" Aiden yelled, concern written all over his face.

"I dropped my iPod in the toilet!" Meryn sounded frantic.

"Pull it out and dry it off, it will be fine," Aiden bellowed.

"You don't understand; I didn't flush yet.... And I went number two." Meryn's tone sounded so tragic that Elizabeth was starting to believe her.

Aiden turned to Elder Evreux his face red. "She's busy, maybe another time..."

"Never mind! Got it!" Meryn yelled triumphantly. Seconds later, she was walking down the stairs wiping her hands on her jeans. Smiling at the Elder, she walked right up to him and offered him her hand to shake.

Elder Evreux looked like he was going to be ill. He stared at her hand as if she were a plague carrier. He spun on his heel to face Aiden. "You know what. You look very busy getting these boys settled. I will come back at a more opportune time." Without waiting for a reply, he bolted for the door as if the hounds of hell were after him. The sound of the door slamming shut echoed in the foyer.

"Can I be just like you when I grow up?" Noah whispered.

Meryn jumped up and down throwing her tiny fists in the air. "Whoo hoo! Meryn two. Douchebag zero."

"Meryn, you shouldn't call Elder Evreux a douchebag in front of our new trainees," Aiden admonished even as his lips were trying not to smile.

"Do not mind us, sir." Lennox and the other trainees gave Meryn a thumbs up sign.

"You little minx. How on earth did you find out that Elder Evreux has to be the biggest germaphobe this side of the Mississippi?" Elizabeth pulled the smaller woman in for a hug.

Meryn looked at her and winked impishly. "I have learned well, Master Yoda," and then held up her phone.

Elizabeth's mouth dropped. "Of course! The history books! You little genius!" She laughed and danced around the foyer with her.

Meryn stopped dancing and turned to Aiden. "And he can't say I wasn't nice. He left all on his own so he can't complain. I am learning about politics."

Aiden shook his head smiling. "I don't think that your version of 'politics' is quite right, but that's okay."

"I like her version, Commander, I say we learn more about her style of politics," Colton joked.

"Okay, enough shenanigans. Alpha Unit, let's get these trainees settled and then introduce them to drills." Aiden's grin was decidedly wolfish.

All the men including the new trainees groaned.

Aiden laughed. "You all didn't think you'd be getting the day off did you? Welcome to the Alpha Unit, you'll soon be missing my brother and his soft ways."

Lennox looked at the other trainees then to Aiden before swallowing. "He was soft?" He looked at Aiden in disbelief.

"Come on, squirts, if Aiden hasn't killed us yet, I doubt you're in any danger. But you may want to leave the name of your next of kin with Ryuu, he's the house squire," Colton said slinging an arm around Lennox's shoulders.

The trainees turned to Ryuu and gave a half bow, which the squire returned. "You are to come to me with any concerns regarding your domestic arrangements. Unit Commander McKenzie has given me leave to discipline you if you get out of hand, but having met you, I don't think that will be a problem. But just to be on the safe side, are any of you especially susceptible to electricity?" Where Aiden had been kidding, everyone could tell Ryuu was not. The newcomers all shook their heads looking dazed.

"Buck up gentlemen, you're here because you scored the highest and wanted to be here. You have what it takes to keep up," Elizabeth said encouragingly.

The trainees all smiled at her warmly. Cedric the fae even winked. Gavriel let out a low, long hiss and moved closer to her. He glared at the paling trainees before taking her hand. "In case you did not know, the rumors floating around Lycaonia are true. A spell was cast to bring all the unit warriors their mates. Any female that lives here is spoken for, and you would do well to remain respectful."

"Absolutely, sir, will not be an issue at all." Lennox and the others shook their heads back and forth.

"Wonderful. Looks like everyone is getting along beautifully. Come on; let's go get your gear so we can start my favorite part of the day. Drills." Aiden grinned at the lot of them before kissing Meryn and walking out the door.

"Look at him; he's like a little boy with a new toy to break in." Meryn sighed happily before her eyes went wide. Wincing, she turned to the trainees. "Sorry."

Keelan, Colton, Gavriel, and Darian joked with the trainees and filed out the door behind Aiden leaving Noah and Jaxon staring at them.

"Meryn, these two were waiting to speak to you, too. The one on the right is Noah Caraway and the one on the left is Jaxon Darrow," Elizabeth explained pointing to the new men.

Meryn turned to them. "What could I possibly do for you?" she asked.

"We want to learn from you!" Noah blurted.

Meryn blinked. "Huh? I'm not a warrior trainer," she pointed out.

Jaxon wheeled closer. "No, but you easily bypassed our sub-routines to take control of the city cameras last month. As you can see, we're not exactly warrior material." Jaxon nodded to his legs. Noah held up his arm pointing to a puny bicep.

Jaxon continued. "You can teach us what you know about hacking. We can help you," he offered.

"It's internet security..." Meryn started.

"Hacking," both Jaxon and Noah said together.

Meryn looked to her. Elizabeth shrugged. This was beyond her. She could organize and run a city, but she didn't know the first thing about computers beyond how to get her reports.

Meryn then turned to Ryuu who was nodding. "I think this is a good idea, *denka*. Teaching others is very humbling and grounding, you need both. Plus, considering your condition, you may need the help."

Jaxon turned to Meryn, concern in his eyes. "Condition?"

Meryn shrugged. "We just found out that I'm preggo."

Jaxon and Noah looked at each other confusion on their faces. Noah turned to her. "How did that happen?"

Meryn shrugged. "Aiden has this thing he likes to do that I just can't say no to..." Ryuu placed a hand over her mouth. Both men blushed furiously.

Without removing his hand, Ryuu turned to them. "If you're to study with Lady Meryn you'll have to get used to her bluntness. To answer your question, she is human. She can get pregnant at any time, which is why she is pregnant out of season." Ryuu removed his hand.

"Oh, that's what they wanted to know." She turned to Ryuu. "I'm hungry."

Ryuu bowed. "Gentleman, we have plenty of breakfast leftover if you haven't eaten," he offered.

Noah licked his lips. Jaxon laughed. "He's a bottomless pit and is always hungry. But I could eat, too. I was so nervous about coming here today, I couldn't eat this morning. When we heard that trainees from the academy were allowed to move to the Alpha estate we thought that it wouldn't be that much different if we came here during the day to learn."

"This way." Ryuu led the way to the dining room.

Elizabeth followed. She wouldn't be of any use outside in the cold carrying gear and she was craving another cappuccino.

When everyone was seated with food in front of them, she pointed to her empty cup. Ryuu nodded and left for the kitchen.

"So, can I ask you something?" Meryn said turning to Jaxon.

He grinned ruefully. "You're going to ask how a shifter can become paralyzed when we can heal so quickly aren't you."

Meryn nodded not even looking embarrassed.

Jaxon blinked. "I fell out of a tree when I was very young, before I could shift. Unfortunately, it has inhibited my wolf so I'm stuck like this. It doesn't bother you, does it? My affliction?" he asked.

Elizabeth could only imagine the kind of life he had led living in a predominately shifter city with a handicap.

"Why would it bother me? I'm kinda jealous; you always have a place to sit." Meryn took a huge bite of her breakfast sandwich.

Elizabeth swatted at her arm. "Meryn!" she admonished.

"Wha'?" Meryn asked with her mouth full.

Jaxon surprised her when he began to laugh. Noah grinned, shaking his head. Finally, Jaxon spoke. "No one has ever looked at me and seen an advantage. Not once. I wasn't sure how this was going to go, but I'm not above begging. Please let us study with you. We'll do whatever you say. We want to learn how to help the warriors like you do." His eyes blazed with passion.

Elizabeth could see that had life been different, he could have easily been one of the trainees outside getting his gear. His body, though seated, was large and muscular. She wondered how many times he had been dismissed and shunted to one side.

"I have minions," Meryn whispered in awe.

"Gods above save us," Elizabeth muttered.

"Ryuu!" Meryn yelled.

He appeared in the doorway almost immediately. "Yes, *denka*?"

"I'm calling dibs on one of the guest suites downstairs for my minions; can you make sure the meatheads know?" She started rubbing her hands together. He bowed and walked out toward the front door.

"You'll teach us? We can actually stay here? Like the trainees?" Noah stuttered his questions.

"Yup! And don't think I'm going to go easy on you either. The things we'll be able to do with three of us." Meryn's eyes shone with excitement.

Minutes later Aiden a frown on his face walked in with Ryuu. "What's this about using a guest suite?"

Meryn nodded. "It's been reserved for my minions. I want them to get the larger guest suite next to the media room, which we will later be tricking out as our command central." Meryn reached down to her ever-present backpack and pulled out her laptop.

Aiden just stared then shook his head. "I'm not going to ask." He turned to Jaxon and Noah. "Welcome aboard and good luck." He walked out yelling to Colton to move Lennox to another room.

"Just like that?" Noah whispered.

"I told you buddy. I had a good feeling about this, like we were supposed to be here." Jaxon punched his friend lightly in the shoulder.

Elizabeth felt a sliver of ice slide down her spine at his words. She looked over at Ryuu and saw that he too had felt something. Jaxon was more right than he knew; they were meant to be here.

"Meryn..." Elizabeth started.

Meryn waved a hand at her. "Shush for a second, my brain is working. I think I have designed a new program; each unit in the future will get a sixth man. He'll be the unit's eyes and ears, their communication link and relay." Meryn tapped away furiously.

"So mote it be," Ryuu whispered from the other side of the room.

Elizabeth clearly saw the important role these two underestimated and overlooked men would play and why Meryn was so necessary to be, who she was, where she was, and who she was mated to.

"Ryuu, I think a bottle of champagne is in order," Elizabeth said, sitting up. She was watching history unfold right before her eyes. She also realized why she had been brought to Lycaonia. Meryn may be the one creating and teaching this program, but it would need someone like her to organize it and keep it running.

"I do believe you are right," Ryuu said and went to the kitchen.

Meryn, Jaxon, and Noah stared at her as if she lost her mind.

Ryuu walked back in with five empty flutes glasses and an open bottle. He poured a glass for each of them, handing Meryn half a glass.

They had just lifted their glasses to toast when the warriors and trainees walked in from carrying in all the luggage. They looked around in confusion. Ryuu nodded to Elizabeth.

She responded the only way she knew how.

She stood and lifted her glass to the room before reciting one of her favorite quotes of all time. *"I wish the Ring had never come to me. I wish none of this had happened. So do all who live to see such times, but that is not for them to decide. All we have to decide is what to do with the time that is given to us. There are other forces at work in this world, Frodo, besides the will of evil."*

"May we perform the jobs given to us well." Ryuu lifted his glass in salute. Together, they both downed their glasses. Meryn, Jaxon and Noah grinning, drank theirs.

"I love that movie! You're like my Yoda and my Gandalf," Meryn said, easily finishing off her half glass.

Elizabeth smiled, she could think of no higher praise from Meryn.

"Whatever needs doing, Noah and I can help." Jaxon said confidently.

"Beth, love, what is going on?" Gavriel walked over to her, taking her glass from her hand and pulling her into his arms.

For a moment, she simply enjoyed the feel of him. His solid frame seemed to anchor her. She thought before she spoke. She had to be careful of what she said; she didn't want to disrupt Meryn's train of thought. She looked up at her mate and shook her head smiling. "Meryn is making history. She has just changed the structure of how units will be run."

"What?" Aiden and Colton asked in unison.

Aiden walked up behind Meryn. "Baby, you can't just change something that has worked for thousands of years. This, whatever it is, needs to be discussed with the council. You need to ask permission before you try to implement changes." Aiden waved at her laptop.

Meryn looked up at him from her laptop. "You mean where I go in and visit with your father the shifter Elder, who loves me, Celyn the fae Elder, who adores me, and Rowan the witch Elder, who admires me and I tell them I have this stupendous idea to save lives. That sort of thing?" she asked.

Aiden groaned. "They have spoiled you too much. Even if you were to get their blessing, this goes beyond Lycaonia. This type of unilateral change needs to be accepted in every pillar city."

Meryn patted his chest. "Which is why, as Unit Commander, you're going to tell them you support me one thousand percent. You can make changes to the units, I know, I looked it up last week just in case I had to pull rank again."

Aiden ran a hand through his hair. "It will never get the support from all the other cities."

Elizabeth faced Aiden. "My uncle will support it if I tell him to and I will. Her idea to add a sixth man to every unit to act as its own command central will save lives, I'm sure of it."

Aiden looked from Meryn to her back to Meryn. "That's just Lycaonia and Noctem Falls."

Darian cleared his throat. "Actually, if Meryn were to suggest it, my queen would also support her. She likes Meryn and has already invited her to the fae city, which is no small feat. She finds Meryn's new outlook refreshing and inspirational. She would have the support of Éire Danu as well."

Aiden looked around a bit wild eyed.

Colton stepped forward and clapped him on the back. "Aiden, it's a good idea, in fact, it's a great idea. I know I, for one, would feel a hell of a whole lot safer if I knew someone like Meryn was watching out for us when we're called out on a mission. Hell! Do you know how much red tape she could slash through by hacking the local law enforcement systems? This could literally save lives, *our* lives. And I don't know about you, but knowing that my mate is on the way, I want to be around to meet her. And you have Meryn 2.0 to raise." Colton elbowed his friend.

"Meryn, can this actually work?" Aiden looked down at his mate with a serious expression.

She nodded and met his eyes. "Yes. I have my first two trainees right here. I'll get them up to speed and then train others. I'm sure there must be more men or even women that will want to join the program." Meryn looked up at Aiden, resolve written on her face for everyone to see.

"Not to speak out of turn, but I would be interested in learning as well, sir. Even when we were at the academy, there were times we were laid up for a few days healing. If I could spend that time watching out for my brother warriors, I would rather do that than stare at the TV waiting for bones to mend," Lennox said taking the initiative to speak. Behind him, all the trainees nodded.

"Okay, Menace. You create this program and make it airtight and I will get the support of the other councils. If you and Elizabeth feel this strongly about it, then I can do no less than make it happen," Aiden said.

Meryn bounced out of her seat and jumped up and down trying to kiss his face.

Laughing, Aiden picked her up. "Why do you hop around like that, you know you can't reach?"

"But I can reach; I just need your help." She peppered his face with kisses.

Blushing, he cleared his throat and turned to the trainees. "Time to start drills."

Grinning at each other, the trainees nodded. "Yes, Sir!" they called out and jogged for the front door.

Aiden groaned, his badass image tarnished. Meryn laughed and nuzzled her nose against his. "My teddy bear."

Colton made the mistake of laughing. Aiden's head swung to him. "Alpha Unit to join the trainees. Let's show them how it's done gentlemen, we go until they drop," he said, smiling at Colton's chagrin.

Gavriel shook his head and turned to Elizabeth. "Try not to take over the world while we poor grunts are training."

She flipped her hair off her shoulder. "We make no promises."

She sat back down and picked up her champagne; they were definitely living in interesting times.

CHAPTER THIRTEEN

Elizabeth listened in as Meryn started describing the different operating systems and computer languages that her new 'minions' would have to learn. She jumped from topic to topic excitedly. After an hour Elizabeth, took pity on Jaxon and Noah who had started to look a little shell shocked and put a halt to Meryn's 'teaching'.

She stood and clapped her hands together; all three looked up at her.

"How about this? Since the two of you will be moving in let's make arrangements to get your things here. I'll put together a rough curriculum with reading materials and Meryn will be on hand for any questions." She almost laughed out loud at the enthusiastic nodding from the men.

"Sounds good to me, I'm not very good at organizing stuff," Meryn admitted. Elizabeth watched as both men looked away, not saying a word.

Bless their hearts.

Noah looked at Jaxon. "We don't have much. I can run to the apartment, get our stuff, and come back. We pay monthly, so we don't have to worry about breaking a lease."

Jaxon frowned and looked down at his chair before sighing. "I wish I could help."

Noah shrugged. "It's not a lot."

"Maybe Sydney and Justice can help. They live in the city." Meryn interjected.

"Sydney Fairfax and Justice O'Malley?" Noah squeaked, turning pink.

Jaxon laughed. "They're Noah's idols; he admires them for living their life on their own terms."

"Plus, they're both hot." Noah mumbled.

Elizabeth looked from Jaxon to Noah and back again. "Are the two of you lovers?"

Noah shook his head frantically. "No, Jaxon is my best friend."

Jaxon ruffled Noah's hair. "I'm straight, but even if I weren't, I'm too ugly. Noah likes pretty boys," he teased.

Noah turned to Jaxon, "You're not ugly, and there's nothing wrong with liking pretty boys," he countered.

Elizabeth agreed, "You're absolutely right Noah, they're my favorite too." She winked at him and he smiled, and then frowned. "But you're mated."

"Mated honey, not dead. Besides you've met my mate, a girl would have to be crazy to do more than window shop with a mate like that," Elizabeth sighed happily.

"He is very handsome," Noah admitted.

Meryn laughed staring down at her phone, her tiny fingers moving a mile a minute. She looked up and gave a thumbs up to Noah. "Justice said he can help you move out. I'll give you his number so you can text him the address." Meryn wrote down the number on a piece of paper and handed it to Noah.

Noah took the piece of paper and held it as if it were the Holy Grail.

"I have Justice O'Malley's phone number in my hand," he whispered.

"And the sooner you use it, the sooner you can get our stuff and the sooner we can move in," Jaxon prompted, nudging Noah.

Noah stood and nodded. "Right. Be back later." Beaming, he practically ran for the door.

When he left, Jaxon shook his head. "It'll be a miracle if our stuff gets here in one piece; he's so excited."

"He seems very young," Elizabeth observed.

Jaxon nodded. "We're both one hundred years old. But he's always been like that. Even though we're the same age, he always seemed like a little brother to me. Since paranormals view our one-hundredth year as the year we become legal adults, Noah and I were promptly kicked out of our homes on our birthdays. My parents no longer wanted to be associated with a son who was broken and Noah's parents don't believe in same sex matings."

"That's very young to be on your own." Elizabeth frowned. Granted, she was only one hundred and fifty, but she had grown a lot in the past fifty years.

"Pffft. I'm only thirty-four so compared to him I must be an infant," Meryn joked.

"Humans age differently than paranormals. You may be thirty-four, but if you were a normal unmated human that would represent one-third of your life span. As a shifter one thousand years to fifteen hundred years represents one-third of our life span. Since you're mated to Aiden, you will live as long as he does. Since I'm mated to Gavriel, I am now immortal," Elizabeth explained.

"So in paranormal to human conversions, I'm older than Aiden?" Meryn asked.

Elizabeth thought about it for a moment and nodded. "If you were going by straight numbers, but in your case I think it may be skewed."

Meryn stuck her tongue out at her.

Elizabeth laughed. "And on that note, I'm going to help Ryuu get their room ready. Meryn, try not to make Jaxon's head explode with explanations while I'm gone." Elizabeth turned to the door.

"He'll be fine." Meryn reached over and patted Jaxon's leg. He shot Elizabeth a look that clearly said, 'Please hurry'.

Elizabeth wiggled her fingers at them. "Have fun."

She walked out and found that Ryuu had already moved a second bed into the guest suite that would belong to Noah and Jaxon and had a stack of sheets sitting on each bed.

"Ryuu, I can make the beds if you have something else you need to be doing," she offered.

He moved the second bed into place and stood back. He faced her and nodded. "That would be most appreciated. I need to start dinner and need the extra time since we're feeding more than twice our usual numbers. I have made arrangements with Aiden that the trainees, including Meryn's minions, will eat two hours prior to the warriors, pushing back your normal mealtime by one hour to begin at seven p.m. That will keep some separation between the two groups and make it easier to serve. As big as the dining room is, I don't think it was meant for seventeen people."

Elizabeth counted in her head and looked at him questioningly. "Seventeen?"

"I have factored for each warrior finding a mate. It's best if we establish separate dining times from the start," he explained.

"Good idea. You go on ahead, I'll finish up here." She walked over and picked up the sheets.

Ryuu bowed. "Thank you. I'll let Meryn and young Mr. Darrow know of our new eating arrangements and let him know I have ordered bars for the bathroom for his ease of use."

"That was considerate of you, I'm sure he'll appreciate it."

"If you'll excuse me," he said and left.

Elizabeth looked around the room. In such a short amount of time Ryuu had done everything he could to arrange the furniture so that Jaxon's wheelchair could maneuver. The man was a credit to his profession.

Humming, she began to make the beds. Chores like this always relaxed her. They were uncomplicated tasks that allowed her mind to wander. She was just finishing the second bed when she heard footsteps behind her. She didn't think anything of it until she heard an unfamiliar male voice.

"Look, my room comes with entertainment." The voice belonged to a tall, well-muscled shifter. He had blond hair and cold blue eyes. He had classic good looks tainted by a sneering upper lip and the lecherous look in his eyes.

"I think you're mistaken," Elizabeth said walking toward the door. She wanted to get to Gavriel and Aiden and find out who this man was. When she went to walk past him, he blocked the doorway.

"Don't be like that; let's get to know each other better," he said reaching out to touch her hair. She pulled back and glared at him.

"Move. Now." She leveled her eyes at him and he smirked. He was enjoying this.

"I have connections, sweetheart; I can make your life easier. Come 'work' for me and you won't have to make anyone else's bed but mine," he offered.

He thinks I'm a servant.

"I've said it before, and I'll say it again. You're mistaken; I'm mated, and I live here. Now move!" She went to shoulder her way past, but he grabbed her and pushed her back.

"I suggest you leave her alone." Ryuu said, walking up behind her adversary, his eyes completely devoid of emotion. Elizabeth had never been happier to see anyone in her life.

"Ryuu, thank goodness you're here." She breathed a sigh of relief.

The man turned and looked Ryuu up and down. Taking in the apron he laughed. "Your mate is a servant. Go ahead and provoke me, China man, my family will bury you," he threatened.

Ryuu looked past him and met her eyes. He raised a single eyebrow in question. She spread her hands and shrugged.

"I have no idea who he is, but he's a complete idiot. And Ryuu is Japanese, you twit, not Chinese." She crossed her arms over her chest.

Snarling, he turned and reached for her again. Ryuu simply extended his hand and wrapped it around the back of the man's neck; a spark of blue flared. The man's eyes rolled back, and he went down. Ryuu let him fall hard. Elizabeth winced as the man's face made contact with the hardwood.

Ryuu extended a hand to help her step over the odious man that now blocked the doorway. Smiling, she took his hand, and he easily lifted her across.

"If you could return to where Meryn and young Mr. Darrow are, I'll fetch Aiden and your mate," Ryuu offered.

"Thank you, Ryuu." Elizabeth followed him out. He went out the front door headed toward the training grounds.

"There you are. We were looking for you," Meryn said walking up. Jaxon wheeled along beside her.

"Meryn, let's go back to the office. It's not safe here." Elizabeth wrapped an arm around her shoulders to steer her back from where they had just come.

Meryn resisted. "What in the hell do you mean, it's not safe?" she asked.

"There you are, you bitch!" An angry voice roared.

When Elizabeth looked up, the blond man was staggering toward them. Moving quicker than she thought one in a wheelchair could move, Jaxon pushed himself between the oncoming giant and Elizabeth.

Just as the blond man was about to pass him, Jaxon reached out a hand and grabbed his forearm. With his other hand, he reached down and set the brake on his chair.

"Out of my way, cripple!" The violently angry man protested as he tried to get his arm free. But try as he might, he could not escape Jaxon's strong grasp.

"It looks like this cripple is stronger than the trainee who placed first in trials. I knew you were an asshole, Sterling. What I didn't know was that you were this weak," Jaxon taunted.

Elizabeth stared. This was a trainee?

"What in the hell is going on here?" A deep male voice bellowed.

"Aiden! Sic 'em, boy!" Meryn pointed to the one Jaxon called Sterling.

Aiden strode forward and grabbed the front of Sterling's shirt, hauling him a good foot off the ground. "Why did you attack my mate?" Aiden growled low in his throat.

Sterling looked around confused. He pointed to Elizabeth. "She's your mate?" he asked.

From behind Aiden, there was a low hiss. Gavriel walked over and pulled Sterling out of Aiden's grasp. "No whelp, she is mine." Gavriel let him dangle as he shook him repeatedly.

Sterling gulped and looked from Aiden to Gavriel wide eyed. "Sir, I think there has been a huge mistake. I thought she was the house servant and flirted a bit. She took exception, and I was about to let her leave when the other servant electrocuted me. When I came out here to find out why I had been attacked, the one in the chair assaulted me."

Aiden turned to them. "Is that true?"

Meryn looked up at Aiden, "I'm sorry all I heard was 'blah, blah, blah, I'm an asshole liar, blah, blah, blah'."

Aiden ignored his mate and looked at Elizabeth.

She took a deep breath and recounted what happened.

"He came into the room set up for Jaxon and Noah just as I was finishing making up the beds. He thought that a servant of this house provided certain benefits. I told him in no uncertain terms that he was mistaken and that I was mated. He still blocked me from leaving the room when I tried to come and get you. That's when Ryuu showed up. This one," she pointed to the man suspended by her mate. "I'm assuming his name is Sterling, made racially disparaging remarks against Ryuu thinking him just another servant. When he started to get violent, Ryuu knocked him unconscious, helped me to leave the room, and set out to find you. Sterling woke and came after me. That's when Jaxon stopped him." Elizabeth wrapped up her story and took a deep breath. Gavriel hissed in Sterling's face, his fangs extended.

Aiden turned to her mate. "Gavriel, I'm putting you in charge of our newest trainee. He's to run until he passes out, and then he's to complete all the drills that the others have done. Make sure you are very through in introducing him to our unit lifestyle."

Gavriel's smile was terrifying. "Come on, whelp, time to break you in." Gavriel simply hauled the struggling man toward the door.

"But I need to change," Sterling protested pointing to his dress shoes and slacks.

"Too bad," Gavriel growled. Ryuu opened the front door for them.

"Thank you, Ryuu. Can I trouble you to make a special menu for this one? Water and gruel for the next week," Gavriel requested as Sterling let loose a string of curses.

Ryuu bowed, smiling. "It would be no trouble at all."

Gavriel nodded. "He is to take all his meals alone in his room."

"I'll see to it personally," Ryuu promised.

Gavriel half carried and half dragged the trainee out the door. Ryuu shut it behind him.

Meryn whistled. "I've never seen Gavriel look so pissed." She looked up at her mate. "I don't want him here. Can we throw him back and get another one?"

Aiden rubbed both hands over his face. "You can't establish a new method of doing things and then change them the second you don't like the results. He scored the highest, and he chose to come here. If we start playing favorites now, it will hurt our case for your sixth man project."

"Aiden, he's unstable," Elizabeth shuddered.

Aiden looked at her pleadingly. "I'll have a one to one with him and make it crystal clear what is and isn't accepted. I'm sure that he was just hyped up about moving in. He'll settle down after a few days. Until then, Gavriel will watch him like a hawk and dog his steps." Aiden turned to Ryuu.

"If he gets out of line again shock the hell out of him, at this point a little brain damage may do him some good." Sighing, he kissed Meryn on the forehead. "Excuse me, ladies, I need to call my brother and ask him why he didn't warn me about that insufferable little prick." Aiden walked past them before stopping next to Jaxon. He laid a hand on his shoulder. "Good work, son. When my mate isn't driving you crazy, come find me. I'll show you some exercises that will really work your upper body." Aiden continued on to his office.

Jaxon turned to them, a goofy grin on his face. Beth had a feeling that the compliment from *the* Unit Commander meant everything to Jaxon, especially a compliment on a physical feat done well.

Elizabeth was about to thank Jaxon when the doorbell rang. Everyone looked at Ryuu who was standing closest. He opened the door and a man in construction gear was standing there. Behind him were two more men in overalls, one holding a clipboard.

"Sir." The man in front brought a hand to his hard hat, greeting Ryuu. "My team was called in by the Unit Commander to build a new closet."

Ryuu looked past him to the other men.

"We have a delivery for an Elizabeth Monroe. Overnight freight from Noctem Falls." The taller of the two pointed to a very large truck in their driveway. Everyone turned to Elizabeth.

Ryuu cleared his throat. "Lady Elizabeth, how many boxes were you expecting?"

Elizabeth winced, walked forward, and looked out the door. "Is it just the one truck?"

Behind her, she heard Meryn whisper. "Seriously?"

The delivery driver nodded. "Yes, ma'am, we got everything in the one truck, but it's packed floor to ceiling, front to back."

Elizabeth started to chew on her lower lip and turned to Ryuu imploringly. She didn't know what to start first.

He sighed and removed his apron handing it to her. "Okay, gentleman, if you would follow me. Your names?" he asked opening the door wide.

"Jensen, I'm the foreman."

"Ed and this is Mattie." The delivery driver said as they all walked in.

Ryuu closed the door and smiled at them. "Here's our dilemma, gentleman. The closet you're to build is for the contents of that truck. We have recently moved seven trainees into our guest suites and each room is at max capacity. So we're in quite a bind as to where to put her things."

Ed looked at Jensen. "How long do you think it will take you to build this closet?"

Jensen rubbed his chin. "I have two fae craftsmen I can call in. We can be done after sunset, but we'll have to start now."

Ed nodded. "Let's do this. You get that closet done today and me and Mattie will leave the truck here overnight. If someone can get us a lift into the city, we can visit with some family and then come back tomorrow to haul everything in," he suggested.

Ryuu looked thoughtful. "Who can we get to drive you to town?"

The front door opened and Noah walked in. "Did you guys know there's a whole bunch of people and trucks out front?" He had a duffel bag slung over each shoulder and was walking on unsteady feet.

Ed reached out and grabbed both duffel bags in one hand.

Ryuu smiled. "Perfect timing, Noah. Could you do us a huge favor and drive these two gentlemen into Lycaonia tonight and pick them up in the morning?"

Noah nodded. "Sure, but I have to get our stuff out of the car before anyone can fit in it."

Ed and Mattie nodded at each other. "Point the way, kid. We'll unload your car so you can drive us into the city."

Noah smiled wide. "Really? That's great; some of that stuff is heavy." He beamed at the older men. Ed ruffled Noah's hair.

"Yeah, come show us what needs to go where." Noah walked off with Ed and Mattie chatting about The Jitterbug and how it was the best place in the world.

Jaxon groaned. "I knew he smelled like coffee. I'll never get to sleep; he'll talk my ear off all night."

Ryuu turned to Jensen. "I'll show you the space you'll be converting, if you'll come with me." They both headed up the stairs.

"I don't know what in the hell is going on anymore. But since Aiden is in my office, looks like we'll have to go to the media room. I wanted to get measurements anyway to see how many feet of cable we'll need to set up servers. Come on, Hulk on Wheels!" Meryn plopped down on Jaxon's lap to his astonishment.

"Mush!" She pointed to the media room.

Elizabeth looked to the ceiling. "Meryn! Do not treat your minion like a sled dog!" She stopped abruptly. Had that just come out of her mouth?

Meryn erupted in giggles and Jaxon laughed. He reached down with both hands and tipped the chair backward, making Meryn squeal as she grabbed him around the neck, pretty much cutting off his air. But he only laughed again and when the chair came back down on the floor, he spun the wheels and they raced down the hall.

Elizabeth couldn't believe the way her life had made a drastic turn.

Don't treat your minion like a sled dog?

Standing alone in the foyer, she began to laugh. How had she survived up until now without these crazy people in her life?

The front door opened, and she was surprised to see her mate walk in.

"Where is your charge?" she asked.

He walked over and pulled her close nuzzling her neck. The gesture sent a jolt of electricity between her legs. "I explained what happened to Colton and Darian; they graciously offered to look after the little bastard while I check in on our renovations. I am assuming that one of the trucks outside belongs to the construction team." He ran the tip of his nose back and forth over her neck.

She relaxed in his arms. This was exactly where she wanted to be. The encounter with Sterling had left her more shaken than she cared to admit, even to herself. She loved how Gavriel always seemed to be able to give her exactly what she didn't even know she needed.

"Yes, Ryuu is showing them the study now. Jensen, the foreman will have to call in two fae craftsmen to get the closet finished by tonight so my things can be delivered tomorrow. Noah is taking the delivery drivers into the city for the night and picking them up in the morning. They are leaving the truck here overnight and complete the delivery tomorrow." She explained and with Ryuu's apron in her hand she wrapped her arms around his waist.

"When I heard that little punk had tried to hurt you, I seriously wanted to kill him. Where is Aiden? I do not want that deviant living under the same roof as you," Gavriel growled looking around.

"He's in his office on the phone with his brother asking about said deviant. Meryn already asked Aiden to send him away, but because of how new the program is, we can't afford for it to seem like we're playing favorites," she explained.

Behind them, Ryuu and Jensen were coming down the stairs. Gavriel stepped back and wrapped an arm around her shoulders. Ryuu walked up and Elizabeth handed him his apron.

"I take it you're the foreman?" Gavriel asked.

"Yes, sir. Nice place you all have here." Jensen said.

"How long would it take your crew to build an addition to the Alpha estate? Big enough for five trainees?" Gavriel stared at the foreman whose jaw dropped.

Ryuu began to chuckle and walked away, tying his apron back on.

"Sir? Are you serious?" the foreman asked.

"Deadly." Gavriel responded.

"That kind of project takes time, materials, man hours..." Jensen thought about it. He looked at Gavriel. "How urgent is the request?"

"If we do not move one of the trainees out of here by the end of the week, I may lose my immortal soul for murdering the little shit in his sleep," Gavriel snarled.

"So kinda urgent then. Okay, let me call in some favors. I'm not going to lie, sir, this might get pricey." Jensen flushed a bit.

"Do whatever you have to. Call whomever you have to. The sooner you get it built, the larger the bonus," Gavriel offered.

Jensen nodded. "Let's get this closet built for your lady and I'll start making some calls." He nodded and headed out the door already yelling for his men.

"You're the most incredible man I have ever met, and I love you." Elizabeth hugged her mate tightly.

"And you are the most important thing in my life, how could I not ensure your comfort and safety. It is best for everyone if they have a space of their own. Maybe after time, the urge to rip out his throat will diminish." He shrugged. "If not, I can always torture him during drills."

"My hero!" she pretended to swoon.

He dipped her down, kissed her lips, and then straightened them both.

"I am going to go make sure Colton and Darian are being harsh enough. Keep Meryn out of trouble."

"That seems to be my new duty in life." She rolled her eyes.

"It could be worse, you could be responsible for training that little bastard." Gavriel's eyes flickered back and forth from red to gray.

"Have fun. Don't kill any of your trainees at work today, honey," she said and stopped. She had done it again! She had said something outlandish, but in this insane house, it made perfect sense.

Gavriel sniffed dramatically. "I make no promises," he said, turning her words against her, and then left.

Don't kill any of your trainees at work today?

And she'd meant it?

Maybe she deserved more than a new closet out of this mating.

CHAPTER FOURTEEN

Elizabeth was about to join Meryn and Jaxon in the media room when the doorbell rang yet again. She looked around; no one else was in sight. She walked over to the door and opened it.

Two men in overalls smiled at her. "Hello, missus, we're here to deliver the office equipment you ordered." The balding man said by way of introduction.

Elizabeth smiled at both men. "Wonderful! Wait right here, that room is in use at the moment. Shouldn't take me a second to clear it out. Be right back." She closed the door and hurried down the hallway. She tapped on the door before opening it. Aiden was just hanging up his archaic phone receiver. He sat back, looking tired.

"What did Adair say?" she asked. She was curious to find out what Aiden's brother knew about Sterling. It wasn't like the academy to allow anyone that could become a possible threat through the system.

Aiden sighed. "He said that Sterling was known for being an elitist and somewhat of a bully, but scored exceptionally well in all the trials and tests. He comes from a very affluent family, so there are politics involved. Adair said Sterling spent half the time at the academy chasing women; he has no real idea how good the little bastard could actually be if Sterling trained correctly. Adair was hoping he would settle down after being assigned to a unit. I don't want to overlook this, but damn if my hands aren't tied."

"So basically he's always been a dick, but now he's a dick that we've actually trained, so he knows better ways to hurt and kill people. Training doesn't make bad men good, Aiden," Elizabeth warned.

Aiden nodded. "I know, trust me, I know." He frowned. "Did you need something?"

"Yes, the new office furniture is here, so they will need access to this room."

"I was done here anyway. I'm going to spend the rest of the day monitoring Sterling. I hope Gavriel hasn't killed him," he muttered, standing.

"Just so you know, Gavriel has asked the construction crew to start on an addition to the Alpha estate for the trainees. He said that his immortal soul would be in danger if he had to live under the same room as Sterling." Elizabeth winced as Aiden's eyes widened.

He surprised her when he broke out in a boyish grin. "Good! And since he requested it, he can foot most of the bill. This is turning out to be a good day, after all. Best of all, since it's Gavriel requesting the renovations, no one can say that I'm treating the trainees differently. Hell, if my father can spin this right, we can make it look like we're spoiling them with new equipment and barracks." He walked past her, practically whistling.

Elizabeth couldn't help but smile and followed him out of the office to the front door. Aiden opened it wide, and both men stepped back startled. To those who didn't know the Unit Commander, he could come across as a harsh military man. But she knew better since she lived with him, the man was a complete marshmallow.

"Gentlemen," Aiden barked and walked past them, toward the training area.

Both men turned to her, looking spooked. She gave them her brightest smile, and they relaxed a bit. "This way, gentlemen. I can't wait to see what the office will look like with the new furniture. We'll have to be careful with the Commander's desk though, it's an antique." She showed them where her future office would be. Both men eyed the huge hand carved desk and gulped. It would be a chore to move.

An hour later, the men tipped their hats and left. She looked around the room. It seemed a lot bigger after they had moved Aiden's wooden monstrosity of a desk to one side to act as a flat surface workstation. The newer desks were smaller but were more functional with technology hutches, filing cabinets, and drawers.

She looked down at the new computers still in their boxes. Smiling, she walked to the media room where Meryn was showing Jaxon and Noah how to strip Ethernet cables to attach new heads. Noah must have slipped back in during all the furniture moving. She was glad he made it back safely.

"Oh Meryn, I have a job for you," she said.

Meryn looked up. "What's up?"

"The new computers are here. Feel like showing your minions how to set them up?" The words had no sooner left her mouth than Meryn was up and moving. She, Jaxon, and Noah followed Meryn to the office where they found her smelling the boxes.

"They have that new technology smell," she said before she began to decimate the packaging.

Elizabeth sat back in her new leather manager's chair, closed her eyes, and listened to their excited chatter. She was exhausted. She would let them work on the computers while she just rested her eyes for a bit.

When she woke, the sun was setting and the room was starting to get chilly. She looked down to see that Meryn had once again lovingly covered her with a red throw blanket. Smiling, she got up. It took her a moment before the dizziness passed and she felt well enough to walk. When she was on steady feet, she followed the sound of voices and found that the men and Meryn were in the family room. Gavriel stood when she walked in and was immediately at her side.

"You could have woken me," she said when he leaned in for a kiss. His lips were warm and soft; the man had no right being so beautiful.

Gavriel shook his head. "I tried to wake you but you were sleeping so well I did not have the heart to move you. If you had not woken up on your own, I was going to wake you in a little bit for dinner."

They walked over and sat down on one of the many love seats. Keelan was reading while Colton and Darian were bantering back and forth over a chessboard. Meryn was sitting next to Aiden, and they were reading 'Macs for Dummies'. She looked around and noticed that there were no trainees around.

"Meryn where are your minions?" she asked.

Meryn looked up. "Lennox came and pulled Noah and Jaxon away so all of the trainees could get to know one another. They finished up their dinner about an hour ago. Ryuu is setting up the dining room for us now."

Elizabeth turned to her mate. "Sterling?"

Colton barked a laugh from across the room. "He said he was too tired to eat and was last seen staggering toward his room. He'll regret not eating tomorrow," he shook his head.

Gavriel nuzzled her neck. "Colton and Darian took very good care of Sterling," he whispered.

"Oh dear," she said then laughed.

She looked around the room; everyone was enjoying their evening. The fireplace was going and cast a warm yellow glow into the room. She snuggled closer to her mate, basking in the fire's warmth.

From the foyer, the sound of the doorbell had them all looking at each other. Everyone then turned to look at her.

She blushed. "All my deliveries already came today."

The doorbell chimed again.

Aiden stood and left to see who was at the door. Elizabeth heard familiar voices before what had to be the entire McKenzie clan walked into the room. Meryn got to her feet and immediately went to Adelaide for a hug. She was then passed to an older version of Aiden who kissed her on the top of her head and passed her to Adam. Adam and two other men hugged her friend and ruffled her hair.

Aiden looked at them. "What are you all doing here?"

Adelaide shot a look in Meryn's direction. Meryn, who was jumping on the blond man's back didn't even notice the scrutiny. Elizabeth smiled. Adelaide might come across as sweet but she was sharp and extremely observant. She was willing to bet money that Adelaide had noticed a change in Meryn during their visit with the sewing circle and had convinced her menfolk to come for a visit so she could check.

Adelaide looked at Marius who stepped forward with a huge basket.

"I brought cookies." Adelaide said and pulled back the red and white gingham towel to reveal a smorgasbord of sweets.

Meryn stopped mid-hop, the good-looking man forgotten, and raced forward. "Cookies!"

Adam elbowed the pouting blond man, laughing. "Looks like you rank below cookies Ben," he teased.

"We can't let our love show too much or Aiden will get prickly," Ben said.

Aiden growled and Ben sighed. "See, he's already getting grumpy."

The man that looked like Adam and Aiden guffawed. "One of these days he's going to maul you, and you'll deserve it, baby brother."

"Adair, don't give him any ideas, I'm the one that has to patch him back together," Adam complained.

Adelaide stepped forward, rolling her eyes. She looked around until she saw Elizabeth. Elizabeth stood and she and Gavriel walked over to her.

Adelaide gave her a hug as well and stood back. "In case you haven't figured it out, these are my sons, Adam, Adair and Ben. This is my mate, Byron and you've met my squire, Marius."

Elizabeth nodded at the men. Byron and Marius gave courtly bows, and Ben winked at her flirtatiously. Gavriel bared his fangs at the prankster.

Ben edged behind his older brother. Adair sighed, but acted like the shield that his brother intended him to be.

Aiden, grinning from ear to ear, wrapped an arm around Meryn. "I think I know why you're here, Mother."

Adelaide turned to look at her son. She took in his wide-open smile and the joy in his eyes. Her hands flew to her mouth, and she gave a low cry. She raced over and pulled Meryn into her arms, crying.

"She is, isn't she? Oh, Byron!" Adelaide was weeping tears of happiness as she turned to her mate, Meryn still in her arms.

"Yes, she is." Aiden looked at his father, his own eyes a bit misty. "Looks like you're going to be a grandfather," he announced.

Aiden's father surprised them all by giving an undignified shout and whooped loudly. He went to Marius, who was beaming and reached into the basket and rummaged around under the towel that held the cookies to pull out what looked to be a very old bottle of scotch.

"This calls for a celebration!" he shouted, his cheeks red and his eyes bright. Beside him, Aiden's brothers were laughing and clapping their brother on the back. The unit members hung back, grinning at each other as they had already known the joyous news.

Byron waved them over as Marius helped Ryuu with glasses. Elizabeth sat with Meryn and Adelaide on the sofa as the men toasted and celebrated. Gavriel turned to her and smiled. She couldn't help the stray thought that maybe one day they would be celebrating their child.

"This festive atmosphere reminds me, are you all going to be able to make it to our house again this year for Thanksgiving?" Adelaide asked the warriors.

All of the men, except Colton, nodded. "I promised my mother I would spend the holidays with them." He heaved a huge sigh. "I'll miss Marius's and Ryuu's cooking," he said, making it sound like an epic tragedy. Darian immediately began to torment him about the food he would miss.

Adelaide smiled at their teasing and turned to her daughter. "Oh Meryn, you couldn't have given us a better solstice present. I wasn't sure earlier when you showed up at the sewing circle. Your scent had changed, but I wasn't sure if that was because you had put on the amulet from Vivian,"

"Nope, just plain ole knocked up," Meryn grinned.

"Speaking of presents." Elizabeth smiled and reached into her pocket. She had been carrying around the keystones all day, but had forgotten to give Meryn hers; now she could give them both to their new owners.

She dropped the keystones into their hands.

"It's so pretty. What is it?" Meryn asked.

"It's a keystone. My fathers had them made for me when I was sixteen. By then, it had become pretty apparent that I was naturally accident-prone. The keystones are connected to the pendant that I'm wearing. If I'm ever in trouble or hurt, I rotate the pendant, and it sends out an alert to anyone with a keystone. So if you see this stone flash that means I might need your help," she explained.

"Neat." Meryn put hers in her pocket.

Adelaide smiled at her warmly. "It's an honor and a gift that you trust me, thank you." She placed hers in the small fabric satchel on her wrist then turned to Meryn. "Oh my! Just think, a baby in the family again," she said, her cheeks flushed.

"I was kinda scared at first, but I'm used to the idea now. I can't wait to meet Meryn 2.0," Meryn said, rubbing her flat stomach.

Aiden frowned. "We're having a boy."

Meryn frowned back. "No, we're not. We're having a girl and I'm going to teach her all about the Doctor and Star Wars and handguns and grenades."

Aiden choked on his scotch. "Like hell! Even if we were to have a wee baby girl, she will be my princess. She'll have pretty pink dresses with lace and dollies!"

Meryn blinked. "Dollies? Lace? Pink? No fucking way!"

"Then have a boy," Aiden countered.

Adelaide clapped her hands together, and they both quieted. "I have the perfect solution." Aiden and

Meryn looked at her expectantly. "Just have twins Meryn, a boy *and* a girl." Adelaide beamed at them.

Both Meryn and Aiden paled and looked at each other. "Just one right?" Meryn asked.

Aiden nodded. "Definitely just one."

Adelaide pouted. "But twins would be so lovely, then triplets next time."

Meryn stared at her mother-in-law in horror before she looked over to Ryuu who was serving impromptu finger foods for their thrown together party.

"Ryuu, ward off bad juju," Meryn said.

Ryuu lifted an eyebrow. "You have nothing to fear from Adelaide's words, *denka*. If Fate decides to give you twins, there isn't much you can do about it."

Meryn sighed. "Fine, but if there's two that's just double the amount of diapers for you and Aiden."

"Hey!" Aiden protested. Adam, Adair, and Ben laughed.

Ben clapped a hand on Aiden's shoulder. "So can I buy the drum set and finger paints now?"

Aiden groaned.

"Yeah, what can Uncle Colton start buying?" Colton asked laughing with Ben.

"Y'all are bad." Meryn laughed at Aiden's expression before turning to her squire. "Ryuu, I'm thirsty. Do we have anything besides scotch?"

Ryuu nodded. "I'll get some juice; it will be just a moment," he said placing a large serving tray down on one of the tables.

"I'll get it, Ryuu," Elizabeth said standing. When she got to her feet, the entire room tilted. Her vision became dim and spots appeared. In the background, she heard Meryn's scream, but couldn't figure out what had upset her.

She heard a crash and felt a sharp pain in her side.

"Bunny!" Meryn cried out.

She blinked up and rolled her head to trying to look up. She couldn't seem to focus. Above her she heard a low growl. Gavriel was crouched over her body, swiping at the hands that appeared at the edges of her vision.

"Dammit, Gavriel, move! She's going to bleed out!" Adam yelled.

"Gavriel, your mate needs help," Aiden said evenly trying to get his second in command to focus.

She blinked up at the men and met Colton's eyes. She blinked again and his frown deepened.

She watched as he walked over to Ryuu. "As soon as we're in the clear, shock him; don't worry about me," he said.

Gavriel leaned down and licked her side as if trying to close her wound. She looked down and saw a large piece of glass from the coffee table sticking out of her side. She let her head fall back, and she closed her eyes.

"Bunny! No!"

She could hear Meryn crying. She wanted to tell her that she really should calm down, she had a baby to worry about, but couldn't get her mouth to move. She opened her eyes and watched as Colton took a deep breath and, with a running start, tackled Gavriel, moving him away from where she lay.

Gavriel hissed and attacked Colton furiously. He clawed desperately trying to get back to her. Ryuu was at their side in seconds. He reached down and grabbed Gavriel by the wrist. Blue flame erupted and covered both Gavriel and Colton. The flames brightened, and both men stiffened and yelled out before slumping down against each other, unconscious.

"Hey there, sweetheart. You weren't kidding when you said we would become friends were you?" Adam asked as his gentle hands pulled back the fabric of her shirt.

"Gavriel?" she whispered.

Ryuu walked over, concern on his face. "Out for now. He'll wake up soon, hopefully more coherent than he was a moment ago."

"It doesn't hurt," she said to Meryn, who had tears streaming down her cheeks. Adelaide had one arm wrapped around her daughter and Marius stood behind the both of them protectively.

Meryn sniffed and swallowed. "That means it's bad. When it doesn't hurt that means it's so bad your brain is shutting it out."

Adam smiled. "Nothing we can't handle. Gentleman some help?"

She closed her eyes as she was lifted onto a blanket.

"Don't let him blame himself," she whispered.

"Let's just concentrate on you right now," Adam said. "Okay men, as evenly and as gently as you can, let's head to the car."

When her vision began to get dimmer and dimmer, she smiled.

"Good," she whispered and gave in to the darkness.

"I don't understand, she's a shifter, she should have started healing by now." Elizabeth woke to Adam's frustrated voice. Exhausted, she kept her eyes closed and listened.

"What do you mean?" she heard her mate ask. She felt relieved that he sounded okay and was close by.

"There's a bruise on her temple that is still healing. As shifters, we either heal or we don't. This looks like she's healing human slow," Adam explained.

"Is she sick? She's been complaining of being tired," Gavriel said.

"These bites, how fresh are they?"

"Those are from last night."

"How often have you been feeding?" Adam asked.

"Once, maybe twice, a day since she's arrived. Last night, I lost control and she lost more than usual," her mate admitted.

Adam made that 'hmmm' sound that every medical healer she'd ever visited made. "I'll run some tests to be sure, but I'd say that the reason why she isn't healing is because she's extremely anemic. That glass in her side tonight wouldn't have helped."

"This is my fault," Gavriel whispered.

"Let me ask you something. Why feed from her so much? I've been sending more than three times the normal transition level blood requirements to the estate."

"Her blood helps more than the other blood combined."

Adam made another 'hmmm' sound. "Interesting."

"I'll stop feeding from her."

Elizabeth turned in her bed and opened her eyes. Both men looked over at her and immediately came to her side. Adam took her wrist between his fingers and looked at his watch.

Gavriel ran a gentle hand over her hair. "I am so sorry, my love," his voice was strained.

"My blood helps. I heard you speaking with Colton when you hurt your head. My blood restores your speed and strength that keeps you safe." She wanted to reach up and touch his face but her hand felt too heavy.

"It is my duty, no, my privilege to protect you and all this time you have been protecting me." Gavriel closed his eyes as if he were in pain.

Adam lay her wrist back down. "Elizabeth, can you think of any reason why your blood would be affecting

Gavriel differently than the blood donated here in Lycaonia?" he asked.

"Could it be because we are mates?" Gavriel asked thinking out loud.

Adam made a sour expression. "Nothing against the metaphysical bonds that tie us together, but this is affecting you on a physical level; I'd like to start there if possible."

Elizabeth thought about how different her life was now. Everything was different. Different house, different food, different routine, different squire... Her thoughts stopped.

"Different squire," she whispered.

"How does Ryuu factor into this?" Adam inquired.

"Not him, Sebastian, my uncle's squire. Every morning he would serve me breakfast in my suite, as I got ready for the day. That included a vitamin designed by my father. I haven't been taking them since I got here, but I bet that is why my blood is helping more than your bagged blood. The council in Noctem Falls asked my father to design a vitamin to help supplement what is now missing from human and shifter diets. We don't eat like we used to. If humans and shifters aren't getting the correct amount of vitamins and minerals, neither are the vampires. It's still in a test phase before being distributed to the other cities." She looked at Adam. "My father could tell you more."

Gavriel turned to Adam. "It would explain why Meryn was so unappetizing. She grew up on junk food and caffeine. She has only been eating decently this past month under Ryuu's watchful eye." Gavriel frowned. "If the vitamin is the reason why Beth's blood helps, it could make other's transitions much easier. The blood I have been drinking does little to satisfy the thirst and might as well be water. No wonder my body is going through blood depravation. I have to ingest three times the normal amount to get the bare minimum required for the changes I am going through, and it is still nowhere near what I actually need."

Adam patted her leg. "I'm keeping you here overnight. Bagged blood may not help your mate, but it will do wonders for you. You should be nearly healed by morning. If you'll excuse me, I have a certain scientist in Noctem Falls to call." Adam turned and headed toward the door.

"Don't tell him about me, he'll just worry," she called after him.

He nodded and closed the door behind him.

Gavriel took her hand and, in silence, ran his thumb over her knuckles. The motion was so soothing she found herself closing her eyes and drifting.

"Do you want me here?" Gavriel asked, breaking the silence.

She opened her eyes and frowned at him. "Of course, I want you here."

"I delayed your treatment because I lost control. I saw everyone as a threat; you could have died and I would still have been fighting them." His face was unreadable.

"You are my mate, I belong with you."

"Are you sure you do not want to go home? Not for good, but at least until my transition is over."

She tugged on his fingers until he looked her in the eye. "You are my home now."

He drew in a ragged breath. "Then all I can do is promise that I will do everything I can to minimize the danger to you, no matter the cost to me."

She brought his hand to her lips and kissed the back of his hand. "Don't make me hurt you later," she threatened with a smile.

His eyes lightened, and he shook his head. "I think I prefer Meryn's blunt and sometimes graphic ultimatums to your polite, smiling threats." He leaned down and kissed her gently. She could feel the depth of his love for her in the barest of touches. "I am going to go next door and apologize to Colton again. He not only got a bit mangled, but he also sustained quite a jolt getting me away from you so you could be treated. Unfortunately, electricity affects shifters more than vampires. He is to be released tomorrow, too."

"Poor Colton. Tell him thank you for me."

"I will, be back soon." He left closing the door softly behind him.

She closed her eyes and pulled the blanket up to her chin. It wasn't long until she was asleep.

CHAPTER FIFTEEN

Elizabeth ended up sleeping through to the next afternoon. By the time she was out of bed and ready to go home, it was almost time for dinner. The house was quiet when Gavriel carried her through the front door. While trying to wake up at the clinic, she'd realized she already missed the zaniness of the Alpha estate. She caught herself wondering if Meryn had threatened anyone at breakfast and what snack of Ryuu's she had missed at tea.

"Where is everyone?" she asked as he walked carefully up the stairs to their room.

"I dropped Colton off this morning after he was released. He went right back to bed. He said he would be down for dinner. Keelan, Darian, and Ryuu have been working with Keelan's brother, Kendrick, via Skype on developing a perimeter spell. Aiden decided to get familiar with his new iMac while Meryn and her trainees played around with some gadgets. The other trainees had the afternoon off and last I heard, collectively decided to catch up on their sleep."

"So it's been a lazy day for everyone then."

"Yes. Meryn did make me promise to tell you that she missed you already and to hurry up and get better."

Elizabeth smiled. She had missed the little terror, too.

Gavriel opened their bedroom door and closed it behind him. He set her down on her feet and watched her carefully.

"I'm fine. Adam said I'm completely healed; the blood helped enormously."

"If you're sure."

"I am. Now. I want to see my closet. I have so much to unpack." She looked around. "Where are my boxes?"

Gavriel steered her toward the door that used to lead to his study. He opened it and she gasped. He had unpacked and hung up all of her clothes. Granted, he hadn't organized it correctly at all since summer tanks were hanging next to winter sweaters, but everything was out and hanging up. The only thing she had to do was the fun part: organize it.

She spun around and threw herself in his arms. "Thank you! Thank you! I love it! When did you have time to do this?"

"My stomach was in knots last night after you fell asleep. I opened the truck and worked on it for a while then went back to the clinic to sleep with you. Then this morning, after I dropped Colton off, I was able to finish. I wanted to do something to make up for yesterday."

"You did nothing wrong, my love. Oh, it's beautiful!" She kissed him gently and then hurried inside. On the far wall of the closet they had installed a three hundred and sixty degree mirror. She could see her outfit from every angle! The shelves and rails were handcrafted wood that went beyond function and bordered on art.

She even noticed that small rune spells had been carved into the wood to maintain a certain level of humidity, temperature, to prevent fire, and to repel bugs. The Celtic knots gave the entire closet a regal feel. Not even her closet at home had been so beautiful.

She walked slowly running her hand along the different fabrics. Beyond the clothes and shoe racks, they'd built a vanity against the wall. The large beveled mirror stood opposite the wall where they had installed a faux window that shone brightly, giving her natural daylight. She could sit here and get ready in the warm rays of the sun.

"I'm never leaving this closet. Ever!" She twirled around exuberant.

Gavriel wrapped one arm around her waist and turned them. He held her in his arms and swayed back and forth. "I have found something that makes you fly. Your father was right, you shine." His nose nuzzled her temple.

"I've always used my clothes as a shield. If I presented the image that I was a polished, refined woman, people assumed that my tripping over my feet was due to a bunched up rug or a highly polished floor. It's my way of defending myself," she explained.

"You do not have to worry about that anymore."

"Why? Do you know of a way to keep me from tripping?" she asked, pulling back to look up at him.

His eyes blazed with the intensity of his feelings. He shook his head. "No, but from now on it will not matter what you are wearing when you trip. Your clothes will not defend you; I will," he promised.

"I love you so much," she whispered.

He pulled her close. "And I love you."

After a few moments of silence, he cleared his throat. "Love? Can I ask a favor?"

Smiling, she looked up and nodded. "Yes, we can have sex in front of the mirror," she answered.

His eyes widened. He opened his mouth then closed it. He turned and looked at the mirror then looked back to her. The expression on his face went from shock to arousal in two seconds flat.

"That was not what I was going to ask, but I will hold you to that. What I was going to ask was if I could see your belly."

Shrugging, she nodded and lifted her shirt. Adam had lent her a boring pair of scrubs that she couldn't wait to change out of.

Gavriel dropped to his knees and proceeded to kiss along the faint pink line. "Did Adam say anything about if... can we still..."

She ran her hands over his hair. "Yes, we can still have children. There was no lasting damage."

His arms circled her legs, and he rested his cheek against her stomach. "Thank the Gods!"

"Already planning an Elizabeth 2.0?" she teased.

He looked up, grinning. In that moment, the years dropped away, his excitement at the prospect of becoming a father made him seem younger. "At least four or five of them. We need to rebuild House Ambrosios."

"Five! No way."

He pouted, and the expression was so out of place on his normally stoic and regal features that it only compounded its effectiveness. How could she say no to that? He was freaking adorable!

"Fine! Whatever. But you have to do diapers." She threw her hands up in defeat.

He kissed her belly one more time and stood. "Deal."

"Okay, scoot. I need to get a shower and change. These things should be burned, I don't see how anyone can wear them." With her finger and thumb she lifted the fabric from her body shuddering.

"I will be reading in my library. Come get me before you go downstairs." He kissed her lips.

"I will," she promised.

He walked out of the closet and shut the door behind him.

Smiling to herself, she looked around for a few more minutes. She loved peeking in the drawers and discovering new places to hang things. Finally, she picked out a comfortable outfit of jeans and a sweatshirt. If they were going to be lazing about the house, she wanted to be in comfy clothes.

With regret, she left her closet and walked to the bathroom for her shower. The hot water felt wanton. They'd cleaned her up the best they could at the clinic, but she still had some blood on her skin. She got out and dried off quickly. She towel dried her hair, braided it, and then wrapped a hand towel around the braid, securing it with a hair tie. The hand towel would soak up any residual water and it would stay off her clothes.

Wrapped in a towel, she padded back into her closet. The smell of cut wood made her smile. She sat down at her vanity and pulled out the center drawer; it was empty. Frowning, she checked the left drawer, nothing. When she opened the right drawer, she had to laugh. Gavriel had simply dumped anything that looked like it was makeup in one drawer.

Shaking her head, she dug through the contents and found her normal beauty routine products. By the time her makeup was done, her hair was dry enough to get dressed. She removed the towel and pulled on her comfy outfit. Slouch socks and fur-lined boots completed her lazy day ensemble.

She left the closet and was about to walk to the library when she heard a 'thunk' sound. She stopped and looked around. The library door opened, and Gavriel walked out with a frown on his face. He had heard it, too. She was about to ask him what the noise was when she heard it again.

Thunk

Gavriel walked to the door of their suite and opened it. He jumped back with a curse when a small toy car raced inside and skidded to a halt in front of her. She stared down and one name came to mind.

"Meryn," she said grinning.

The small car raced around her feet. "Hurry up, I'm bored!" Meryn's voice sounded funny coming from the speakers of the small car.

"Coming, dear."

The tiny car turned and bolted out the door.

Gavriel was rubbing the space between his brows. "How did she do that?" he asked.

"There's a camera and microphone on the car. The wheels are large enough and are designed to be all terrain. I imagine it took a while to get up the stairs. Going down however..."

In the distance, they heard a small crash, then laughter.

"See."

Gavriel was shaking his head, but she caught his small grin. She knew he absolutely adored the petite human and she could see why. He had probably never experienced anything like her in all his years. That had to be refreshing to someone like him.

"Let's go downstairs. There's no telling what she'll do if I take too long." She walked up and hugged his arm.

They walked downstairs and found that the unit warriors, Meryn, Ryuu, and Meryn's trainees were in the family room. The glass table she had crashed into had been replaced with a small wooden one and no sign of the previous evening lingered.

"About time! Where have you been all day?" Meryn demanded.

"I was catching up on my sleep." Elizabeth winked.

"Oh." Meryn blinked. "Yeah, some days all I want to do is sleep. All the sex wears me out," she confessed.

Noah stared, and Jaxon just shook his head. Looked like one of them was already acclimating to their teacher.

"Meryn, come here baby before you scandalize the room," Aiden said, patting the space next to him.

"Sure, but I wanted to show Bunny that Ryuu was able to get all the blood out of the floor," she said walking over to where Elizabeth had lain the night before.

The room got silent. Aiden covered his face with his hands, Colton groaned; Darian and Keelan stared, waiting for her to breakdown.

She walked over to where Meryn pointed. She looked down and was surprised. Ryuu had done an amazing job; there wasn't a single speck of blood anywhere.

"He's a miracle worker," she said.

Meryn nodded. "Yeah, considering you were bleeding all over the place."

"Meryn!" Aiden barked.

Elizabeth looked down and saw the way Meryn's fist was clenched at her side. Her words were flippant and jovial, but they hid a deeper emotion. She remembered very little about the night before, but she remembered the way Meryn had cried and the fear in her eyes.

She reached down and took Meryn's hand in her own. Meryn looked up and for a split second, the fear was there again. Elizabeth could handle Cranky Meryn, Angry Meryn, Spazzing Meryn, even Crazy Meryn, but she could not stand the fear in her friend's eyes.

Smiling, Elizabeth bumped hips with the small human. Meryn grinned, the anxiety leaving her face. Smiling, she bumped her back. Elizabeth bopped her again, this time toppling her over onto the love seat. Meryn sat up and chucked a pillow at her. Elizabeth ducked and sat next to her.

Aiden looked from her to Meryn and back. From the look on his face, Elizabeth could tell he didn't understand how they could be laughing, but that was okay. This was between sisters.

Aiden shook his head and mumbled. "I don't get her sometimes."

Gavriel sat down in the wingback chair next to them and picked up a copy of the Lycaonian Herald, the city's newspaper. "We are not meant to. Only get concerned if they are not smiling," he advised.

Aiden brightened. "Sounds good to me."

Meryn looked at Elizabeth and rolled her eyes. "Men!"

Elizabeth had to agree. She looked over to Aiden. "Aiden, did you have a chance to look over the templates I created for you?"

He nodded, and then frowned. "I think I'm missing something though. It's too easy."

"It's supposed to be easy. If you follow that format and turn it into me, I can input the forms into the database. After a few years learning about your computer, and when you can open a browser window, I might show you how to input the information directly into the database. But for right now, just fill out the printed forms."

Aiden looked relieved. "I prefer the printed forms, you can keep your databases."

Ryuu walked in and bowed. "Ladies, gentlemen, dinner is ready."

Everyone stood and started toward the dining room when Aiden's cell phone rang. Everyone froze.

He answered. "McKenzie here."

Elizabeth clearly heard Aiden's father over the phone. "Son, over a dozen ferals have been spotted north of the city."

"We're on it."

"Be careful," Byron commanded.

"Yes, sir." Aiden ended the call.

"Colton, Darian, you're in charge of the trainees. I don't want to include them, but we have to start somewhere. If things get bad, get them out."

Colton and Darian ran to the stairs yelling for the trainees to turn out.

Aiden turned to Gavriel. "In or out? I'm leaving it up to you."

Gavriel stepped forward. "I am in. Even if the only thing I can do is keep your retreat path open, I am going."

Meryn began to shake.

Aiden kissed the top of her head "It will be okay, baby, just like us doing drills. We'll be back before you know it." He stepped back and looked at Ryuu.

Ryuu stepped forward and pulled Meryn to his side. "Nothing will come near her, I swear it."

"I'll hold you to that," Aiden said. They nodded at each other.

Aiden turned to the last member of the Alpha Unit. "Keelan, looks like you can try some of those visibility spells sooner than you thought." Aiden's smile was dangerous.

Keelan's answering smirk was just as deadly. "I can't wait."

Aiden looked around. The trainees were breathing hard and pulling on their gear in the foyer. The Alpha Unit members were pulling out their gear to be put on in the car while en route and checking the large duffel bags that held their weapons and ammo.

Gavriel pulled Elizabeth close. "I have to go," he whispered.

She nodded without saying a word.

"I love you." He stepped back and kissed each eyelid gently.

"I love you, too! That's why you have to come back to me," she said, her heart in her throat.

"I will," he promised.

Aiden strode toward the door. "Alpha Unit. Move out."

Elizabeth prayed to anyone listening to watch over her mate.

Gavriel stood to the south and took aim. Multiple rounds were going off all around him. Some of the ferals were visible, some weren't. With the extra manpower provided by the trainees, the prospect of taking out a dozen ferals was not impossible, but that did not rule out fatalities. Over the radio, he heard Gamma's Unit leader, Sascha, report that a fresh wave of ferals was heading their way and that Gamma was right behind them.

"Aiden! Ferals coming up on our six," he called out.

Gavriel brought his gun up and fired. He took out the feral that had been running up behind Keelan. The more they killed the more there seemed to be.

"Not too long now. Then you'll be like us," a voice taunted. Gavriel turned and fired several rounds into empty air. Heinous laughter surrounded him. Growling, he felt his fangs burst through his gums.

Not now, please Gods not now!

Taking deep breaths, he focused on the sights at the end of his gun barrel and kept firing. He was reloading when more ferals spilled out of the woods from the south.

"Sonofabitch!" Aiden roared.

The ferals ignored the unit warriors and ran past them, heading north toward the mountains. Sascha burst from the tree line at a dead run and began yelling out his report. "Delta and Beta got called out to take down a pack northeast of the city. Zeta and Epsilon are about fifteen klicks east of here taking down another reported dozen."

"Let's get these fuckers!" Oron yelled.

Gavriel stopped as Sascha's words sunk in. "Freeze!" he yelled. The men stopped their forward advance and fell back to surround him.

"Talk to me, Gavriel, why did you stop us?" Aiden demanded.

"All the feral packs are converging to the north, I think they are leading us into a trap. Delta and Beta are to the northeast and Zeta and Epsilon are to the northwest. I think they have something designed for us in those mountains," he explained.

"Why would they want all the units together in the mountains?" Keelan asked thinking out loud.

Gavriel felt ice flood his veins. He turned and looked back.

"Oh Gods! We're not being led into a trap, we're being led north." Gavriel began to shake.

"What is south of here that is so special?" Christoff asked.

"Meryn," Aiden whispered.

"The Alpha estate," Colton replied at the same time.

Gavriel threw his head back and roared.

Beth!

They were after his mate. Gavriel felt his fangs descend even further as blood began to pour from his fingertips as longer, sharper claws emerged.

"Fuck! It is his apex!" Christoff turned to the men. "Stay back and no matter what you do, do *not* get in his way!" he yelled.

Gavriel was beyond caring. Under the surface of his skin, his muscles were ripping apart. Each tendon snapped and lengthened; the pain was immeasurable.

"Keep the ferals off him!" he heard Aiden yell.

Gavriel opened his blood-filled eyes. The ferals had realized that they weren't being followed and had doubled back to attack them en masse.

He opened his mouth and released a sound that thundered through the mountains. Around him, even the ferals stopped to stare at him in horror. He used every ounce of pain, every spasm that set his body on fire, to fuel his rage. His fangs dropped to their full battle length and his shirt ripped as his chest expanded. He was taller, broader, faster, stronger.

Laughing manically, he moved forward. Everyone was moving so slowly. Cackling, he used his new claws to rip the throats out of the ferals who seemed like they were standing still.

Kill! Kill! Kill!

He wanted blood and death. No one harmed his mate!

When he looked around, and the only bodies that stood were his fellow unit members, he hesitated. He tried to remember why he should not kill them.

"Gavriel, if you're in there, look at your belt. Look down! Elizabeth is in trouble, we have to get home!" Aiden yelled, pointing.

He looked down and saw a bright blue flashing light.

Keystone. Beth. Mate. My mate. Beth! Beth is in trouble!

He turned toward the direction where his mate waited for him and, unable to wait for the others, he began to run. The ground flew under his feet and the trees became a blur.

"Fuck! How fast is he now?"

"Get to the vehicles!" he heard the men shout.

BethBethBeth

The litany of her name drove him forward.

Elizabeth checked the safety on the gun. She slid it off and held it facing up. All around the house ferals snarled and growled.

"Where are they?" Meryn asked, sitting on the sofa clutching hands with Noah, both were pale as a sheet. Jaxon sat in his chair in the doorway facing the foyer. The taunts outside grew louder and Meryn covered her ears.

We're coming!

We're coming to rip your baby from your stomach, you human whore!

"Fuck off, assholes!" she yelled.

Elizabeth knew that it was just bravado; Meryn was scared to death. So was she. She looked over to where Ryuu sat back in the recliner speaking the same phrases in Japanese over and over again under his breath. Sweat ran down his temples and saturated his shirt.

Outside, the ferals were held back from the house by a faint blue glow. Whatever Ryuu was doing was working, but it was exacting a terrible price. The squire looked like he was in agony.

She held up her glowing bright blue pendant. She'd activated it the second Ryuu detected the ferals approaching. That was five minutes ago.

"Please hurry," she whispered.

Ryuu groaned, and Elizabeth heard a loud crash in the foyer. Ryuu's eyes opened.

"I can't hold this one back," he choked out, fighting for breath.

Meryn stood as if to go check out the noise.

Elizabeth pushed her back down to Noah. "Stay here! Think of the baby!" Elizabeth yelled and ran past her.

She ran into the foyer where Jaxon was staring at the opened front door in horror. Without hesitation, Elizabeth leveled the small revolver and began shooting. When the gun was empty, the feral was bent over clutching at its chest.

Grinning, he staggered to a standing position. Jaxon wheeled forward placing himself between the bleeding feral and Elizabeth.

"Jaxon, no!" she cried.

"What are you going to do you little crippled shit?" Blood and drool dripped from the feral's chin.

"This!" Jaxon extended his left arm and moved the small brass charm inside the spell circle. Elizabeth had to shield her eyes as a huge fireball shot forward, engulfing the feral in white-hot flames.

His screams filled the air as the stench of burnt hair and flesh permeated the foyer. Jaxon rolled backward, coughing on the smoke. Elizabeth pulled his chair backward, away from the screeching blaze, back to the family room.

"Who told you that you couldn't be a warrior?" she asked, gasping for air.

Jaxon grinned as he coughed. "Good thing Ryuu showed Noah and I the alarm spells yesterday."

Suddenly, the ferals disappeared from view. They were no longer trying to get in through the windows and couldn't be seen anywhere. The silence was eerie and unsettling. In the distance, she heard the sound of a car screeching to a halt and a deep bellow.

"That sounds like a bear," Elizabeth said, moving back to the opened front door.

"Aiden?" Meryn asked, coming to her side.

"Nope. Byron. Oh dear. Did you know that was physically possible?" she asked, unable to look away from Byron's carnage.

"No, but fuck if that isn't the coolest thing I've seen in a while." Meryn watched unblinking.

The sound of an inhuman cry sent chills down her spine.

Meryn looked up at her, terrified. "What was that?"

Elizabeth shook her head. "I don't know. I've never heard that sound before."

Outside Byron stopped, his eyes widened. He threw down the body parts in his hands before he and two other men leapt for the porch. Elizabeth darted forward and disarmed the front door spell. The men ran inside the house looking spooked.

"What the fuck is that, Byron? A new monster the ferals created?" a tall man with a graying, shaggy beard asked.

"No idea, John, but I'm staying out of its way." Byron wrapped an arm around Meryn and kissed the top of her head. "Thank all the Gods you're safe. When we pulled up and saw them swarming the house I thought the worst."

"Ryuu kept them away," Meryn said, pointing to the family room.

"And it was not easy," Ryuu joked. Noah helped him forward, holding him up on one side with Jaxon steadying him on the other.

Elizabeth edged toward the door and caught a glimpse of the savage monster that was stalking the ferals outside.

"Oh sweet Gods above, Gavriel. Oh my poor mate," she whispered, tears in her eyes. He had hit his apex during the battle and was now drowning in bloodlust.

"That's Gavriel?" Byron whispered.

Two SUVs pulled up, keeping a distance from Gavriel. The unit warriors poured out of the vehicles and trained their guns on her mate.

"No they don't!" she yelled.

She jumped from the porch and ran over and placed herself between her mate and the men, her arms outstretched.

"Leave him alone! How could you?" she screamed.

"Get out of the way Elizabeth!" Aiden yelled.

"No! Never!"

A low growl had her turning to face the monster that was her mate. His fangs were soaked in blood and extended four to five inches past his chin to his chest. She stared at their impressive lengths. Vampires grew approximately half of an inch of fang for every thousand years of life. Though most older vampires only extended their fangs part way to feed or show aggression. It was only during instances where a vampire felt threatened did they extend fully. There was no hiding his age now; it was on display for all to see.

"If you think you're biting me later with those things you have another think coming." She put her hands on her hips and faced him down. She hoped levity and humor would break through the killing haze in his mind.

He paused and tilted his head at her. She was getting through to him.

"Sexy fun time will only happen if you retract those suckers, mister," she said, her voice trembling.

"Beth. My mate." His voice sounded harsh and deeper than she had ever heard it before.

"That's right, my love, it's Beth, your Bunny." She swallowed hard against the knot in her throat; she couldn't lose him now, not when she had finally felt what it was like to be complete.

Gavriel's mouth twitched and his fangs began to recede. He took deep breaths and, within seconds, they were retracted completely. When he looked up, his eyes were back to their normal gray color and focused.

"My Beth, my Bunny," he whispered and opened his arms.

Crying out, she collapsed against him, sobbing.

"Shh, my love, I am okay, it is over. Thank the Gods, it is finally over." His lips were dry and cracked as they pressed against her forehead.

"They almost shot you," she cried. Then she remembered; they had almost killed her mate. She whirled around and flew at Aiden, punching wherever she could reach.

"How could you? How could you try to kill him?" She could barely see through her rage.

"Aiden, seriously, what the fuck?" Meryn kicked Aiden in the shin.

"Ow! Ow! Dammit! Someone get her! Colton, you deranged shit, get them off of me!" Aiden did his best to block her blows.

An arm came up behind her, pulling her away from the Unit Commander.

"I hate you! I hate you!" she cried.

"Beth! Beth! Baby, they had tranquilizers!" Gavriel croaked, trying to get her to hear him. She stopped fighting.

She turned. "Really?" she sniffled.

"Yes, baby. Though, now that I think about it, even if they had shot me, I think I would have been okay."

"Sorry, baby!" Meryn apologized looking up at her mate contritely.

Aiden frowned at everyone. Colton began to laugh. Aiden flipped him off, and Colton wheezed harder.

"You went against an army of ferals and didn't get a scratch on you. You come home and piss off the women and they almost take you out!" Colton had to put a steadying hand on Sascha's shoulder. The Gamma Unit leader was laughing so hard he had to lean against Colton to stay upright. The pair of them howled and slapped their legs. It wasn't long before all the men were laughing, expelling a lot of built up stress and tension. In the background, Oron reported that all the units had returned with no casualties, that the ferals ran away around the same time Gavriel had arrived at the Alpha estate.

"You know son, you shouldn't be upsetting Meryn like this," Byron chastised.

Aiden stared open mouthed at his father before turning to bark at Meryn. "Don't touch that!" he pulled her away from the body of a feral.

"But it's still twitching," Meryn said.

Elizabeth turned to Byron. "Thank you for coming so quickly; I don't know what would have happened if you hadn't come when you had."

Two grizzled warriors clapped Byron on the back. "Good thing we were visiting for drinks, eh, Byron," one laughed.

The other cracked his knuckles, grinning evilly. "I haven't had this much fun since I retired," he admitted.

Aiden stepped forward and shook hands with both men. "John, Abraham, I'd like for you to meet my mate, Meryn. Meryn, this is John Younger and Abraham Carter, the retired leaders of the Gamma and Epsilon Units. Let me add my thanks to Elizabeth's. Thank you for coming as quickly as you did."

"Looks like things have changed quite a bit since we retired. I don't remember ferals running together like this." John turned one of the ferals over with the toe of his boot.

Elizabeth stared down and gasped. At least twelve different sets of guns were trained on the dead feral.

"What is it, Beth?" Gavriel asked, turning her away from the corpse.

"I know that man," she whispered.

Aiden knelt down and stared at the dead man's face. "I do not recognize him. Do you know him from Noctem Falls?"

Meryn pushed past Aiden to look down. She inhaled and covered her mouth with both hands. "Oh, no!" Her eyes filled with tears. She turned and buried her face in Byron's chest. Aiden stood and went to her concerned.

Rubbing Meryn's back, Aiden looked back to Elizabeth. "Who is he?"

"I don't know him from Noctem Falls. I know him from scanning in pictures of the missing couples; this man was one of them. The second couple on the list," she whispered.

"Poor bastard turned feral after his mate was killed," Christoff said in a soft voice.

Darian took off his jacket and covered the man's face.

"Oh Gods!" Elizabeth moved away from Gavriel toward the dead bodies.

"Beth, baby, let me." Gavriel said moving her away from the enemy dead.

One by one they were turned. "You can stop now." She looked up to see Meryn standing next to Byron looking just as shaken as she felt. Suddenly, she wanted her own father very much.

Gavriel steered her back to the group of warriors.

"I recognized two more. Can someone take pictures before the bodies are disposed of? I don't trust myself and I don't want someone going unidentified."

"We'll take care of that Commander, why don't you get the ladies inside," Sascha recommended.

Gavriel tensed up beside her. "He said I would not have a choice." He turned to her. "They did not come after me tonight, they came after you." His words silenced the men.

"This wasn't a random attack, they deliberately tried to turn you," Aiden growled.

"They also said they were coming for my baby. How did they know? We haven't made an announcement." Meryn wiped her tears with her sleeve. Aiden plucked her from his father's arms and held her close.

"How did you keep them out of the house?" Aiden asked.

"Ryuu," both she and Meryn answered together.

They all turned to see the squire sitting on the porch steps; he waved at them.

"Damn good squire you have there, little lady." Abraham complimented.

"I know. He's the best!" Meryn preened.

"They almost won, didn't they?" Elizabeth said turning to her mate.

He shook his head. "Even if the worst came to pass, I would follow you. I would never let you face the unknown alone."

Beth watched as he, Aiden and the rest of the men exchanged looks. She knew what words were left unspoken.

After I slaughtered all those responsible for your death.

CHAPTER SIXTEEN

"Happy Thanksgiving, everyone!" Adelaide said as they walked into the Shifter Council estate. Everywhere Elizabeth looked, the house was tastefully decorated for the holiday. The smell of roast turkey, pumpkin, and cinnamon had her sighing blissfully. All the Alpha Unit members were able to make it except for Colton and the trainees; they had returned to their respective homes for the holidays. Adam, Adair, and Ben sat talking with Byron. Adelaide was fussing over Noah and Jaxon in a motherly fashion and both young men were soaking it up. Darian and Keelan were checking out each covered dish excitedly and Aiden was trying to keep Meryn out of the food.

"You never told me how much you loved Thanksgiving," Gavriel said, nipping at her neck.

"I love the food! It's all my favorite comfort foods put together in a huge feast, how can you not love that?"

"I was there for the first one, remember," he teased. They sat at the dining room table enjoying the chaos around them.

Elizabeth noticed the subtle differences in her mate. To his disgust, none of his clothes fit him anymore. He had to have a tailor come to the estate for new measurements. He had grown two inches, putting him close to Colton's height at six foot six, unheard of for a vampire. Where he had been lean and long before, he now carried more muscle, but it was compact unlike Aiden's larger, bulkier frame. To her, he was now walking sin. Every inch of him was sculpted, defined muscle. His hair was longer, as were his fangs when he fully extended them.

In private, he also admitted that he had to work with Aiden to create a new regiment for training. He was now working out using a routine similar to the larger fae. But the changes weren't just physical. Elizabeth was starting to see what Meryn had meant about her mate being a charming gentleman. He rarely got surly anymore and smiled more often. The only thing left unchanged was his possessive nature, for which she was grateful.

"Meryn, darling, we're eating soon." Adelaide laughed as Meryn ran from dish to dish wanting to try a bite of everything. Aiden had given up keeping her out of the food after she informed him the baby wanted it, he was now telling her to try all his favorite foods.

Darian and Keelan were glued to Marius's side trying to wheedle whole pies from the squire.

Ryuu was nearly back to normal and helping Marius in the kitchen. For a few days after the attack, he had been stuck in bed while he had regained his strength. Ultimately, it was not only the men begging him to act as a buffer between them and an un-caffeinated Meryn, but also the nursing attempts by Meryn herself that hastened his recovery.

"Oh, I just remembered!" Meryn said suddenly, looking at Gavriel.

"Yes?" he asked.

"Can you please tell Elizabeth that I'm right? Neither she nor Sydney believed me when I told them what you said about that shifter commander going home after the battle where the Dark Prince saved his life." She made a face at Elizabeth.

Elizabeth had to turn her head. She knew that Meryn was right since she now knew that Gavriel had actually been there.

Gavriel leveled his gaze at Elizabeth, his eyes twinkling. "You should listen to Meryn; she is getting to be an expert regarding paranormal history."

"Wait? What story? That is the first time I heard that ending, too," Aiden said.

Meryn beamed up at her mate. "Gavriel said that after the vampires healed the shifter commander, he turned his back on the war and walked all the way back to Lycaonia to see his newborn son."

"Why weren't we ever taught that?" Aiden asked, looking at his father.

Byron shrugged. "It's the first time I've heard it, too. Lots of stories were lost after the Great War; two whole generations were wiped out before it came to an end."

"Are you sure about this, Gavriel?" Byron asked.

Gavriel nodded and sat back. "The shifter was tired of fighting. He knew his mate had died giving birth to their son and, to him, it would dishonor her if he were to die before making sure the baby would be okay. Once healed, he thanked every vampire who treated him and began walking. The Dark Prince knew that the shifter would never make it to Lycaonia on his own so he traveled with him. Many times, the Dark Prince saved the shifter's life on the long journey back to the shifter city.

"When they arrived, the shifter did not stop to rest, to eat, or drink. He went directly up to the nursery to meet his son. When he asked the nurse if his mate had named the baby, she shook her head and said that his mate had requested that he name their son upon returning home. The shifter held his son close; the tiny child was the last link he had to his mate. He looked up at the Dark Prince and asked him what he should call his son.

"The Dark Prince was honored to be asked such a question and answered with the name of the godson he had lost centuries earlier, 'Mikhail'. Once father and son were settled, the Dark Prince left, promising that he would look after Mikhail and his descendants."

Aiden chuckled. "Mikhail was my great- great grandfather's name," he said before shoveling a small quiche into his mouth. Meryn elbowed him.

He looked down at her. "What? They can't be the same. Can they?" He looked around.

Byron was nodding. "Dear Gods, this needs to be added to our family journal," he whispered.

"Let me get this straight, the Dark Prince from vampire legend saved my great-great-great grandfather's life, named my great-great grandfather and promised to look after his descendants? Come on! It's not like there's a five thousand year old vampire sulking around helping to defend this family." Aiden protested then stopped as all blood drained from his face. He turned to look at Gavriel.

Gavriel smiled and wiggled his fingers at him. Aiden collapsed into the dining room chair next to his father.

"Holy shit," Jaxon and Adair whispered at the same time.

"It's why you volunteered to become a unit warrior isn't it? I never could figure out why someone as strong as you would take orders from me." Aiden stared down at the table.

Adelaide walked over and pulled Gavriel in for a hug and kissed him on the cheek. "Thank you for watching after my son."

"He has not been so bad," Gavriel teased.

Darian cleared his throat. "I thought you didn't want anyone to know."

Gavriel shrugged. "This is not everyone; it is family. Besides, I have a feeling the ferals knew who I was, and that is why I was targeted. It may only be a matter of time before my age comes out."

"They don't stand a chance, not with you on our side," Keelan said smiling at Gavriel.

Her mate shrugged modestly, grinning.

Elizabeth felt her heart swell. Her mate had lived for thousands of years and had shaped the very fabric of their history. He had been fighting for so long and for the most part doing it alone. She could give him the one thing she knew he desired. The one thing that, should anything happen to her, could possibly save his soul.

"I want to have a baby!" she announced.

Unfortunately, she hadn't counted on her mate taking a huge gulp of wine at that moment. Sputtering and gasping for air, he turned to her.

"Do you mean that? Truly?" The joy on his face made her wish she could get pregnant that night!

"Yes, when the time comes, I want to have a baby!" she promised.

He pulled her into his lap and held her close. "Thank you," he whispered against her neck.

"We have all winter to practice making a baby," she said and winked when he pulled back to look at her.

"Another baby! Oh, I can't wait! I need to start on their blankets now!" Adelaide clapped her hands together excitedly.

"You're going to have a jackalope!" Meryn said and collapsed against her mate giggling.

Elizabeth felt her jaw drop. "My baby will not be a Jackalope! Meryn, you take that back!"

Darian frowned. "Isn't a jackalope a bunny with antlers?"

Elizabeth shot him a look of death. He held up his hands defensively.

"A bunny with killer saber tooth fangs! Awesome!" Meryn said, smiling.

Elizabeth thought about it for a second, that didn't sound too bad. "That's actually kind of interesting," she admitted. She turned to Gavriel. "If anything happens to me, you'll need to stick around to make sure our little vampiric bunny grows up big and strong."

Gavriel rested his head on her shoulder. Around them the festivities continued, as Adelaide got the men to help Ryuu and Marius carry the food to the table.

"You're always thinking of me, of ways to save me. I am supposed to look after you." He pulled back and looked into her eyes.

"It's my job to take care of you, no matter what," she said stubbornly.

"My Bunny. My Protector."

"And don't you forget it," she said pulling him down for a kiss.

He broke off their kiss and looked at her with heat in his eyes. "We will start practicing tonight," he whispered.

"Sneaky vampire."

EPILOGUE

Colton sat up in his childhood bed at his parents' house and fought back the bile trying to climb up the back of his throat. He had dreamt of his mate again. Her face had been contorted in pain and worry. The smell of sickness and death surrounded her.

He flung himself backward and covered his eyes with his arm. Why would Fate be showing him his mate in so much pain when he wasn't able to be with her? He tried to hold on to the nebulous fading images from his nightmare. She had dark circles under her eyes and she had been too pale.

Everywhere his mate turned was sickness, blood, grief, waste, fear, and death. What kind of hell was she trapped in?

"Please. All I ask is for a chance to meet her, to show her some joy in this life before we join you," he whispered his prayer as two scalding hot tears escaped, racing down his temple to disappear into his hair.

"Please."

Thank you for reading!

I hoped you enjoyed My Protector.

For a full listing of all my books please check out my website www.alaneaalder.com

I love to hear from readers so please feel free to follow me on Facebook , Twitter, Goodreads, AmazonCentral or Pinterest.

If you liked this book please let others know. Most people will trust a friend's opinion more than any ad. Also make sure to leave a review. I love to read what y'all have to say and find out what your favorite parts were. I always read your reviews.

Don't forget to sign up for my newsletters so you will receive regular updates concerning release information and promotions.

OTHER BOOKS BY ALANEA ALDER

Kindred of Arkadia Series

This series is about a shifter only town coming together as pack, pride, and sloth to defend the ones they love. Each book tells the story of a new couple or triad coming together and the hardships they face not only in their own Fated mating, but also in keeping their town safe against an unknown threat that looms just out of sight.

Book 1- Fate Knows Best
Book 2- Fated to Be Family
Book 3- Fated For Forever
Book 4- Fated Forgiveness
Book 5- Fated Healing
Book 6- Fated Surrender
Book 7- Gifts of Fate
Book 8- Fated Redemption

Bewitched and Bewildered Series

She's been Bewitched and he's Bewildered...

When the topic of grandchildren comes up during a weekly sewing circle, the matriarchs of the founding families seek out the witch Elder to scry to see if their sons' have mates. They are shocked to discover that many of their sons' mates are out in the world and are human!

Fearing that their future daughters-in-law will end up dead before being claimed and providing them with grandchildren to spoil, they convince their own mates that something must be done. After gathering all of the warriors together in a fake award ceremony, the witch Elder casts a spell to pull the warrior's mates to them, whether they want it or not.

Each book will revolve around a unit warrior member finding his destined mate, and the challenges and dangers they face in trying to uncover the reason why ferals are working together for the first time in their history to kill off members of the paranormal community.

> Book 1- My Commander
> Book 2- My Protector
> Book 3- My Healer
> Book 4- My Savior
> Book 5- My Brother's Keeper

Made in the USA
Monee, IL
28 July 2020

37165072R00163